Freaky Sights

A MYSTIC CARAVAN MYSTERY BOOK 13

AMANDA M. LEE

WINCHESTERSHAW PUBLICATIONS

Prologue

18 YEARS AGO

"Look at her. She's so weird."

Poet Parker clutched the books she'd collected from the library closer to her chest and did her best to ignore the three girls standing beneath the shade of a weeping willow. She kept her shoulders squared and her eyes down as she started along the sidewalk.

They were talking about her. They were *always* talking about her. She'd long ago opted to ignore them — her mother told her picking a fight with catty girls was a waste of time — but it was getting harder as she got older. Of course, the girls were getting more obnoxious as they got older.

"She's not just weird. She has a stupid name," Jenny Galbraith said, her voice carrying. She wasn't even trying to be surreptitious. She wanted Poet to hear her. "I mean … who names their kid Poet?"

"Circus freaks, that's who," Carrie Conners replied. She was the follower of the group and went along with whatever the other two said. "That's what she is, right? A circus freak?"

"She's not even good enough for the circus," Jenny replied. "They wouldn't have her. She's more like a carnival freak. My dad says carnival people are perverts and cousin-humpers … I'm not sure what that's supposed to mean."

"I think it means they hump their cousins," Carrie offered helpfully.

"Thanks for that," Jenny said dryly.

Poet refused to look at them. She knew that would give them the sort of power she would forever regret. It took effort, especially when she had enough magic to knock them over and make them cry. She couldn't use it. Her parents had warned her for years now. The kids already thought she was strange. If they figured out she was magical … well, her life would be over.

Okay, maybe that was a little dramatic, but her parents were terrified people would find out that she was more than just a twelve-year-old girl. They'd warned her — over and over — that nothing good would happen if the wrong person found out. They'd even said that she could be taken away. She hadn't understood before, she'd been too young, but now … let's just say she'd had more than one nightmare about what could happen if things took a turn.

"What do you have there, Poet?" Lexie Burns called out. She had a lollipop in one hand and twirled her dark hair around a finger of the other. "Are you reading those because you have no friends?"

Poet dutifully put one foot in front of the other. If she could make it to the end of the block the girls would give up following. They wouldn't risk going into the neighborhood because the kids on Poet's side of town didn't like the girls from the other side. You wouldn't think there would be a class system in Michigan, but there was, and Poet was happy to live on the side where kids weren't afraid to throw punches if arguments got too testy. She could fight with the best of them, and Jenny and her merry band of jerks wouldn't risk being on the receiving end of a fist that could mar their perfect faces.

"She's acting like she can't hear us," Lexie said. "I bet she's afraid of us."

"I think she's just jealous," Carrie supplied. "She knows we're friends and she doesn't have any."

Poet gripped her books tighter. She'd made it to the main sidewalk. If she turned right, she could take the long way around the block and reach her house in ten minutes. If she turned left, she would have to cross in front of the girls but be home in five minutes. It seemed embracing the longer walk, despite the heat, was in her best interests. She turned right.

The sound of scampering feet on the sidewalk made her cringe. She didn't have to look over her shoulder to know that Jenny and her friends had decided to follow. They would stick to the main road, not follow when she turned right down Jefferson Street, but for now they weren't giving up on their torture. There was still a half block to traverse before she reached the turnoff — and that would feel like a lifetime.

"Hey, Poet," Jenny called out in the singsong voice she adopted when she was about to embrace her title as snottiest girl in school. "What's your hurry? We just want to hang out with you. I would think you'd want that because no one else wants to hang out with you."

"I heard even her parents don't want to hang out with her," Carrie said. "That's why they're never at home."

Poet gritted her teeth. She was close to saying something even though she knew it would backfire. She couldn't help herself. Her father said she'd inherited the need to run her mouth from her mother. Of course, her mother said it came from her father. Poet didn't know which of them had imbued her with the urge to say snarky things, but it had gotten her in trouble more than once.

"I heard that her parents are going to leave her at the fairgrounds the next time the carnival is in town so they take her," Lexie said.

"Well, I heard that they left her there last year but even the carnival freaks didn't want her," Jenny offered. "I mean … how bad do you have to be for the carnival freaks not to want you? I think it's because Poet's parents are worse than carnival freaks. What's worse than carnival freaks?"

"Those women at spas who pop zits," Carrie offered.

The girls cackled like mini-witches on the hunt … and that's when Poet snapped.

"Well, I heard the mailman makes a stop at Jenny's house every afternoon before lunch so he can deliver something special to her mother," Poet said. She couldn't turn back now. "I heard that Jenny's father doesn't want to touch her mother because he's afraid he'll get another Jenny, so the mailman has to deliver his package to her mother instead."

Poet understood most of what she was saying. She was repeating things she'd heard her parents say in jest over glasses of wine, but she was aware of the power of the words. Still, she was surprised when she felt a hand wrap in her black hair and yank.

She let loose a growl when her head snapped back, dropping the books and throwing a vicious elbow before swiveling. Her elbow made contact with Jenny's nose, causing the girl to scream as she released Poet's hair and slapped her hands over the throbbing area.

"You broke my nose!" she screeched.

Poet felt a burst of grim satisfaction as she saw the blood seeping through Jenny's fingers. She wasn't sorry. Not even a little. "Maybe you should've kept your hands to yourself."

Lexie, her eyes wide, glanced between Jenny and Poet. "You're going to get in trouble," she said. "We're telling our parents you attacked us."

"Go ahead," Poet said. "Tell your parents that it was three on one but you still lost. That makes you guys look all sorts of awesome."

"We didn't do anything to you," Carrie snapped. "You came after us. We were minding our own business."

"If you say so." Poet turned to collect her books, fervently hoping they hadn't been damaged when she dropped them. She had money saved from her birthday, but she didn't want to use it to replace the books.

"I hate you." Jenny moved her bloody hand from her nose and caught Poet on the side of the face as she was bending to retrieve the books. "You're such a freak. I just … hate you so much."

Slowly, Poet straightened and fixed Jenny with a death glare. She reacted without thinking, the magic she always kept tethered flaring to life as she lashed out and smacked the girl with equal force.

Jenny might've had righteous indignation on her side, but Poet had magic and might. A burst of flaming power exploded when Poet contacted the girl's face, the force of the blow strong enough to rock Jenny back on her heels.

The purported broken nose forgotten, Jenny's eyes widened as a series of bumps appeared in the form of a hand on her cheek.

"What was that?" Jenny cradled her face, her voice a breathy whisper. "What did you do?" She made a sound like a wounded animal when she felt the bumps. "Omigod! What is that?" She was desperate when she turned to Lexie.

For her part, the other girl looked more confused than worried. "I think it's just a zit," she said, peering close.

"I can't have zits." Jenny was beside herself. "I go to a doctor for zits."

"Well, you've got them now." Lexie shrugged. "They kind of look like a pattern."

"There's more than one?" The shrieking Jenny unleashed seemed inappropriate for what was happening, but Poet barely reacted.

"There's like fifty of them," Lexie confirmed. She almost looked giddy at her report. "And they all look like they're ready to be popped." As if to prove it, she reached over and did just that, making a face when the pus exploded outward. "Ugh! Now that is gross."

"It really is." Carrie gave Jenny a wide berth as she took a step back. "How did that even happen?" Her eyes tracked to Poet after a few seconds, recognition dawning.

Poet's expression didn't change.

"You did this to me!" Jenny reached out to slap Poet a second time, but Poet caught her wrist and squeezed, putting an extra jolt of magic into the motion. "You want to be very careful," she warned in a low voice. "If you touch me again, I'll make you pay."

Jenny very slowly, very carefully, withdrew her hand. Much like Carrie, who was already halfway down the sidewalk, she started to back away.

"I'm going to tell my mother," Jenny warned when she finally found her voice. "She's going to call your mother and you're going to be in big trouble."

Before Poet could respond, Lexie did. "What are you going to tell her?" Lexie asked. She was much calmer than the others as she trailed behind them on the sidewalk. "Are you going to have her charged with giving you zits?"

"Shut up, Lexie!" Jenny barked.

"We should leave," Carrie insisted. She was at the end of the block now. "I think I hear my mother calling."

"Your house is three miles away," Lexie pointed out.

"Then she must be really mad," Carrie spat.

Poet watched them for what felt like a really long time. It wasn't more than twenty seconds. Each one of those seconds dragged to infinity and back, however, and when she finally felt comfortable enough to avert her gaze, the first thing she checked on was the books. Thankfully, they seemed fine. After she'd collected them, she looked up again to track the girls. They'd disappeared.

Guilt set in almost immediately as Poet started trudging home. There was no way this incident wouldn't be reported to her parents. There would be hell to pay. Perhaps she should out herself right away when she got home. She'd found it was better to own up to her mistakes than try to hide them.

The answer had been made for her. Her mother, a phone pressed to her ear, arched an eyebrow as Poet let herself into their ranch house.

"Yes, I understand that Glenda," she said in an even tone. "I don't know what you want me to do about it. I guarantee that Poet isn't handing out zits as some form of punishment, no matter what Jenny says."

Her mother listened for another several seconds and then let loose a heavy sigh. "I don't know what to tell you," she said. "If you want to report it to the cops, I can't stop you. I'm not sure they'll believe that a twelve-year-old girl managed to give another twelve-year-old girl a face full of zits."

More silence.

"I'm not calling you crazy," Poet's mother insisted. "I'm just saying that the story seems to be lacking something … like proof, or rationality."

Poet pressed her lips together as she watched her mother roll her eyes. She sensed she was about to get into a boatload of trouble. That didn't mean she regretted what she'd done to Jenny. Odds were that her actions would mean several weeks of quiet because Jenny wouldn't want to risk facing off with Poet a second time.

"Well, you have to do what you have to do," Poet's mother said after a few more seconds. "No, I don't think I will be punishing Poet for giving Jenny zits." Another beat of silence. "Because that's not a real thing. Yes, well, I'm sorry you feel that way. Have a nice day, Glenda."

Poet had trouble meeting her mother's gaze as the phone call ended.

"Do you have something you want to say?" she asked when Poet didn't offer a comment.

"Not really." Poet scuffed her foot against the floor.

"Did you give Jenny Galbraith a face full of zits?"

If any other mother had asked her daughter that question it would be considered ludicrous. That wasn't the case here.

"Um ... ."

"That's what I thought." Her mother continued staring. "Did they go after you again?"

"She pulled my hair. I elbowed her in the nose to get her to let go. Then she slapped me and I ... just ... don't even know how it happened. I didn't know I was going to do that until I'd already done it."

"I see." Her mother's tone was clipped but there was amusement in her eyes. "I guess that will teach Jenny to keep her hands to herself."

Hope surged through Poet. "I'm not in trouble?"

"You need to be careful," her mother cautioned. "You can't just do ... the things you can do ... whenever things get tough."

"I know, but ... they're so mean."

"That's why you're not in trouble." Eyes twinkling, Poet's mother slipped an arm around her daughter's shoulders. "You could've done a lot worse. A face full of zits isn't the worst thing ever ... and it's not as if Jenny didn't have it coming."

"What if she tells people?"

"That you gave her zits? I'm not too worried about that. To be safe, you need to stay away from her for a bit. It's important that you not give her more fodder for her outlandish stories."

"I didn't want to be around her in the first place. They were waiting when I left the library."

"Yes, well, I guess they learned a lesson about minding their own business, didn't they?"

Poet was taken aback by her mother's amusement.

"Let's have some popcorn and iced tea, and you can tell me all about it," her mother suggested. "I want to have all the facts in case Glenda calls again."

"That's it?" Poet was dumbfounded. "I thought you would punish me."

"I'm not going to punish you for protecting yourself. There's going to come a time when you'll have to protect yourself regularly. I want you prepared. What you did today ... well ... it was the smartest thing you could've done."

The older woman leaned down to Poet's eye level. "We don't want you being aggressive with other people. That won't benefit you in any way. But you must protect yourself. You won't have a choice as you get older.

"What you did today was the smartest thing you could've done," she continued. "You hit her where it hurts — her vanity — and you didn't do anything to draw attention to us. If she tries telling that story to anyone, nobody will believe her."

"Carrie and Lexie were there."

"They're not exactly reliable witnesses, are they?"

"I guess not." Poet chewed the inside of her cheek. "I'm really not in trouble?"

"The only way you'll be in trouble is if you don't tell me the story. I don't want you to leave out a single detail so I can picture it forever."

Poet smiled. "It was kind of fun."

"I'm sure it was. Let's get that popcorn and iced tea."

CHAPTER 1

One

PRESENT DAY

"I think I'm going to be sick."

My best friend Luke Bishop gripped the ship's railing so tightly his knuckles turned white, and he leaned so far over I feared he might fall into the churning ocean. I wrapped my arms around his waist and tugged backward.

"Don't go over," I snapped. "This is not the time to drown."

Luke slapped my hands away. "Don't grab on to my stomach. Do you want me to puke on you?" His glare was vicious when it landed on me … and his face a little green.

I instinctively backed up. If it was one thing I hated, it was being puked on. I, Poet Parker, was a sympathetic puker of the highest order. If he threw up, I would follow suit. I wouldn't be able to help myself. That would totally ruin my street cred on top of being really gross. "Don't you dare," I warned, extending a finger.

"Then don't grab my stomach." Luke weakly slapped at my hand again. He was far too weak to give me the grief he normally flung around like confetti at Mardi Gras.

"What's going on here?" Kade Denton asked as he joined us. He was one of the few people on the ship who hadn't felt a single twinge of motion sickness as we sailed between Florida and Moonstone Bay, a paranormal island we were eyeing as a permanent location for Mystic Caravan Circus when it was time to stop taking it on the road.

"Luke is sick," I said, my hand automatically going to Luke's back when he faced the railing again. As much as I enjoyed messing with my best friend — and I did — there was no joy to be found in his discomfort. It was better to mess with him when he could mess back.

"Seasick?" Kade asked, cocking his head as he gave Luke a fresh look. He didn't appear to be brimming with sympathy as much as amusement. "Are you going to lose it over the railing, bud?"

I elbowed Kade and shot him a serious look. He might've been enjoying his status as head of security, and all-around sailing aficionado, but I didn't want to encourage him. "Don't make things worse," I chided. I moved directly behind Luke and rubbed both hands over his solid back. "What can I do for you?"

"Kill your boyfriend," Luke hissed. "Make it hurt."

"Fiancé," Kade corrected with a grin. "I'm her fiancé now. I no longer acknowledge the boyfriend tag."

My lips quirked at the way he puffed out his chest. We'd been engaged for several weeks now — each day seemingly more blissful than the previous as we enjoyed our downtime in Florida — but now it was back to reality. In addition to serving as a scouting mission, we'd turned our trip to Moonstone Bay into a working vacation of sorts. Mystic Caravan Circus would be setting up on the island for an entire week. It was an audition, for the island and us, to see if we had anything to offer — and vice-versa — and everybody looked forward to the excursion.

"You're an awesome fiancé," I reassured him as I leaned in for a quick kiss.

Kade caught my chin in his hand and lengthened the exchange, letting loose an exaggerated sigh when we finally separated. "That's the stuff."

I winked at him and then turned my attention back to Luke. "Seriously, what can I do for you?"

"I just told you. Kill him. I'll feel better the second you do that."

"Oh, somebody sounds grumpy," a male voice said as another figure slid closer. This one belonged to Cole Ryan, Luke's boyfriend and the newest member of Mystic Caravan Circus. He'd joined our team in Cleveland, after we crossed paths during a magical battle, and he'd been enamored with my best friend ever since. Luke wasn't the easiest person to get along with — and I say that as someone who loves him — so I was fairly certain Cole was some sort of saint. Not only had he embraced Luke's oddness, he'd also helped rein in some of his theatrical overindulgences. They were a good match, and I looked forward to a lifetime watching them banter their way to happily ever after.

Well, if we could find a permanent location for the circus.

"I got you some ginger ale," Cole said as he handed Luke a plastic cup. "See if that helps settle your stomach."

Luke glared. "Ginger ale? That's your solution?"

"I don't have a solution." Cole kept his voice even. "You're seasick. I'm actually surprised because you're the sort of guy who loves amusement park rides — the faster the better — but it is what it is. We'll be docking at Moonstone Bay within the hour. Until then, we just have to get through it."

"Awesome." Luke's eyes were almost black with disgust as he snagged the cup and sipped.

"You'll feel better as soon as you're on dry land," Cole said pragmatically. "And next time we know to pump you full of motion sickness medication before leaving Florida."

"There won't be a next time." Luke's tone was grave as he sipped the ginger ale. "I'm never getting on a ship again. They're evil."

"What if we move to Moonstone Bay?" Cole was clearly ready to indulge Luke, but only to a point.

"We're not moving to Moonstone Bay." Luke was adamant. "It's off the list. I cannot deal with … *this* … ever again."

"You'll be fine." Cole absently patted Luke's shoulder and then left him to stew at the railing as he lowered himself to a bench and fixed his attention on me. "I contacted my cousin. She knows we're arriving today. I told her we needed to oversee the delivery of the equipment and tents before stopping at her bar for dinner."

"Sounds good." I bobbed my head. "I want to get the lay of the land as quickly as possible, and it's always good to have an inside person."

"Is nobody listening to me?" Luke asked mournfully. "Am I already dead and you can't hear me?"

"You'll be fine," Cole soothed. "You're just a baby when you're sick. You'll be fine as soon as we dock."

"Yes, it's not like one of those other sicknesses you've had where you get spots in unfortunate places," Kade teased.

I grabbed Kade's hand and dragged him away from Luke before my friend — a shifter with dangerous claws — could lash out and cause the sort of damage we'd be forced to heal for days. "Don't push him when he's sick," I warned, directing Kade to the bench next to Cole. "You don't like when people mess with you when you're sick."

"I don't get sick," Kade countered. "I'm in peak physical form. Getting sick is for weaklings."

"I'm going to kill you as soon as I'm feeling better," Luke warned. "I'm just going to … ." He mimed ripping the head off an invisible man. "Poet can't do it. She's convinced she loves you. I'll have to do it for her."

"Oh, you can't take my Kade from me," I countered as I rested my head on Kade's shoulder, smiling when I felt his lips brush my forehead. "I'll be sad forever."

Luke didn't miss a beat. "No, you won't. I'll find you a new guy, maybe even on this island. A better guy."

"You're just grumpy," Cole chastised. "It won't be long now." He fixed his eyes on me. "So, how will the hotel situation work? Without the trailers, we're not going to be setting up the fairgrounds as we normally would. I'm not sure what to expect."

"We've booked rooms for everybody," I replied. "At a smaller hotel, the one your cousin recommended. It's run by a woman named June Seaver. She's supposed to be a witch, so we don't have to hide who we are from her. That itself feels like some sort of miracle."

"If Lilac recommended her, she must be a good person," Cole said.

"I still can't believe your cousin's name is Lilac Meadows," Kade mused. "She must hate her parents."

Cole hesitated and then shrugged. "She doesn't interact with much of the family these days. It's a whole big … thing. She's one of the few members of my family I can tolerate. Well, other than my immediate family. She didn't have the same warm upbringing I did. My mother insisted we distance ourselves from the other members of the family when I was a kid. Lilac was different. She didn't want any part of the nonsense. She stayed with us one summer when her mother was … doing whatever it was her mother did. I'm not even sure. I liked her right away, and my mother made sure she could always call us if she ever got in trouble."

"What sort of trouble?" Kade asked. As chief of security, he was always on the lookout for things that might trip us up.

"Fire magic is … difficult … sometimes," Cole explained. "Lilac grew up on this island and her half-demon status didn't endear her to the population. It's rare for all four elementals to settle in the same place with one another. Usually, a location is overrun by one sort of elemental. Moonstone Bay is different."

"That's why you think we'll fit in?" I asked.

"I haven't visited since I was a teenager," Cole cautioned. "I remember it being a great place. The stormy season lasts only a couple of weeks. Other than that, it's hurricane free. You can be yourself there. The island is predominantly populated by other paranormals. You have to be careful with the tourists, but you can be yourself most of the time."

I flicked my eyes to Kade to read his reaction. "Sounds like a pretty good deal," I said. "Think they'll welcome us?"

"That I can't answer." Cole's smile faded. "I wish I could say they'll open their arms to us, but we need to feel it out. Given the number of festivals they have, a permanent circus would be a big draw. I just don't know if they'll be open to it."

"That's why we arranged this trip," Kade pointed out. "We can scout out the island and get paid at the same time."

"It's going to take at least a year to secure the move," I added. "We have contracts to fulfill. If Moonstone Bay wants us, we'll have to start planning in earnest."

"It could be worth it," Cole said. "We could have permanent homes here. No more living out of trailers, or constantly moving around. We could have yards ... and pets ... and kids." His smile was rueful. "Isn't that what we all want?"

Kade slung his arm around my shoulders. "It's what I want."

"I just want to die," Luke complained.

He was almost neon he was so green. I had no doubt he was going to lose his lunch. "Max called ahead to get clearance," I explained. Max Anderson was the head of Mystic Caravan Circus. He also happened to be Kade's father, a fact that Kade wasn't aware of until nearly a year ago. "They'll have equipment to move all our stuff. Apparently, vehicles are at a premium on the island."

"How do people get around without trucks?" Kade asked.

"Moonstone Bay is essentially one big city and then outlying rural areas," Cole explained. "The rural areas are predominantly farms — cattle and produce. I guess there's a siren stronghold out there too. Lilac just breezed over that part. In the city, most people use carts for transportation."

"Like golf carts?" Kade asked.

Cole nodded. "Yeah. I think it sounds fun too."

"What about housing?" I asked. "Do they have room to accommodate an entire circus?"

"I guess we'll find out." Cole extended his legs and flicked his eyes back to Luke. "How are you feeling, baby?"

"Like I hate all of you," Luke whined. "I don't understand why I'm the only one who is sick. I'm in the best shape of all of us."

"Um ... excuse me?" Kade's voice ratcheted up a notch. "Who are you including in this 'us' you just mentioned?"

"I'm definitely in better shape than you," Luke fired back, his eyes igniting with competitive spirit. "If you don't believe me, we can strip right here and start flexing."

"Ah, the game of kings," Cole drawled.

"Cole is in the second-best shape too," Luke insisted. "If it weren't for me, I would say he's the apex of men."

Cole drawled, "That could be the nicest thing you've ever said to me."

"I'll say nicer things when I don't feel like I'm dying."

"Drink your ginger ale."

I pressed my lips together to keep from smirking. Cole handled Luke better than anybody I'd ever met. He somehow managed to marry fun with the appropriate amount of responsibility, and Luke always responded.

"I have a question," Kade interjected, his hand landing on my knee. He was a tactile individual, loved hugging more than anybody I'd ever met, but since the engagement he'd been even more touchy-feely. I wasn't complaining, especially since we were about to spend a week on an island paradise. Sure, we had work in front of us, but I expected plenty of time for play.

"Shoot," I prodded.

"What happens if we do settle here?" he asked. "Let's say every-thing works out exactly as we hope. We fall in love with the island, and make arrangements to settle in a year or so. What happens to the rest of the group?"

I was confused. "What do you mean?"

"It's what's best for us. We're magical. Living on a magical island sounds great. Do we think that all the others — the midway folks, the general workers and the clowns — will feel the same way?"

"Oh." Realization dawned on me, and I nodded accordingly. "I don't think all of them will come with us. Some will. Some will decline and move to other jobs. We won't know how many until we're much closer to the move date."

"Keep in mind, most don't know why we're really here," Cole cautioned. "We're keeping that to ourselves for now. We don't want to work people up about circus operations, at least as they know them, ceasing. We need a firm plan in place before we can move forward."

"I get it." Kade nodded in understanding. "I'm not saying we should make an announcement over dinner or anything. I've just been thinking about the logistics. The trailers will be gone, right? We'll have to sell them because they won't be necessary here."

"I'm guessing that's how it would go," I agreed, my eyes keen as they searched his face. "Is that what you're worried about? Will you be sad to see the trailers go?"

He shrugged, noncommittal, and kept his gaze on the ocean expanse. Even though we couldn't see land in any direction, it was an absolutely breathtaking view. "That will be a little sad. It's our first home together. I'm just trying to picture things."

Kade was a planner. It made sense that he would want things spelled out. Unfortunately, I didn't have the answers. "We're going to have to play it by ear. I'm sorry that I don't have the answers."

"Oh, it's okay." He squeezed my knee. "I guess I'm a little excited to check out the island. This could be our home."

"I think we'll know relatively quickly if it's something we want to entertain," Cole said, cringing when Luke heaved.

I followed his gaze, frowning when it became apparent that Luke was indeed losing the contents of his stomach over the side of the ship. "Crap." I averted my gaze and tried to hold back my gag reflex. "Stop making that noise, Luke."

"You stop making that noise," Luke hissed, his shoulders hunching again as he prepared to launch another assault on the ocean. "Ugh. This is the worst. I can't ever deal with this again. Island living is out."

"We'll medicate you next time," Cole insisted. "It will be better. I promise. In fact … ." He didn't get a chance to finish because his eyes were on me as I lurched to my feet. In typical fashion, Luke throwing up had triggered the urge in me. "Oh, no. Not you too."

"Out of the way!" I slapped Kade's hand when he reached for me. I was in no mood for the lovey-dovey game now. "Just … don't touch me." I hurried to the railing, making sure to keep at least ten feet from Luke.

"Not so funny now, is it?" Luke demanded as he wiped the back of his hand across his mouth.

"It wasn't funny when it was happening to you," I snapped, squeezing my eyes shut. *Don't do it. Don't do it. Don't do it.* I tapped into my magic, hoping somehow I could hold it back.

Luke retched again.

Ugh. "Maybe I'm going to need the medication too." I joined Luke in worshipping the sea, hating myself — and him, quite frankly.

"Yeah, we're definitely going to have to get water travel under control before we head back," Kade lamented. "This is not good for any of us."

"It was fine when it was just me," Luke snarled.

"Yes, well, what can I say?" Kade replied. "I love her more."

"It won't be long," Cole said. "Just … do what you have to do. We'll be right here when you're done."

He was trying to exert some calm over the situation, but his words had the opposite effect. Now I just wanted to slap him around, which was likely how Luke felt when I tried to console him. "We need to reach land," I said after my second round of vomiting.

"Soon," Cole insisted.

No matter what he said, it wouldn't be soon enough.

CHAPTER 2

Two

I was a limp rag, and Kade practically carried me off the ship. He deposited me on a bench on the shady side of the dock, purchased a bottle of water for me, and left me with a kiss to the forehead to oversee the unloading of the equipment.

Luke insisted on walking off the ship under his own volition but was more than happy to settle with me on the bench once away from prying eyes.

"Still want to move to an island?" he drawled as he guzzled his water.

"I was fine until you got sick," I insisted, shooting him a dirty look. "This is all your fault."

"Yeah, yeah, yeah."

We sat there an hour, at first too pouty to engage in anything other than sarcasm. But after that we began to feel better.

"It's pretty," Luke noted as he stretched his arms above his head and scanned the town. "Who doesn't love a good kitschy downtown? I bet they have like ten tiki bars."

He loved a good tiki bar. Truth be told, so did I. "We'll find one before bed tonight."

"Sounds good." Luke extended his hand to pull me to my feet just as Cole and Kade returned. "How goes work, boys?" he taunted in a twangy voice.

Kade made a face. "I take it you're feeling better." He headed straight for me and brushed my hair from my face. "How are you feeling?"

"I'm fine," I reassured him. Now that the puking was in the past, I felt a little guilty for being so mean to him when he tried to hover. "Sorry I yelled at you."

"It's okay. I'm used to it."

Now it was my turn to frown. "You're used to me being mean to you?"

He smiled. "I like when you're mean to me."

"We're going to talk about this later," I warned, averting my mouth when it looked like he might try to kiss me. "What are you doing?"

"Making up with my beautiful bride-to-be." His eyebrows collided. "Is that not allowed?"

"I haven't brushed my teeth since puking."

"Good point." He laced his fingers with mine and gave me a little tug. "The luggage is on the way to the hotel, along with our people. We told them to get settled and then report to the fairgrounds. By the time we get there all the equipment and tents should've been delivered."

"Sounds like a plan." Honestly, a hot shower and access to my toothbrush sounded heavenly. "We should be able to meet everybody there in an hour."

"We gave them two hours," Cole said. "We weren't sure how long it would take the hotel to check everybody in and then there's the walk to the fairgrounds."

Now that my stomach no longer felt like it was riding a Tilt-a-Whirl, I was up for anything. "Let's hit the hotel."

THE MOONSTONE BAY CABANA CLUTCH HOTEL WAS NICE, but nowhere near as opulent as the huge monstrosity of a resort down the beach. There had been debate when we were arranging lodging regarding which hotel to select. Even though the other resort was clearly nicer, and this one was undergoing renovations, I decided we'd made the right choice.

The hotel owner was a nice woman named June Seaver. She insisted that I come to her if I had any problems. Apparently, Cole's cousin Lilac had paved the way for us — and in fantastic fashion — so I felt comfortable with our choice. I immediately hopped in the shower when we got to our room, which had a lovely view of the downtown area. After thirty minutes of washing the dregs of the ship ride off me, I exited the shower to find Kade had placed my toothbrush and toothpaste on the counter. I was only too happy to oblige him.

I changed into shorts and a T-shirt and pulled my long hair back in a loose bun. Kade pinned me to the wall by the door to make up for his lost kiss, and by the time we met Cole and Luke in the lobby I was breathless.

"You look like you did the dirty," Luke complained as he studied my face during the walk. "You didn't have enough time for that." He shot an accusatory look to Kade. "Are you falling down on the job? Five minutes is not enough time to love a woman properly."

Kade's death glare was straight out of a horror movie. "Keep it up."

Luke didn't look bothered in the least. "We'll find you a new man here, Poet," he insisted as we crossed the street. "Island men are so much better looking. In fact … well, hello." His voice dropped to a low rumble, and he practically preened as he straightened.

"What are you looking at?" I demanded as I studied the fairgrounds. Most of our equipment had been delivered, scattered haphazardly. That was to be expected when dealing with people who weren't familiar with how the circus would be laid out. Ah, well. Without trailers, our job would be easier when it came to organization.

"I believe I found my backup," Luke whispered, his eyes drifting to a tall man standing next to the sidewalk. The piece of eye candy was big, broad-shouldered, and ridiculously good-looking. "Don't tell Cole, but if things don't work out, I'm totally going to make that guy my trapeze partner."

I rolled my eyes. "That is too much man for you."

"Excuse me?"

"You heard me. Heck, I think he's too much man for me."

It was almost as if he heard us, because the man slowly turned his eyes in our direction. He had a phone pressed to his ear and a badge attached to his belt.

"Uh-oh," Luke and I said in unison.

"Shifter," Luke added after a few seconds, his nostrils flaring. "Wolf."

I glanced at my best friend and then back at the man. "You're sure?"

"Yeah. He's … very masculine."

I made a face. "He's also a cop." My stomach clenched. A shifter cop on a paranormal island? That had to be good, but I was always nervous dealing with law enforcement. I'd been on the wrong end of pointed questions more than once. "It does make sense that you're hot to trot for him," I said.

"The dude is gorgeous," Luke replied, offering up a cheeky wave as the man started in our direction. "Oh, yay. He's coming. How do I look?"

I risked a glance to my right and found Cole glaring at his boyfriend.

"I'm right here," Cole growled.

"I know," Luke replied. "How can I miss the third most handsome man on the island?"

"Oh, well, now I'm third." Cole shook his head and skirted around me so he could be first to greet the newcomer. "Have you considered that maybe I'm actually first and you and the new guy are second and third?"

"Not even for a moment," Luke said.

"Hello." The shifter cop had a ready smile as he crossed. His gaze bounced from face to face, and he shook Cole's proffered hand. Finally, he looked me square in the eye. "You're in charge, right?"

I was taken aback. Most people assumed the men were the leaders. Not all of them were sexist — at least inherently so — but there was always a level of "She's a girl so somebody else must be in charge" in most locations. "Poet Parker." I extended my hand, a flurry of images clouding my mind when we made contact. The emotions associated with those images were powerful, but I kept my face impassive so he wouldn't know I'd breeched his mind.

"Galen Blackwood." His smile was warm. If he realized I'd gotten a peek inside his head, he didn't show it. "I'm the sheriff."

"Oh, that makes him even hotter," Luke muttered. He was a shifter, just like the sheriff, so he was well aware the man could hear him. He didn't seem to care.

"Ignore him," I said, shaking my head at Galen's unasked question. "He likes to be the center of attention."

Galen's smile didn't diminish. "I know a few like him. By the way, if you're determined to be the hottest one on the island, you're going to have competition."

Luke blanched. "I have no competition."

"We'll see what you have to say after you meet our resident cupid." Galen turned back to me. "You guys are setting up here but staying at June's hotel."

I nodded. I found it interesting that he had so much information on us. "We already checked in."

"June is a great woman. Don't give her a hard time." His voice was stern but there was a glint in his eyes. "I'm here to welcome you and answer any questions you might have. I understand that you're the sort of circus that will fit in on Moonstone Bay."

"And we heard Moonstone Bay is the sort of island that would fit in with us," I teased.

He grinned. "Either way, we're glad to have you here." He glanced at his phone, frowning at an incoming message. "I'm not sure what the protocol is here, but I'll leave the setup to you," he said as he rubbed the back of his neck. Upon second inspection, he looked tired, as if he had other things on his mind. "If you need anything, don't hesitate to call my office. Moonstone Bay can be confusing to newcomers."

"I've been here before," Cole volunteered. "I visited one summer when I was a kid. My cousin owns a bar here."

"Really?" Galen's expression didn't change. "Who is your cousin?"

"Lilac Meadows."

"Seriously?" Galen grinned. "Lilac is a good friend. We grew up together. She and my girlfriend are like giggling schoolgirls with one another quite often. I'm sure I'll be seeing you, but duty calls."

"Anything we can help you with?" I asked. The visions I'd seen in his mind had been jumbled, overlapping, and occasionally vicious.

"I don't think so but thank you for the offer." He managed a smile as he started toward his official vehicle. "I hope you guys have fun. We haven't had a circus here in years."

"Oh, he even looks hot walking away," Luke gushed. "I can't wait to get to know him better."

"Again, I'm right here," Cole snapped.

"Of course, you are." Luke squeezed his hand. "How could I forget you?"

I pressed my lips together as my gaze drifted to Kade. "Ready to get to work?"

"Yup, but only because I have visions of you walking with me on the beach after a few tiki bar cocktails this evening."

I beamed at him. "I think that can be arranged."

AFTER SEVERAL HOURS OF SETUP, WE had the main attractions in their proper locations. There was still a lot of work to do, but that would progress faster tomorrow. We cut the workers loose early so they could enjoy the tropical paradise and then went to meet Cole's cousin.

Cole was the first through the door of the kitschy tiki bar, his excitement growing with each step between the fairgrounds and his cousin. When he walked into the bar it was as if a spotlight was shone directly on him, and the pretty blonde behind the counter immediately zeroed in on him.

"Well, well, well," she drawled, her hands landing on her hips. "I expected you hours ago. Better late than never, eh?"

Cole laughed as he hurried to her. Her arms were already open as she stepped out from behind the bar and wrapped him in a bearhug.

"I missed you," he enthused as he held her. "I didn't even realize how much until we got here."

"I missed you too, handsome." Lilac grinned before focusing on the rest of us. "Are you going to introduce me to your friends?"

"Absolutely." Cole ran through the introductions, smirking when Lilac decided that Luke needed a hug too. By the time he finished, he looked happier than I'd ever seen him. He obviously adored his cousin, but he didn't talk much about the rest of his family.

"Get settled," Lilac instructed, inclining her head toward a table in the corner. "I'll bring some drinks and you can catch me up on everything." She didn't ask for our orders, but the pitcher of daiquiris she brought when she returned were just what we needed.

"The island seems really cool," I noted as I sucked down my drink. It was delicious, which seemed somehow miraculous given the fact that I'd been puking only hours before. "Cole said you've been here your whole life."

"Well, when you live in paradise it's hard to leave," Lilac replied. She'd left her employees to run the bar and seemed content to hang out with us. "Everybody is excited to have a circus in town. The regulars have been talking about it nonstop since it was announced you were coming here two weeks ago."

"Well, we're here to serve," I said.

"Speak for yourself," Luke countered. "I'm here for the daiquiris. Oh, and maybe that sheriff. We met him a few hours ago. He is just all sorts of hot."

"My boyfriend, ladies and gentlemen," Cole deadpanned.

Lilac's smirk lit up her entire face. "You met Galen?"

I nodded. "He wanted to welcome us, but he seemed a bit distracted."

"He's good at his job, but he's been dealing with little fires the last two days," Lilac explained. "I guess that's better than big fires — we get a lot of those — but Hadley told me he's getting frustrated."

"Who is Hadley?" I asked.

"His girlfriend. She's my best friend. She lives in the lighthouse down the way."

A quick flash invaded my mind, an image I'd picked up when shaking Galen's hand: a pretty woman, long black hair and piercing blue eyes. When she'd invaded Galen's head she was smiling. That's how I saw her now. "Are they a cute couple?" I asked the question in an effort to quench Luke's insatiable lust for the sheriff.

"Definitely." Lilac bobbed her head. "I look for them to get engaged soon. They live together. I've known Galen my whole life and never saw him care about a woman more than a few months. He fell head-over-heels for Hadley in record time. They're inseparable."

"Poor Luke," I said as I poked my pouty friend's cheek. "I guess you've been thwarted again."

"No random chick is a match for me," Luke countered.

"Hadley isn't a random chick," Lilac warned. "She's ... more."

I wanted to ask what that meant. Lilac barely knew us. Maybe after a few days she would be more comfortable sharing gossip. "You said that the sheriff has been putting out little fires," I prodded. "Anything we should be worried about?"

"I don't think so, but I can't say for sure." Lilac's face fell. "Apparently there's been a run of vandalism. It's the local kids, acting out of sorts. It's like spring fever or something."

"What sort of vandalism?" Cole asked, his law enforcement training kicking in. Much like Kade, he liked to be on top of things when it came to security concerns.

"The normal stuff." Lilac shrugged. "There's been some graffiti, someone stole a gnome from Meg Flanders's yard. There's been some eggs tossed. Oh, and I guess a group of kids terrorized Norman Flagg a few days ago. He's kind of a jerk, though, so we're not sure he didn't have it coming."

I smiled. "Sounds like stuff that could happen anywhere."

"But it rarely happens here," Lilac acknowledged. "The community is small. Everybody knows everybody. I'm sure Galen will handle it, and because he's kind of a softie when it comes to kids, he'll probably make them do community service and call it a day. He got into a fair bit of mischief when he was their age."

"There are worse things than mischievous kids," I agreed. Still, it was cause for concern. We didn't think we'd need the magical dream-catcher we erected when traveling. Perhaps I'd been hasty when declaring it unnecessary this time.

I slid my eyes to Kade and found him watching me with unreadable eyes. "Maybe we should swing by the fairgrounds on our way back to the hotel. Just in case."

He squeezed my knee under the table. "We can do that. But let's enjoy ourselves here first. A bunch of bratty kids aren't anything to worry about."

"Daiquiris and dinner first. We'll worry about the other stuff later."

"That should always be the rule."

CHAPTER 3

W e walked the beach back to the fairgrounds, studying the
town before erecting the dreamcatcher. I had to call Raven,
Nixie and Naida to join us — a call that wasn't welcomed by the pixie
twins, who felt their time was better served stalking the beach — but
they grudgingly came.

"I don't understand why we need this," Raven admitted as she
studied the expansive fairgrounds. "I mean … it's a magical island.
Three-quarters of the people who come here are paranormal, so the
dreamcatcher won't work."

"That's why I want to modify it," I explained. "Apparently a group
of kids have been up to mischief. Instead of drawing in paranormals, I
want to set it to repel mischief makers and alert if anybody has nefarious ideas."

Raven made a face. "You're going to have to be a bit more specific
than that. Nefarious ideas could be anything, including getting down
and dirty on the beach once everybody is asleep."

It took everything I had to keep a straight face. "Are you talking
about yourself?" I asked.

"Oh, don't be such a prude." She rolled her eyes. "I'm a bit old for
beach shenanigans."

I waited because I didn't believe her.

"There's supposed to be a private beach by a new resort they're building," she added. "I thought I might take a walk down there later with Percival."

Percival was her clown. No, really. She was a centuries-old lamia who'd fallen in love with a clown. The dude faked a British accent, but she didn't seem to care. I found the entire thing fascinating. "Well, then how about we set the dreamcatcher to alert if something violent is going to happen on the fairgrounds?" I asked.

"That could work." She blew out a sigh and nodded. "Just be fore-warned: This island is crawling with paranormals. We might get questioned about the dreamcatcher at some point."

"If we're questioned, we're questioned." I shrugged.

It took us twenty minutes to erect the dreamcatcher. As soon as we finished, the pixie twins took off for the water. Naida loved swimming at night, and I figured she would entertain herself in the water until almost dawn. As long as she didn't cause trouble, I didn't see the harm in it. The Moonstone Bay shallows were likely swimming with paranormal water lovers. Naida knew how to take care of herself.

"Ready?" Kade asked as he appeared at my side. He looked happy and relaxed, the daiquiris Lilac served up doing their job.

I nodded as I slipped my hand into his. "Did Cole and Luke already head back?"

"Yup. They were bored and there was no reason for them to be here. It's not as if this is the typical dangerous, isolated location we set up shop in."

He was right. Still, I had reservations. "What if that makes us complacent?"

Kade's eyes lit with amusement. "That's what you're worried about?"

His steady gaze left me squirming. "I don't want to lose our edge. This place is beautiful, but what if that's a facade? What if there's something ready to strike under the surface?"

"We'll be ready. We're always ready. Try to unclench, baby." He sent me a sidelong smirk. "We're in a tropical paradise for an entire week. I'm going to be really annoyed if you don't enjoy yourself."

"What does one do when they have a quiet evening to themselves in a tropical paradise?"

His eyes lit with a wicked gleam. "I'm glad you asked. I have a few ideas."

"Somehow I knew you would say that."

I SLEPT HARD, SOMETHING ABOUT THE SALTY air wafting through the open window lulling me. Even though we'd spent the last month not working, I still got up with the sun most days. But I managed to sleep ten hours, something I rarely did.

"What are the plans for today?" Luke asked as he shoved a huge forkful of waffle into his mouth.

"You could cut the waffles and take more bites," I noted as I watched him try to swallow the hunk.

Cole thumped his back when he coughed. "Try not to choke over breakfast and die. That would make for a bummer of a day."

When Luke finally managed to swallow, he sent his boyfriend a rueful smile. "Just a bummer of a day?"

Cole snickered. "Well, the sheriff is quite attractive. I thought I might see if he was interested once my mourning period is over. That's only three days, so I think I can tough out the wait."

Luke replaced his smile with a scowl. "I don't think I like you."

"Oh, don't be petulant, Snickerdoodle." Cole's grin widened. "I would mourn hard those three days."

Even though I knew Cole was pushing things — Luke was nothing if not intolerable when pouting — I couldn't hide my laughter. I dug into my omelet and considered the original question. "We have to set up today. If we knock out the big stuff, that just leaves the little stuff for tomorrow. It shouldn't take more than a few hours."

"Then we can hit the beach or something," Kade suggested. "I want a lazy day with my future wife."

Luke's eyebrows drew together. "You just like referring to her as your 'future wife.'"

"Guilty."

"She's not a possession. She's her own person."

"Oh, stuff it." Kade had been in a glorious mood since the proposal. He was almost giddy these days, which made me happy because he was prone to brooding on occasion. Things had eased for him since we'd met. He was still getting used to the paranormal game, but he was also getting good at wielding his magic. On top of that, he was forging a real relationship with Max. Things had been tense between them when Kade first learned Max wasn't just a family friend who popped in once a year to dote on him and his mother growing up. Now they voluntarily spent time together.

"I believe one thing that should definitely be on the menu today is couple time," I interjected. "Kade and Luke have been spending a bit too much time together."

"No doubt," Cole agreed. "I'll make sure to keep Luke away from you guys this afternoon. It's smart to focus on the big stuff this morning. The temperature is supposed to skyrocket around noon."

"That was my feeling," I agreed as I sipped my coffee. "Even the lattes are better here," I said. I hadn't meant to say it out loud, but I earned triple smirks from the men in my life. "What?"

"I get that you're trying to temper your enthusiasm for Moonstone Bay because you don't want to get your hopes up in case things don't work out," Kade said. "But it's okay to have a good time. If things don't work out, we'll find another place to settle. I just want you to have a good time."

"I'm having a good time." It came out defensive. "Oh, just stuff it. I don't need your encouragement to have a good time. I'm a fun person."

"You're an absolute delight," Kade agreed.

"Totally." Cole sent me a knowing look. "I know when I think of Poet Parker, I think 'relaxed' and 'fun.'"

"I don't need this abuse." I sipped my latte again, my eyes narrowing when I saw two of the servers standing about five feet away with their heads bent together. They looked intense. Before I even realized what I was doing, I extended my magic to bolster my ability to hear them.

"What are they saying?" Cole asked.

"Hmm?" I dragged my eyes to him. "I wasn't eavesdropping." Whoops. I was being defensive again.

His lips curved. "Of course, you were. We all want to hear the dirt. Spill. Is there some big island to-do?"

"I'm ... not sure." I glanced back at the women, which included our server. "I think they said something about a body."

Cole's expression turned serious. After a few seconds of contemplation, he pasted a fake smile on his face and raised his hand to get our server's attention. She immediately crossed to him.

"Do you need something?" she asked.

"I could use more coffee," he replied. "Just out of curiosity, were you talking about a body?" He acted as if it was the most normal question in the world.

"Oh, you heard that?" The woman turned sheepish. "I didn't mean to be so loud. They're saying there are four bodies at the fairgrounds."

I immediately went rigid. "At the fairgrounds?"

"Four dead bodies?" Kade asked at the same time. He was already reaching for his wallet for a tip.

Cole remained calm. His background in law enforcement made him good in a crisis. "Are they tourists or locals?"

"Nobody is saying anything," the woman replied. "Sorry."

"It's fine." Kade shoved the bill and a huge tip in her hand. "Sorry we have to run. Breakfast was great. We'll be back."

The woman beamed at him when she saw the size of her tip. "Thank you so much. I'll look for you guys when you come back."

"We'll see you soon." Kade pressed his hand to my back to usher me toward the door. "Let's get over there. There's no reason to freak out — unless we have something to freak out about."

It was too late for that. Trouble had found us ... again. Now we had to mitigate it.

"NOW IS IT OKAY TO FREAK OUT?" LUKE demanded as we stood on the sidewalk and watched the crime scene techs work. The flashing lights from the emergency vehicles had been visible from the hotel, and we'd practically run to the fairgrounds. Unfortunately, the gossip from our server had been spot on. There were indeed four bodies near the fairgrounds. They'd been arranged in the shape of a cross.

"That's two body drops with religious overtones in as many months," Cole mused.

"At least the bodies aren't technically on the fairgrounds," I said. The bodies had been dumped across the road from the fairgrounds.

"It's close enough." Cole was grim as he made eye contact with Galen. "I think we're going to be questioned regardless."

I followed his eyes, squaring my shoulders when I realized the sheriff was coming to intercept us. He had a dark-haired woman with him, one I recognized from the brief flashes I'd gotten inside his head. "That's his girlfriend," I said, internally cursing myself for blurting it.

"Who?" Cole's gaze roamed my face. "The woman? Are you sure she's not part of his team?"

"She might be," I replied. "I saw her in his head when we met. He's not good at shuttering his emotions — or maybe he wasn't trying because his mind was on other things — but she's all over the memories I saw."

"Were the memories dirty?" Luke asked.

I shrugged. "They were … intimate. Nobody was naked," I added hurriedly when I saw Kade glaring at me. "I saw them laughing on the beach. He caught her when she was playing around in the surf and kissed her senseless. I think it was a memory from the night before he met us. That's why it was at the forefront of his brain."

"She's pretty," Kade mused.

Now it was my turn to glare.

"Not as pretty as you," he reassured me with a chuckle. "It makes sense that they're together. She's clearly not here in an official capacity and yet she's sticking close to him. I bet they work together in an unofficial capacity."

It made sense. "That means she's paranormal."

"I guess we'll find out." Cole shifted so he was the center member of the group. "Let me answer the initial questions. I want to feel him out on this."

It took Galen two minutes to reach us because he was continually waylaid by people working the crime scene. He answered their questions, feigning patience, but he almost looked relieved when he finally reached us.

"So, this probably isn't the scene you wanted to find when you headed here this morning," he started.

"We heard they found bodies on the fairgrounds," Cole replied. "The waitstaff was buzzing about it. That's why we're here so early. We weren't quite done with our breakfasts yet."

"Sorry about that." Galen shook his head. "Gossip spreads like herpes on this island."

"That's a lovely visual," Luke drawled.

Galen held out his hands. "I was still sleeping when I got word." He didn't introduce us to the woman with him, but I was interested enough to focus on her. Power practically radiated off her. It wasn't of a malevolent nature, it was … flowery. That was the best way I could describe it. There was a lightness about her that rarely manifested when an individual boasted so much power.

"What happened here?" Cole asked. He was grim as he regarded the bodies. "That seems like a rather pointed message."

"It does," Galen agreed. "We don't have anything other than what you see right now. I'm concerned that the bodies were dropped so close to the fairgrounds. It's an odd location."

I thought about the dreamcatcher we'd hastily erected the night before. Had the fairgrounds been the original target for the tableau? The dreamcatcher could've forced the killer to change course.

"What do you need from us?" Cole asked. He was all business now.

"I just have a few questions." Galen patted the front of his shirt, clearly looking for something. He frowned when he didn't find it.

"Here." The dark-haired woman handed him a small notebook that she'd procured from her pocket. "It was on the nightstand when I ran back up for my sunglasses this morning. I thought you might need it."

Galen shot her the sort of smile that could set curtains — or perhaps panties — on fire. "I knew there was a reason I loved you."

"Ugh." Luke groaned. "What a waste."

If Galen was bothered by the complaint, he didn't show it. "This is

Hadley Hunter." He inclined his head toward his girlfriend. "She helps me on cases sometimes."

"Hello." I spoke for the first time. As handsome as Galen was — and he was handsome — I was much more interested in her. The power that continuously moved through her aura made my skin hum. My magic was attracted to her magic. "I'm Poet Parker." I extended my hand.

Hadley took it without hesitation, and when our hands met there was an instant spark, powerful enough to make us both jerk our hands back.

"What was that?" Galen asked, his eyes on his girlfriend.

"Static," Hadley replied, although she didn't look certain of her response.

"Static?" Galen arched an eyebrow and focused on me.

I considered lying but given the fact that he was a shifter in love with a powerful witch, it didn't seem necessary. He lived on a paranormal island after all and knew more than most. "Our magic reacted," I replied, not thinking twice about telling the truth.

"In a bad away?" Kade asked.

"No." I flashed a smile. "It wasn't bad. It's just … a lot of power."

"Is your whole circus magical?" Galen asked. "I was told only certain members were."

"Not everybody," Cole replied. "Most of the performers are magical. The midway workers aren't. The clowns aren't. The janitorial staff isn't either. Only about a third of our people."

Galen pursed his lips and nodded. "Okay, well … I was told several members of your team were here late last night. Did you see anything out of the ordinary?"

Well, that answered that question. We hadn't seen a soul when we'd been working on the dreamcatcher. Apparently, we'd been seen, though. We would definitely have to be more careful.

"We were just checking on things," Kade replied. He knew better than to bring up the dreamcatcher without a serious discussion first. "We're not used to sleeping so far from our equipment. We wanted to make sure everything was okay before heading back to the hotel for the night."

"So you didn't see anything out of the ordinary?"

"Nothing," Kade replied. "It was quiet. We all commented on it. We thought it was awesome."

"Well, looks can be deceiving," Galen replied. "This island is rarely quiet. I might have more questions later, but we're good for now. If you have work to do, go ahead and hit it. We won't be here for very long. They don't like when we draw attention to bodies."

That was a weird thing to say, but I nodded all the same. "I hope it comes together for you fast."

"You and me both."

CHAPTER 4

"What do you think?" Cole asked when we were safely ensconced on the fairgrounds.

"I think that it's entirely possible this has nothing to do with us," I replied.

Cole snorted. "Since when have we ever been that lucky?"

"Poet is right," Kade interjected. "The bodies weren't found on the fairgrounds. This wasn't directed at us."

I felt the need to correct him, even though I was loath to do it. "Except we modified the dreamcatcher and made it so no violence could be carried out on the property. It's possible we forced the killer to adjust his or her plan."

Kade worked his jaw. "You think that's possible?"

I held out my hands. "Anything is possible."

"So, what do we do?" Cole blew out a sigh and shifted his attention to the other side of the road, to where Galen was hurrying his team along while Hadley gave him an earful about something.

"I don't know," I said. "If someone did try to drop the bodies here, there was a reason … and that reason can't be good."

"If it's any consolation, Galen seems like a straight shooter," Kade noted. "I don't think he's just going to assume we're to blame because we're members of a circus. His girlfriend though … ."

I felt Kade's eyes on me. "His girlfriend is a witch," I replied to the unasked question. "She's … powerful. She's somehow flowery at the same time. I don't know how to explain it."

"So she's not evil," Cole surmised. "That's good for us."

Was it? I didn't have an answer.

"Of course, she's evil," Luke countered. "She snagged that fine hunk of man for herself when he's clearly playing for our side."

I couldn't contain my laughter. "Clearly," I said dryly.

"He is." Luke insisted. "I have immaculate gaydar. He wants me."

"Don't let your imagination work overtime," I said, patting his head. "If you want to dream, he doesn't seem to care. As for Hadley … ." I blew out a sigh. "She's interesting. They're a strong unit. Even though she's not law enforcement, he brought her along because he wanted her take on the bodies. He trusts her."

"Lilac trusts her too," Cole offered. "She mentioned her last night. They're best friends. Lilac wouldn't be suckered in by an evil person."

"Maybe Lilac doesn't understand how insidious she's being," Luke suggested.

"Or maybe you're being ridiculous." Cole shook his head. "He's not gay. He loves his girlfriend. Get over it."

"But he's so hot," Luke whined.

"He can be hot without being into you."

"No." Luke shook his head. "That's against the rules."

"Well, clearly nobody explained the rules to him." Cole's eyes were probing when they landed on me. "I'll keep my ear to the ground. We need to be careful, but I don't think we should change our routine. We don't have enough information."

I agreed. "Until we know more, it's business as usual. Let's get set up. I want all the tents up by noon."

KADE WAS ANTSY SO HE SPENT THE morning running the perimeter. The proximity to the ocean bothered him. He said anyone could come from the water and infiltrate our safe haven. I wanted to argue that wasn't likely, but because it had happened once before —

with dire consequences — I let him be. It was better to let him obsess about that than go off on a tangent.

I dropped my personal belongings inside my tent when the crew had finished erecting it. The island was hot — stiflingly so — and we had to break out the fans. I was certain we'd packed them, and I just needed to find them so I could start doling them out. I headed toward the midway with that intention. It would be just like Mark Lane — the tool who ran the midway — to hoard them.

I pulled up short at the sound of voices as I rounded the corner of the ticket booth. One of them belonged to Mark. I wasn't afraid to throw down with him — it had happened multiple times over the years — but it sounded as if he was already engaged in an argument, and I wanted to hear that out before I moved on him.

"I'm not stupid," Mark insisted, causing me to roll my eyes. He was often stupid, and deliberately so. He was also manipulative, to the point I didn't trust him one iota.

The answering voice was a surprise. Max normally didn't bother helping with setup operations. He was more of a figurehead than anything else these days. He left the day-to-day operations of the circus to me. The fact that he was here now had my curiosity sensors burning.

"I didn't say you were stupid, Mark," Max replied in an even voice. I had to crane my neck to see him. They stood between two of the game booths, and Max's stance told me he wasn't happy with the direction of the conversation. "I said you were being stupid. There's a difference."

"Not really," Mark replied dryly. His hair was like a grease pit, and I cringed when he ran his fingers through it and then sniffed them. That wasn't gross or anything.

"I'm not sure why you called me here," Max said. His tone told me he wasn't in the best of moods. Of course, that could have nothing to do with life and everything to do with the fact that Mark was an oily bastard who rubbed everyone the wrong way.

"I called you here because you refuse to schedule the meeting I've asked to be put on the books the past three weeks." Mark's voice was shrill. "I'm sorry I had to use underhanded methods to get you down here, but you refuse to engage with me otherwise."

"First, I didn't put the meeting on the books because we were enjoying our downtime," Max shot back. "I was in and out of Florida for the duration of the month and I had people I wanted to spend time with while we were there. It's our downtime for a reason. We enjoy life and don't think about work."

"Whatever." Mark made a face. "I know what you're doing, Max. I know what we're doing here."

"Here in the fairgrounds?" Max's face remained blank. "I believe if you don't know what we're doing in the fairgrounds at this point then we have bigger worries."

"I'm talking about this stupid island," Mark snapped. "I know you think I'm oblivious to the other part of this circus, the part your son and his pretty little girlfriend run together, but I'm not. This island has a certain reputation, same as that Romani girl you continue to favor, and you're not hiding anything with this visit."

I bristled but remained in the shadow of the ticket booth to listen.

"Her name is Poet, and I don't care for your tone, Mark." There was warning in the way Max shifted. "As for Moonstone Bay, I'm thrilled you did your research. That shows real growth. Most of the time you only care about yourself. Kudos."

"I still only care about myself," Mark fired back. "That's not going to change. That's why I called you here. I want you to know that I know what you're up to."

Max folded his arms across his chest. "And what's that?"

"You're planning on disbanding the circus."

"I don't believe that conversation has ever been held. Why would I disband my own business?"

Mark threw up his hands in frustration. "Fine. Maybe 'disband' is the wrong word. You plan to keep it operational, but you won't travel any longer. You're eyeing this location as a permanent spot."

"What makes you think that?" Max's inflection didn't change but his gaze grew stronger. I'd often wondered why he insisted on keeping Mark, who was a complete and total jerk. He was vague with his responses, always sticking to the money angle. Mark brought in the most money. That often earned him a pass. Today, though, Max looked as if he'd had his fill of the midway chief.

"Not to repeat myself, but I'm not an idiot. Your son's girlfriend and her merry band of morons aren't nearly as sly as they think they are. That blond one, the one with the big mouth, the gay one … ."

Max held up his hand to silence Mark, and even though the midway chief was bold, he wasn't stupid. "You want to be very careful about what you say next," he warned. "Luke's sexuality has nothing to do with anything. If you believe it does, we're going to have a different sort of problem."

Mark glowered at him. "Oh, give me a break. I don't care if he's gay."

"And yet you brought it up."

Mark threw his hands in the air, frustration getting the better of him. "Knock it off, Max. I heard rumors in Florida. Apparently, Luke was chatting with Nellie and people heard him mention settling on this island permanently. That is not going to happen."

"Oh, really?" Max's lips twitched in amusement. "Since when do you tell me what I do with my circus?"

"Since I'm the one who brings in the most money."

"There are more important things than money."

"Say that again when you're broke," Mark seethed. "We're staying on the road for as long as humanly possible. I'm not moving to some paranormal stronghold so your pet freaks can play with the local freaks. I'm putting my foot down. We are not moving here.

"Now, if you want to talk about a permanent location, I insist on being part of the team that makes the decision," he continued, tugging on his shirt to smooth it. "I'm thinking Vegas is the place to be. It has a comfortable climate and even when it gets hot it's not humid to the point of dying … like this horrible place." He made a face as he gestured toward the ocean. "You need to let go of whatever dreams you have planned for this place."

Max didn't move a single muscle. "Are you done?"

I recognized the tone and shrank back. He was angry. This wouldn't end well.

Mark, ever stupid, didn't pick up on the signs. "I guess I'm as done as I'm going to be."

"Then let me tell you something," Max said in an icy voice. "You're not in charge of my circus. You don't get a vote. You don't dictate terms. If I want to settle in one location, I'll settle there. If you don't like it, you can find another job."

Mark let loose a scathing snort. "Excuse me? I'm the only reason you make money."

"Your position can easily be filled by another individual."

"Oh, really? You might want to be careful, Max. If you keep pushing me, I'll call your bluff."

"Won't that be interesting?"

"I've had enough of this." Mark shook his head. "We're not staying here long term. That's all there is to it." He took off in a huff, not looking over his shoulder to meet Max's gaze. He was clearly unnerved. But that didn't mean he would back down.

"You can come out now, Poet," Max sang out, jolting me back to reality.

I was sheepish when I emerged from the side of the ticket booth. "I wondered if you sensed me." I sent him an apologetic smile. "I was looking for the fans. It wasn't my intent to eavesdrop, but I couldn't help myself when Mark started going at you."

"Mark is … Mark." Max leaned in to hug me when I was close enough. "How is my girl?"

He'd plucked me off the streets of Detroit and changed my life as a teenager. I'd used my magic to pick his pocket and was shocked when he caught me. Instead of punishing me, he'd offered me the chance of a lifetime. I grew up with a father, one I'd lost at a young age, but Max had slipped into the role of surrogate father without a single word of complaint. Sure, it was weird to think of him as my father when I was engaged to his son, but I tried not to dwell on it too much.

"I'm good." I offered a smile. "Well, other than the bodies discovered across the road. I'm assuming you heard."

"I did." Max prodded me with his hand to walk toward the big top. He seemed eager to get away from the midway. "Do we have any reason to assume the bodies have anything to do with us?"

"No, but ... well ... coincidences aren't really a thing in our world."

"Keep an eye on the situation. If anything crops up that I need to know about, I'll be around." He lightly grabbed my wrist and held up my hand to study the amethyst ring there. "How is engaged life treating you?"

"Pretty well. Kade is ... really excited. He keeps referring to me as his future wife and told Luke that he could no longer call me his girlfriend."

"Have you made any wedding plans yet?"

I shook my head. "We figured we would get this visit out of the way before focusing on that. Kade really likes to plan. He doesn't mind traveling like we do, but he's still new to it. I think we both want a permanent home at some point."

"And you think Moonstone Bay could be it?"

"It's far too soon to tell."

He released my hand. "What about the other thing?"

The hair on the back of my neck prickled. I didn't have to ask what he was referring to. He'd been the first one I called when the letter arrived in Florida. Even before I told Kade about it, I had Max on the phone.

"You mean my uncle?" I had to force out the words. I hadn't seen Uncle Sidney since I was a child. When my parents died, he hadn't been around. Even though I wasn't particularly close with him, I'd assumed he would swoop in at the last minute and save me from the system. Instead, he fell out of my life as if he'd never been there. Now he'd written a letter and informed me he would be in New Orleans when we arrived in two weeks. It was like a bomb ticking down in the back of my mind.

"Yes." Max slowed his pace, his eyes roaming my face. "You're upset."

"I'm not upset." The denial escaped before I could think better of it. Max could read me and would know I was lying. It was too late to haul the words back, so I simply held out my hands. "I don't know him. I have nothing to say to him. If he shows up in New Orleans, I'll make sure he knows that I want nothing to do with him and send him on his way."

Max didn't look convinced. "Poet ... ."

"It's fine," I insisted before he could get up a full head of steam. "I don't need reassurance, Max. Sidney was my father's brother. He was part of my life a long time ago. He's not part of my future."

"He clearly has an agenda."

"He probably wants money. I kind of remember him borrowing money from my parents when I was a kid. They tried to keep that stuff from me but there's one memory in particular ... ." I trailed off, frowning.

"If he's looking for money, direct him to me. I'll handle him."

That made me laugh. "I'm an adult, Max," I reminded him. "I'm marrying your son, for crying out loud. I'm also magical and can tap an elemental to set him on fire if I feel like it. I don't need you to protect me."

"I don't think of it as protecting you." He brushed my hair from my face in a fatherly manner. "I think of it as standing with you. I'm not afraid to handle this man. You were a child when you last saw him. If he is after something that you don't want to give, it's my place to see him off."

"He's my uncle."

Max sighed. "We'll figure it out when we get to New Orleans. For now, enjoy the island. Treat it like a pre-honeymoon with Kade. Have some fun."

"That's the plan." I flicked my eyes back to the road and saw Galen's team loading the bodies. A crowd, including two children, stood on the sidewalk watching the show. The boy and girl looked about ten years old. They held hands and for a moment I thought they were crying. When they looked up, I saw they were laughing.

A chill ran up my spine as the kids slowly tracked their eyes to me, almost as if they sensed me watching.

"That's weird," Max said after a few seconds. He'd noticed the children too. "I'm surprised they're allowed at a crime scene."

"It's a magical island," I reminded him. "The rules here might be different."

"I can't see them being that different."

"I guess we'll learn more the longer we're here." I shook myself out of my reverie. "Either way, I have work to do. We want all the big stuff up today."

"And have fun," he prodded.

"And have fun. That's tops on my list. I promise."

I filed my misgivings about Sidney's imminent visit away. Max was right. Now wasn't the time to dwell on it. Now was the time for sun and relaxation. The hard stuff would always be waiting.

CHAPTER 5

S etting up took a bit longer than I would've liked — the beach served as a distraction for almost everybody — but we finished by one o'clock. As predicted, I had to fight Mark for the fans. I knew what he was really agitated about when he refused to hand them over. Then Kade and Cole stepped in and Mark relented, though he remained surly as he watched the fans removed from the midway.

"That's one jerk of a dude," Cole noted as he wiped his forearm across his face, the last of the fans being placed in the tents. The heat had come in like a wall, oppressive and overbearing. "We're done. We'll have to account for each one of those fans tomorrow morning because I wouldn't put it past him to steal them back."

"If he does, then I'll have a different sort of meeting with him."

"Do you have the authority to fire him?" Cole almost looked hopeful. He wanted to take over the midway operations. I couldn't just hand him the job, however. Mark had a contract. If we could break the contract, things might shift in a way that would benefit all of us. Well, everybody but Mark.

"I don't, but he and Max were arguing today. He knows that we're looking at Moonstone Bay as a permanent home. He told Max he wouldn't allow it, and that irritated Max. We might be able to approach Max with our plan sooner."

"I still want to meet with Max on my own."

"Then schedule it." I turned to face him, hands on hips. "You're an adult and Max likes you. He won't give you a hard time over it."

"I planned on doing it after our trip here."

"I suggest doing it sooner. Now is a good time. Max is irritated. You're offering him a solution to his problem."

"Yeah." Cole rubbed his chin. "I'll set up a meeting for the next few days. Until then, how does lunch sound? I thought we could go back to Lilac's bar. She wants to make plans to hang out later. She has a full menu and I hear the food is great."

As if on cue, my stomach let out a ruthless growl. "Let's grab Kade and Luke first. I'm sure they're both starving."

"If you believe Luke, he's dying of starvation and has been for days. He could keel over at any moment."

"Then we'd better save him."

LILAC'S BAR WAS MOSTLY EMPTY WHEN WE ARRIVED, which surprised me. Then I reminded myself that we were having a late lunch. Given the heat, it was entirely possible mealtimes were earlier on Moonstone Bay.

"Hey!" Lilac hopped up from a long table she was sitting at with three other people. Two of them were recognizable faces — Galen and Hadley — but the third belonged to a handsome guy in a plain white T-shirt and a pair of well-worn jeans. "I was hoping to see you guys today."

Cole immediately headed for his cousin and gave her a hug. The guy I didn't know watched the exchange with speculative eyes. That's when it hit me: The guy was Lilac's boyfriend. He had a protective air about him as he watched her, but he didn't look as if he was going to hop to his feet and throw down with Cole, even if his girlfriend's affections for another man clearly bothered him. It was an interesting struggle to watch.

Lilac tore through introductions quickly. "This is Booker." She gestured to the guy in the white shirt, who was busy trying to steal fries from Galen's plate. "And this is Hadley. Guys, this is my cousin Cole and his friends Luke, Poet and Kade."

"I'm a little more than a friend," Luke replied, his lips curling.

"His boyfriend," Lilac corrected.

"I was going to say, 'the center of his world,' but sure." Luke's nose flared as he darted his eyes around. "What is that smell? Are you baking a cake?"

Booker straightened in his chair, alarm racing over his features. "What did you just say?"

Lilac let loose a choked laugh and waved her hand in front of her face, as if trying to cool herself.

"Cake," Luke repeated, oblivious to the others' reactions. "It smells … awesome. Red velvet cake. My favorite," he said as he began to prowl around the table.

I opened my mouth to ask if we should sit at a different table, but Luke caught my attention by moving closer to Booker. In that instant, everything I was going to say fell out of my head as Luke leaned close — so close his chest was practically plastered to Booker's back — and inhaled deeply.

"It's you." He looked both appalled and delighted as he pulled back and stared at Booker. "You're the cake."

"I'm not a cake," Booker shot back, jabbing a finger at Galen when the other man's shoulders started shaking with silent laughter. "It's not funny."

"What's not funny?" I was genuinely at a loss as I edged closer to Booker. I couldn't smell anything but piña coladas. Luke's sense of smell was keener than mine, but I could always smell cake. "I don't … understand." I unfurled my magic, something nudging at the corners of my mind. Booker was clearly a magical being, but he was somehow different from every other magical being I'd ever encountered. "What are you?" The question was out of my mouth before I could register how rude I sounded.

"He's a tool," Galen replied, wiping his mouth with a napkin. "He just refuses to acknowledge it."

"He's delicious." Luke rubbed his cheek against the back of Booker's dark head, reminding me of a cat that desperately wanted to be stroked. "Oh, you are … just the best thing ever."

Cole put up with a lot from Luke when it came to suggestive comments and overt flirting, but this was too much. "Seriously?" There was no amusement in his eyes as he watched his boyfriend fawn over Booker. "I'm right here … for now."

Luke jerked up his head, seemingly confused. "What do you mean? I just … seriously, do you not smell that? I swear my mouth is actually watering."

"It's not his fault," Lilac said hurriedly, placing her hand on Cole's arm to stop him before he could storm out of the restaurant. "I'm sorry. I didn't realize that he would be affected. He can't help himself."

Cole's fury wasn't diminished by his cousin's words. "We're supposed to be together and he's rubbing that guy."

Booker grabbed Luke's wrist and gave it a vicious twist. "And if he doesn't stop, I'll have to kill him."

"I don't understand," I interjected, stepping between Cole and the door before things spiraled out of control. "What's happening?" I grabbed Cole before he could sidestep his cousin. "Let's hear her out."

"You always take Luke's side," Cole complained. "I should've known this wouldn't be any different."

"I'm not taking Luke's side," I insisted. I meant it … mostly. "I'm confused. I've never seen him act like this."

"He's a cupid," Lilac volunteered quickly, ignoring Booker as he emitted a series of growls. "Luke can't help himself. If Booker was a female cupid, Luke wouldn't react. Luke is attracted to men, though … ." She trailed off, fixing a pleading look on her cousin. "It really isn't his fault. As soon as he's away from Booker's pheromones he'll return to normal and feel like an ass."

I was officially intrigued. "I've heard of cupids." I moved closer to Booker and stared into his annoyed eyes. "I think I've crossed paths with one or two — at least they claimed to be cupids — but I was never sure. This is … fascinating."

"I can think of a few other words to describe it," Kade said as he snagged the back of my shirt. "Are you attracted to him?" He looked worried at the prospect.

I took a moment to consider the question, my gaze bouncing between Kade and Booker. It was a fair question. From what Lilac was saying, I should be feeling the same as Luke. But I didn't. "No. I'm only attracted to you." I smiled. "Promise."

Kade looked back to Lilac. "I don't understand."

"I don't either." Cole's tone was still cold. "Perhaps your cupid is defective."

"I don't need this." Booker threw his napkin on the table and started to rise. Luke was still so close to him there wasn't enough room to navigate, and they bumped chests. "Dude, give me some space if you don't want me to kill you."

Luke looked as if he was ready to risk it. "You smell like the best thing ever. I can't stay away from you."

"It's not his fault," Lilac repeated, again for Cole's benefit. "As for Poet, that's a good question. Elementals can usually ignore the lure of cupid scent. But you're not an elemental." She cocked her head as if seeing me for the first time. "What are you?" The question wasn't meant to be rude. She was genuinely curious.

"I'm not exactly sure," I replied. "I was the only magical one in my family. They had no idea why I manifested. My parents died when I was a teenager, and I was on my own. I never had access to my family tree or anything. I guess you could say I'm an enigma."

Lilac smiled. "There are worse things to be." When she turned back to Cole, she was determined. "I swear this isn't his fault. Just … give me a second. I'll mix him a special drink. It should diminish what he's feeling, at least for a little while."

Cole didn't look thrilled, but he nodded as he sank into the chair next to Hadley. "I don't know how I feel about all of this," he admitted.

"I was confused at first too," Hadley offered. She was mowing her way through a plate of tacos and seemed to be enjoying the show. "I've seen it a few times now — always with women — so I'm kind of used to it."

"It never stops being entertaining," Galen drawled as he leaned back in his chair and slipped his arm around Hadley's back. "This is what you get for being the island sex symbol, dude."

"I really am going to kill you," Booker threatened. "I'm going to sneak into that lighthouse tonight and smother you with a pillow."

"You guys need to play your kinky games another time," Hadley warned, snickering when Galen pinched her hip. "What? I've always said that the snarkfest you guys share borders on sexual tension occasionally."

"Let's not go there," Galen warned, making a face when Luke encroached on Booker's territory yet again. "Okay, I'm going to save you because I can't deal with hiding a murder for Booker." He stood and grabbed Luke around the waist, lifting him and placing him in the chair next to Cole. "Stay there," he warned.

Luke looked pained. "But he smells so good."

"No." Galen shook his head. "You just think he does. He really smells like rancid fish and gym socks."

"Thanks, man," Booker said.

"Just trying to help." Galen pressed his hand to his heart and grinned.

Booker rolled his eyes until they landed on me. Unfortunately, I was still staring … even though I'd told myself it was rude and I should stop. "Do you have something you'd like to say?" he asked blandly.

"I have a million questions." I opted for the truth. "I might give you a list later."

When Booker smirked, it lit up his entire face. "Okay, you might not be so bad."

"She's engaged," Kade said. "To me. Just in case you were wondering."

Booker's grin grew broader. "I'm with Lilac." He pointed for emphasis. "You can breathe easy."

Kade turned sheepish. "Sorry. I'm confused."

"Perpetually," Luke said. He looked to be straining to get a better sniff of Booker. "Why red velvet cake?"

"Because it's your favorite," Booker replied, sighing when Lilac appeared with a tall glass of blue liquid and placed it in front of Luke. "Drink all of that, bud."

For a moment I thought Luke would fight the order. One look at Cole had him gripping the glass and downing the contents. He finished quickly, briefly shutting his eyes before letting loose a tremendous belch. "I'm sorry." He looked horrified. In Luke's world, bodily functions were not something to display. "That tasted like sewage."

"Drink a lot of sewage, do you?" Lilac grinned as she leaned in close to study his eyes. "You're already looking better. Your pupils are half of what they were a few seconds ago. Tell me how you feel."

"Um … ." Luke cocked his head, as if trying to ascertain the answer. "I feel pretty good," he said finally.

"Do you smell cake?"

"No, it's more like licorice now."

Lilac shrugged. "It's the best I can do." She shot an apologetic look to Booker. "I'm still working on the correct formula. If I want my boyfriend to be able to visit, I've got to have it at the ready most days."

"Yes, otherwise Booker has to run for his life," Galen teased. It was obvious he and Booker were friends, though not exactly friendly. It was a weird dynamic. They were almost like brothers. I was willing to bet they would fight to the death for one another. "There's nothing worse than having to peel a pile of teenage girls off him when they get a whiff. It's embarrassing."

"Says the guy who goes gooey whenever his girlfriend makes the water dance," Booker replied grumpily.

I had no idea what that meant but figured now was the time to redirect the conversation. "Do you mind if we join you?" I asked Galen.

"Knock yourself out." Galen smiled for my benefit as I settled with Kade on the opposite side of the table. "I assume you have questions about what happened near the fairgrounds."

"We're … concerned," I acknowledged. "We want to keep our people safe. Do you know anything?"

"Not really. The medical examiner has the bodies, but there are no marks on them. We have no idea how they died."

"Must be poison," Booker said. "I mean … that's the only thing that makes sense."

"Or magic," I mused, thinking back on the way the bodies had been arranged. "It looked ritualistic in fashion."

Hadley's eyes were keen when they locked with mine. "You know about ritualistic murders?"

"We've seen a few over the years," I replied. "We travel to a lot of different places, which means we've seen quite a few things."

"Have you ever seen anything like this?" Galen asked.

"Not exactly. I don't know enough about what you found to really comment, though," I said. "Who were the victims?"

"We don't have identities yet," Galen replied. "We're still working on that."

Cole shifted. He was still angry with Luke, who kept shooting adoring looks toward Booker, but he was also invested in keeping our group safe. His background in law enforcement made him curious. "So they must be tourists. You obviously know all the people who live on the island."

"In theory," Galen confirmed. "They could be tourists. We're checking the hotels. They could be construction workers. We've had quite a few move here temporarily because of the big resort construction project. They live in trailers in the woods in that area. I'll be stopping in after lunch to see if any of them have gone missing."

"Were they all men?"

"Yup."

"Seems someone should be missing them," Cole said. "When will you know cause of death?"

"Hopefully by the end of the day. We only have one medical examiner."

"Right." Cole rolled his neck, his mind obviously working at a fantastic rate. "And if you find out it was poison?"

"Then I start digging. Unfortunately, on a magical island, there's more than one type of poison."

That wasn't surprising. I wanted to offer our services to help but refrained. If he thought I was too eager to get involved, he might start looking at us harder.

"Let us know if you need anything," I said. "I hope this is a one and done for you guys."

"Me too." Galen shifted his eyes to Hadley. "There are other things I'd rather be doing than investigating ritualistic murders."

"Oh, baby," she cooed, batting her eyelashes in theatrical fashion. "You say the sweetest things."

He laughed, as I'm sure she'd intended. "That's my goal in life. Always."

CHAPTER 6
Six

"How about a tour?" Lilac asked when we'd finished lunch. She'd kept a firm eye on Luke for the duration and I had a feeling it was to protect him, not Booker.

"You want to give us a tour?" Cole's eyebrow arched as his gaze drifted to us. "Sounds pretty good to me."

"I'm in," I confirmed. I wanted to see what Moonstone Bay had to offer. On the surface, it was beautiful. Every place had secrets, though, and there was no one better to get them from than a longtime resident.

"I think it sounds fun," Kade confirmed with a grin as he focused on Booker. "Although ... ." He didn't finish what he was saying. He didn't have to. The problem was apparent.

"Oh, don't worry about me," Booker said as he stood, digging for his wallet. He pulled out a hundred-dollar bill and dropped it on the table. "I have to get to work. I've already stayed longer than I should have."

Lilac frowned disapprovingly at the money. "What did we talk about?" she prodded.

When Booker smiled at Lilac it lightened up his entire face. I'd been wondering what she saw in him — other than looks — until that moment. The air positively zinged between them. "We talked about the fact that I'm going to over tip you because otherwise it's weird."

"No, we talked about you eating here for free and not tipping because otherwise it's weird," Lilac corrected.

"Well, I can't do that." His smile never diminished. "I don't expect you to wait on me."

"I brought you lunch and a drink. I hardly consider it servitude."

"I'm not taking it back." He took a step toward her, jabbing a finger in Luke's direction as he crossed. "Don't even think about it," he warned before tapping Lilac's chin to get her to look up. "I'll see you later?" He looked worried that she might turn him down.

Instead, she let out a long sigh. "I guess."

He gave her a quick kiss, but the look they shared suggested he wished he had more time to drag things out. "I'll text when I know what time I'll be finished."

"I'll walk you out," Galen said, his hand landing on Booker's shoulder. It was clear he had something serious he wanted to talk with the other man about in private. "Hadley, I'm assuming you're going on the tour with Lilac?"

Hadley bobbed her dark head. "I'm not going to miss the chance to meet magical people."

He leaned in and gave her a kiss. "Don't get into trouble, okay?" He was serious. "I've got a lot going on and I don't need extra distractions."

Hadley's eye roll was pronounced. "I don't ever find trouble."

Galen's snort was loud. "Right. I'll text when I know what time I'll be done. We'll talk about dinner then."

"Yeah, yeah, yeah." Hadley's wave was breezy. "I expect a massage later for that 'trouble' remark. I'm a pillar of this community and want to be treated as such."

Galen might boast a gruff exterior but his love for his girlfriend made him look like a marshmallow in my book. "I'll treat you accordingly later."

Lilac didn't even wait for the men to exit before turning talk to the tour. "I figured we'd walk. It's hot, but if we take bottles of water, it will be fine. Plus, other than Booker's van, we don't have a vehicle big enough for all of us."

"Can we see everything if we walk?" I asked.

"Not everything," Lilac replied. "If you want to see the wilds, you'll need a vehicle. But we can see everything in town."

That was good enough for me. "Lead the way."

WE STARTED AT THE LIGHTHOUSE, wandering inside to our hearts' content. I wasn't certain what to expect but it was actually homey. It was obvious Hadley and Galen weren't sticklers about cleaning. Their stuff was spread all over the place. It wasn't dirty, though. It was ... welcoming.

"We're having a standoff," Hadley explained to my unasked question as I studied the pile of clothes next to the oversized chair in the far corner of the room. "Galen likes to tease me about being domestic so I'm trying to see how bad things have to get before he does the laundry."

I scratched my cheek, trying to imagine Kade letting a pile of clothes hang out for more than twenty seconds. "How is that working out for you?"

"It's turned into a game," Hadley admitted. "He doesn't mind doing housework, but this is more than that. It's about one of us winning."

"What does the winner get?"

"Bragging rights ... and a massage ... and maybe something else." She averted her gaze quickly, her cheeks turning pink.

"Hadley and Galen play weird sex games," Lilac offered. "Half the island wants to strangle them because they're so obnoxious. I think they're cute."

"We are cute," Hadley said.

"Yes, but you're easy to amuse." Lilac winked at her before focusing on Cole. "You seem more intense than I remember. Is something going on?"

If Cole was surprised by the question, he didn't show it. "I don't know what you mean."

"You're not here just to work." Lilac was blunt — something I liked — and she clearly had no intention of backing down. "You're here to scope out the island."

Cole darted his eyes to me. "I think you're seeing something that isn't there," he hedged.

I decided to save him from himself. "We're looking for a permanent place to settle," I interjected, drawing Lilac's attention. "We realize that staying on the road isn't feasible for the long haul. We all love working for the circus. The idea of settling on a paranormal island holds some appeal."

"Really?" Lilac looked delighted at the prospect. She sidled closer to Cole and beamed. "I would like it if you were here."

Cole returned her smile. "I've missed you. You're one of the few relatives I genuinely love. You can't tell people what we're considering yet." He was stern. "Poet was supposed to keep her mouth shut until we'd talked to our boss. That's what we agreed on."

"I didn't want you to have to lie — and badly — to your cousin," I shot back. "She should know what we're considering. We still don't know if Moonstone Bay will be a good fit."

"What are your concerns?" Hadley asked. "I'm one of the newest residents here, so I might be a good person to tap for information."

"Well, how openly can you wield magic here?"

"Two weeks ago, we had plane doors opening everywhere and Godzilla appeared on the beach," Hadley replied, not missing a beat. "A shark shifter changed on the fly and took him down. Nobody said a word."

I laughed at the picture she was painting. "Godzilla?"

"Baby Godzilla."

"Interesting." I felt comfortable sharing with Lilac. "Not all of our people are magical. We have … an eclectic bunch."

Lilac looked directly at me. "You said you don't know what you are."

"I don't, but I'm guessing it's a mixture of witch and a few other things. My mind magic is stronger than that of other witches. It's possible I'm just a magical mutt."

Kade growled. "I don't like when you put yourself down."

"It wasn't meant as an insult," I said. "More like a magical observation."

"I still don't like it."

"We have a variety of magic at our disposal," I explained for Lilac's benefit. "We have several shifters, a lamia, a set of pixie twins, a dwarf from another plane, a magical strongman, two mages and Cole."

Lilac nodded. "We have all those here. I don't see how you guys moving here will be a problem. It's the permanent circus that will be an issue. You'll have to get it past the DDA."

"Will that be a problem?"

Hadley grumbled.

"They're always a problem," Lilac replied. "But they might like the idea. A circus is a draw. You guys are paranormal, so that should make things easier. You need a plan to pitch, and we need to get one of the DDA members on our side." She turned to Hadley. "I'm thinking Galen's mother is our best shot."

"Galen's mother is on the DDA?" That seemed unusual.

Hadley bobbed her head. "I'll talk to Galen about it tonight."

"Maybe we should make sure that we really want to consider this place first," Cole suggested. "We need to know the ins and outs before we decide. We need to know the things you don't include in the brochure, Lilac."

I didn't miss the furtive glances Lilac and Hadley shared.

"The island is mostly straightforward," Lilac said. "The sirens have a stronghold on the far side of the island and keep to themselves. There's a coven of witches on that side who occasionally cause a few issues, but they've been quiet lately.

"The plane doors were a significant issue," she continued. "You can't open plane doors here. If members of your group do that, it won't be tolerated."

"That would only affect Nellie, Naida and Nixie," Cole noted. "They're all from different planes ... though I don't think they visit home very often."

"Not ever," I confirmed. "We can make sure they don't break the rules. What else?"

"There will be little things that throw you," Lilac said. "Our local salon owner is a koala shifter, for example, so she's clingy. The wolves run the beach ragged during the full moon. There is one other thing." She looked uncomfortable. "I think it's better to show you."

"The cemetery?" Hadley asked.

Lilac nodded.

THE WALK TO THE CEMETERY SEEMED to take forever. In reality, it was only ten minutes, but the heat made it feel like years.

"You'll get used to it," Hadley said as she trudged along the sidewalk next to me. "The heat, I mean. I thought I was going to die when I first got here. Dehydration is a real thing. You'll figure out pretty quickly that you need to drink water throughout the day if you don't want to get cramps."

"Good to know." I shot her a small smile. "Do you like it here?"

"Yeah. I wasn't sure I would at first. When I got word that my grandmother had left me a lighthouse, I didn't know what to expect. I realized relatively quickly that I'd found my home."

"Galen?"

Her smile was instantaneous. "I love Galen. I feel like we belong together. We somehow … fit. It's more than him, though. My grandfather is here. He owns a farm inland. I've made friends. This place feels like home if you know what I mean."

"I haven't had a home for a long time," I said. "We're always on the road. I didn't think I wanted a home until recently."

"Kade?" Hadley teased, mimicking my tone from when I brought up her boyfriend.

"I guess he's part of it," I confirmed. "We're happy. There was a time in my life I didn't know if that was possible. The engagement got me to thinking. We want children … eventually. You can't take children on the road. They need roots."

"I get that." Hadley bobbed her head. "How much of a hurry are you in?"

"We have time. We have contracts that run through the next year at least. We would want to strike a deal with your DDA and then plan for the future. Not all our workers would want to move here. It would take time to get all the pieces in place."

"So, at least a year," Hadley mused.

"I'm guessing more like eighteen months, but we'll see. I … ." We rounded a corner and I smacked into an invisible wall of dread. My inner danger alarm dinged in fantastic fashion, and I turned swiftly, grabbing Kade by his shirt and shoving him away from whatever was incoming.

He caught me before he fell off the curb, his eyes wide. "What is it?"

"Evil," I replied, my heart clogging in my throat. "There's evil here."

Cole reacted without thinking, his hands catching fire as he scanned the bushes. Luke's fingers elongated into claws as he prepared for battle. Lilac hopped between us before we could start battling invisible forces.

"Don't," she instructed, shaking her head. Her hand closed over Cole's fingers, forcing him to extinguish the fire. "Nothing will attack."

"This place is evil," I insisted, my eyes going to a large wall constructed of coral. "What is this?" I asked.

"It's the cemetery," Lilac replied, glancing around to make sure nobody had witnessed our collective freak-out. "Come on." She linked her fingers with Cole's and tugged. "I promise it's okay. I won't let anything hurt you."

We followed Hadley and Lilac in silence as they led us to the rear of the cemetery wall, where a huge window allowed us to peer inside … except there was nothing to see. The cemetery was quiet, nothing but the pervasive feeling of evil I'd picked up as we approached the property.

"Several years ago, someone hexed the cemetery," Lilac explained. "We have no idea who or why. All we know is that every night at dusk, the residents crawl out of their graves and wander. At dawn they crawl back into their graves. It happens every night like clockwork."

I was dumbfounded. "Zombies?"

"Yeah." Lilac rubbed her cheek.

"And there's a window," Luke noted. He didn't look as bothered as the rest of us as he moved near the glass and lifted his nose to scent the area. "Ugh. You can smell the death. What's with the window?"

"Residents have loved ones here," Lilac replied. Her gaze was on

Hadley. "The locals like to sit on the bench sometimes and see the people they buried here."

That was beyond morbid. "You can't be serious." I said "Zombies are dangerous. The people you loved are long gone. You can't let zombies wander unchecked. You have to destroy them."

Lilac pinned me with a serious look. "Before you go any further, you should know that Hadley's mother is one of the zombies."

I felt sick to my stomach. "I'm sorry." When I turned to Hadley, she was standing at the window, her face blank. "That's terrible. I didn't mean … I didn't … ."

"It's okay." Hadley held up her hand. "There are times I think it's best to take all of them out. But when I really think about it, I feel sick at the prospect."

"The zombies are contained," Lilac insisted. "We're still trying to find a way around the hex. It's a work in progress. No new bodies are buried in the cemetery. We've built another one on the other side of town. I just thought you should know about this one in case it affects your decision regarding the island. Not everybody is okay coexisting with zombies."

She had that right. I rolled my neck. "We should probably talk about it as a group," I said.

"That's exactly what I would do in your position," Lilac said. "In fact … ." Whatever she was going to say died on her lips when a bolt of magic — a big purple ball of doom — slammed into her. The magic hit with enough force that Lilac was knocked against the wall. Her shoulder absorbed most of the blow, but her head grazed the frame of the window, and she looked dazed when she hit the ground.

"Lilac!" Hadley raced toward her friend. She advanced only two feet before she was hit with a similar barrage, causing her to trip and smack her head into the cement bench. She went down hard enough that the sound echoed.

Then I heard it. Laughter. Only it wasn't the sort of laughter that warmed the soul. No, this was the sound of diabolical hatred … and it sounded as if it was coming from children.

"Duck!" Cole roared as another burst of magic hurtled toward us.

He deflected the magic to a nearby tree, his fire mixing with whatever was being lobbed at us and causing a willow to go up in purple flames.

I did the only thing I could do and covered my face. I didn't have enough magic to shield us from whatever our attacker had planned, and there seemed to be no end in sight.

"Here it comes again!" Luke screamed.

I braced for impact, telling myself that I needed to find the source the second there was an opening. This time, the outside magic ran into a magical wall. The explosion was terrific, and yet nothing made it through to endanger us. When I glanced up, I found Kade had erected a shield. His face was fierce, his eyes wild, and the power radiating off him was out of this world.

"There!" Cole pointed to a small hill on the opposite side of the road.

I had to squint to see through the smoke, and what I found staring at us was chilling. Children, a boy and a girl, laughed as they watched us hunker down behind Kade's shield. They sounded demented, as if they were having a grand time pulling wings off butterflies.

"We need to give as good as we get," I said as I crawled to Cole. "Kade, keep that shield up until we tell you to drop it," I ordered.

He nodded, a muscle working in his jaw.

I pressed my hands to Cole's shoulder, meeting his gaze for a split-second. I could amplify his powers. We'd done it before. "Are you ready?" I asked.

He nodded. "Let's do this."

"Now!" I roared at Kade.

He dropped the shield the same moment he fired a volley of magic toward the kids. The girl — I recognized her from the fairgrounds earlier — looked momentarily stunned when Kade's magic hit her square in the chest. She pitched backward, her legs flying into the air. When she hit the ground, she turned into a plume of smoke and disappeared.

The boy seemed shocked. His mouth was still open when Cole's fire magic engulfed him. He went rigid, a silent scream frozen on his face as the fire consumed him. When he exploded, a similar plume of violet smoke escaped.

"What the hell was that?" Luke demanded as he crouched protectively next to Hadley, who appeared unconscious.

That was a very good question. What in the ever-loving fairy freak was going on here?

CHAPTER 7
Seven

W e called Galen as Kade used his healing magic to bring her around. She was dazed, but the confusion quickly gave way to fury.

"Who was it?" she demanded as she rubbed the side of her head, frowning when her fingers came back covered in blood. "I didn't have a brain injury, did I? You didn't like … see brain matter anywhere?"

Kade arched a speculative eyebrow.

"You're fine," I reassured her, hunkering down in front of her as Kade went to help Lilac. "Galen is on his way."

"Where is Cole?" Lilac asked, her eyes wary as Kade tentatively reached out to touch her shoulder. "No funny business," she warned.

Kade made a face. "I'm engaged."

That made Lilac smile despite the pain. "That doesn't stop most people from getting handsy."

"Well, I love my fiancée. Even if I didn't, I'm not the sort of guy who gets off touching a woman for no good reason."

"Oh, you're cute." Lilac pressed her finger into Kade's cheek, ignoring his grimace, and smiled at me. "He's like a big, loyal watchdog."

"He's way more than that," I said. "Let him heal you. He's getting good at it."

"Getting?" Lilac went back to staring at Kade. "Is this something new?"

"Kind of," he said. "Just hold still."

I pushed Hadley's hair from her temple to study the spot where she'd struck the bench. "Other than the blood, you can't tell anything happened." I attempted a smile. "How do you feel?"

"I'm okay," Hadley reassured me. "I'm just afraid that my brains are smeared all over that bench. If so, I'm going to have to collect them. Of course, I don't want to touch brains, which complicates things."

"It's a conundrum," I agreed on a smile. "Just ... sit still for a few minutes. I'll get you some water." I turned, intent on finding one of the bottles we'd dropped when the kids attacked, but my attention was drawn to pounding footsteps from the east side of the cemetery wall. I wasn't surprised to see Galen rounding the corner.

"There he is." Hadley beamed at him from her spot on the ground. "I almost died. You're going to have to massage me for hours tonight to make up for it."

Galen's chest heaved when he saw her, relief temporarily taking over his expression. "You're okay."

"I'm great," she reassured him. She almost sounded giddy. "I think my brains might've been spread all over the bench, but I'm fine now."

Galen dropped to his knees next to her, his nostrils flaring. "Where did this blood come from?"

"My head," Hadley replied. "I just told you I lost brains."

Galen pulled her to him for a hug, bewilderment clouding his eyes as he pressed his cheek to the top of her head.

"She seems a little ... happy," I noted.

"It's the euphoria that comes from almost dying," Lilac volunteered as she rotated her shoulder. Kade had clearly healed her when I wasn't looking because she seemed much more mobile than she had a few seconds earlier. "That's a pretty neat trick you've got, buddy." She grinned at Kade. "What's up with that healing magic?"

Kade glanced at me, uncertain.

"He's part mage," I volunteered, "and part human. He's learning about his mage half, which apparently can heal. He's been practicing."

"The practice seems to be working," Cole said as he appeared from the other side of the cemetery. He looked frustrated. "There's nobody else out here. Those kids were either alone and somehow transported themselves to another location ... or they're dead."

"What kids?" Galen stroked Hadley's hair, holding her so tight I was surprised she could breathe. "I need to hear the story from the beginning."

I opened my mouth to respond but Lilac sent me a small, almost imperceptible headshake. "Let me," she said as she slowly got to her feet. She kept one hand on Kade's shoulder to balance herself — she seemed to be testing her strength — and then sent him another smile before releasing him. "I want you guys to settle on Moonstone Bay for that healing ability of his alone."

"Lilac, I need to know what happened," Galen insisted. "If someone needs to be killed for hurting my Hadley, I want to know who I should be looking for."

"I don't know that there is anybody to look for," Lilac said. "I think Kade and Cole killed them ... I'm not sure." She rubbed her chin, as if debating, and then focused on Galen. "We brought them here to tell them about the cemetery. They might want to relocate here permanently, and we thought it best they know about the island's quirks."

"I don't need to know why you brought them here," Galen growled. "I need to know what happened."

"I'm not exactly sure." Lilac chose her words carefully. "We were talking, explaining how the cemetery works, and then it happened. It hit me first. It came out of nowhere. I didn't sense anything before it happened."

"What happened?" Galen demanded.

"A magical assault," Cole explained. "The magic was purple. I've never seen anything like it. It slammed Lilac into the wall. Hadley tried to run to her, but it hit her next ... hard."

"Really hard," Hadley agreed. "The last thing I remember is my face hurtling toward that bench. I thought I was a goner."

Galen gripped her tighter. "Please don't say things like that. You're fine."

"Because Kade healed me." She smiled at Kade. "My hero."

"If you keep fawning over him, I'll have to kill him," Galen warned.

"Step back, big guy," Hadley said, patting his chest. The more she talked, the more drunk she sounded. I was starting to think there was something to Lilac's euphoria theory.

"It was kids, Galen," Lilac said, drawing the sheriff's attention back to her. "They were on the hill over there. Kade threw up a shield that kept us protected and gave us time to mount an assault. Well, gave them time, I should say. I was still out of it and Hadley was unconscious. They saved us."

A muscle worked in Galen's jaw. "How did it end?"

"Kade took out the girl." Lilac was matter-of-fact. "He fired magic at her and she kind of … exploded into smoke. Cole did the same to the boy."

"They're dead?" Galen craned his neck to see the spot Lilac indicated. "I don't see any bodies."

"They didn't leave bodies behind. They just … poofed. The smoke dissipated. I'm not sure if they died or if we're dealing with something else."

Galen prodded. "Did you recognize them?"

"No." Lilac shook her blond head. "I've never seen them. I don't think they were local."

"Then someone brought them to the island." Galen turned his eyes to Hadley, who was tracing her fingers over his cheek.

"You're so pretty," Hadley cooed. "Have I mentioned how much I love you? It's a lot. Like this big." She held out her arms as far as they would go. "Not just because you're pretty. You have a big heart and you're really good in bed."

"Thank you, baby." Galen smiled indulgently before pressing a kiss to her forehead. When he looked up again, his gaze was on Kade. "How long will this last?"

"I don't know." Kade shrugged. "I've never quite had this reaction after a healing."

"I'm telling you it's the euphoria." Lilac was full of determination when she crossed to Hadley. She was all smiles when she squatted down in front of her friend. "I'm going to kiss your boyfriend if you don't snap out of it," she warned. "He's going to like it, even though he'll deny it."

Hadley snorted. "You're not going to kiss Galen. You're too in love with Booker, even though you guys are determined to pretend you don't love each other." Hadley struggled to a sitting position that wasn't contingent on Galen holding her up. "I'm feeling a little more normal now. I'm really hungry. If you feed me, I'll be back to my old self by the time we're done."

"Now there's an option." Galen smiled as he rubbed her back. "How does dinner sound to everybody else?"

"We should have dinner at the fairgrounds," I said. My mind had been working at a fantastic rate since the attack ... and I had some questions. "We'll be alone there. We have barbecue equipment. We can handle steak, corn, potatoes and salads for everybody."

Galen hesitated and then nodded. "I guess that sounds good. We do need to talk."

"We do," I agreed. "Whatever happened here today was just the start. We're nowhere near done with this."

Galen's lips firmed into a hard line. "Let me take Hadley home and get her changed. We can be at the fairgrounds in two hours."

I checked the clock on my phone screen. "Perfect. I'll get our people there so we can break things down. We need to be prepared next time. I'm guessing the next attack will be more coordinated."

"That's a sobering thought," Galen said as he touched his fingers to the blood drying on Hadley's forehead. "I don't want this happening again."

He wasn't the only one.

BY THE TIME we reached the fairgrounds, most of our team was present thanks to a mass text. None of them looked happy.

"Kids attacked you?" Raven demanded as she helped me shuck corn. She was a centuries-old lamia and yet she never put up a fuss when it came to helping with dinner.

"I don't know that they were really kids," I said, my eyes drifting to the street. Galen had just parked, and he, Hadley, Booker and Lilac were approaching. "They poofed — like they were made of magic. I've never seen anything quite like it."

"What about the magic they hit you with?" Naida demanded. "You said it was purple. What kind of magic was it?"

"That I don't know." I held out my hands. "I didn't get up close and personal with it. Whatever it was, it knocked Lilac for a loop and almost killed Hadley."

"Hadley was almost killed thanks to the collision with the bench," Cole countered from his spot at the picnic table. "We don't know what the magic would've done to her. It was the head injury that almost did her in."

"Yeah, let's not say things like that, huh?" Galen growled as he arrived at the table. He ushered Hadley to a spot at one end and cracked a bottle of water before handing it to her. "Drink up, baby."

"Is she better?" I asked. I was almost afraid of the answer.

"She's no longer drunk," Galen replied as he squeezed his girl-friend's shoulder. "She feels like she has a hangover."

"I'm fine," Hadley insisted. "I'm just a little … slow, if that makes sense."

"I'm hoping a good night's sleep gets her back to normal." Galen kissed the top of Hadley's head and then drifted closer to us. "I've had uniforms looking for the kids you described the past two hours. Nobody has seen them. I think they're dead."

"If they were ever alive in the first place," Cole said. "We don't even know what we're dealing with. All we know is those kids packed a wallop and they turned into smoke when we used our magic on them. That doesn't mean they're dead. It just means they stopped throwing magic at us."

"Fair enough." Galen sat next to Hadley and prodded her to drink her water, his eyes narrowing when he caught sight of Nellie wandering past several tents as he patrolled the fairgrounds. "Is that dude wearing a dress?"

"That's Nellie," Cole said. "He's a dwarf from another plane."

"He likes cross-dressing," Luke added. "He says that his bits need to breathe. He doubles as our bearded lady."

"Awesome." Galen shook his head. "He's not supposed to be walking around with an ax."

"I look forward to you telling him that," Luke said with a grin.

"I think I'll pass," Galen said. "As for the kids … I don't know what to do about them. Nobody has filed a missing person report, so it's not as if I can broadcast what happened."

"You've been having trouble with kids," I pointed out, my mind going back to the previous day. "Lilac told us that you were dealing with a bunch of mischief complaints."

Galen balked. "Yeah, but those were nothing. Graffiti, off-color chalk drawings — and there were some water balloons being thrown. That's not the same as magically trying to kill you guys."

"No, but maybe your general mischief is tied to our magical assault," I suggested.

"I … don't … know." Galen flicked his eyes to Booker, frowning when he realized the fire elemental was using Lilac as a human shield. Nixie and Naida had abandoned their work in the kitchen and were busily sniffing him from the other side of his half-demon lover.

"Uh-oh," I muttered when I realized what was happening. "This isn't good."

"He's a cupid," Raven noted as she studied Booker. "They can't help themselves from being turned on. He has that effect on people."

"Yes, and it's the bane of my existence," Booker snapped. "Down, girls."

I had to bite back a laugh at his growl. "Isn't there a way we can turn this off?" I directed the question at Lilac. "You have that special drink."

Lilac nodded. "I do, but they're pixies. It won't work on them."

"He smells fabulous," Nixie purred as she tried to edge around Lilac. "Like peanut butter cups."

"He smells like sushi," Naida countered.

I pressed the heel of my hand to my forehead. "There must be a way to fix this. We need to work together to figure this out."

"I have an idea on that front." Lilac raised her hand when it looked like Naida might run her over to get to Booker. "Please don't make me set you on fire. It's the last thing I want, but I won't have a choice if you keep throwing yourself at my man."

"That might be the hottest thing you've ever said," Booker said, jutting out a finger when he saw Luke crossing toward him. "No!"

"Tell me your idea," I demanded. This was quickly getting out of hand. "We need to focus on those kids, not … whatever is happening here."

"It's called hormones," Hadley offered helpfully. "Booker kicks everybody's hormones into overdrive unless they have elemental blood or some other form of magical barrier."

"Lovely." I met Lilac's steady gaze. "What's your idea? Seriously. Naida can create tornadoes if we're not careful. You can create fire out of thin air, so I'm guessing that's a bad combination."

"Your boyfriend," Lilac sputtered, her eyes burning as her hair flashed pink. "Don't make me hurt you, little fairy," she snapped at Nixie when the pixie made a grab for Booker's butt.

"Kade?" I was beyond confused.

"He can shield," Lilac gritted out. "Make him shield Booker. That will at least allow us to get through a meal without a murder."

I looked at Kade with renewed hope. "Can you do that?"

It was obvious the idea had never occurred to him. Now that it had been brought up, however, he appeared intrigued. "Can't hurt to try."

"Do it fast," Booker ordered, his chest pressed to Lilac's back. "I do not want to start a war between magical factions."

We had to put an end to this, and now. "Kade, this is getting ugly."

"I'm on it." Kade moved to the other side of the table. "Just … give me a bit of room."

"I want to dip my sushi in soy sauce," Naida argued. "Why would I wait to do that?"

"Move faster," Booker hissed. "I hate soy sauce."

This was definitely getting out of hand.

CHAPTER 8

K ade had to try three times before the shield worked. The first time he managed to encase Booker in a bubble, but it didn't exactly play out as he hoped because Booker couldn't interact with the outside world and kept bumping into Lilac and repelling her when he tried to touch her.

"This is not happening," he declared, fury obvious.

The second time, Kade conjured a bubble that moved. Unfortunately, Nixie crept directly inside the bubble and got her hands on Booker's chest before Cole hauled her out.

Finally, on the third attempt, it appeared to work exactly as designed.

"What do you smell?" Cole demanded of Luke, who had a peculiar expression on his face.

"Nothing," Luke replied. He looked disappointed. "It's almost as if there's a void. It's odd but … he no longer smells like red velvet cake. How depressing."

Cole scowled at him. "You and I are going to have a very long talk later about what is and is not acceptable to say to the man you supposedly love."

"That sounds like the exact opposite of fun," Luke drawled.

I fixed Naida and Nixie with a curious stare. "What about you guys?" I asked. "What do you smell?"

"Dead cow carcasses." Naida had completely lost interest in Booker once the barrier had been erected. She now stared at the steaks on the grill. "It really is disappointing."

"Yeah." Nixie bobbed her head. "Now he's just a man."

"I'm way more than that," Booker groused as he slid his arm around Lilac's waist. He looked relieved to be able to touch her, and my heart did a little dance for him. He really wasn't a bad guy. He just had an unfortunate affliction that made him standoffish. "This is better."

Lilac grinned at him as she poked his face. "It's weird. They're right about you suddenly being a void. I can usually feel you — like, sense you when you're near — but now there's nothing."

Booker studied her face. "That doesn't sound good."

"It's good for dinner," she insisted. "You need to be able to eat without having Luke planted in your lap. And I really prefer not to have to kill anyone to keep them from putting their hands on you."

He cocked his head, considering, and then nodded. "Good point." He gave her a quick kiss before sitting at one of the picnic tables. He opted for a spot on the end so he could make a quick getaway should the spell suddenly fail. "I'm going to want you to drop this thing when it's time to leave," he said to Kade. "I have plans tonight that don't include my girlfriend finding a void when she wants to cuddle."

"Did you just say 'cuddle' with a straight face?" Galen demanded. "I'll never let you live this down, man."

If looks could kill, Galen would be dead. "I've had to listen to your crap about Hadley for months … and I guarantee the word 'cuddle' came out of your mouth at least ten times."

"It did not."

"Oh, yes it did." Booker's annoyance was palpable. "I once heard you tell Aurora that morning was your favorite part of the day because Hadley was warm and cuddly. Don't bother denying it."

"Did you tell Aurora that?" Hadley beamed at Galen. "That's kind of sweet."

"Drink your water," Galen instructed, his tone gruff even as his lips curved into a smile. "I'm taking you home early for bed tonight. We can talk about the cuddling then."

Booker coughed a word into his hand that sounded suspiciously like "pushover" and then smiled at Raven as she delivered a plate of steak to him. "I'm glad to see you're not a slave to your hormones. Are you an elemental?"

Raven smirked. "Lamia."

"Seriously?" Booker's smile disappeared in an instant. "Can you really turn into a snake?"

"There are a number of things I can do."

Booker kept his gaze on her a moment longer before focusing on Nellie. "What's your story?"

"I'm from a different plane, buddy," Nellie replied. "Your cupid voodoo doesn't work on me."

"It works on them." Booker pointed to the pixie twins. "Unless I'm mistaken, they're from another plane."

"That's a good point," I said. "But Nellie isn't gay. He just likes dresses."

Booker pursed his lips, as if thinking hard, and then dug into his steak. "So what's the deal with these magical kids?"

"We were just about to ask you that," Cole said. "My understanding is that you were having problems before we even arrived," he said to Galen.

"Not the sort of problems you had this afternoon," Galen said as he massaged Hadley's neck. She looked as if she was ready to pass out. I still had questions regarding her reaction to Kade's healing magic, but they could wait for another time. I didn't want to drain her.

"There were a lot of reports," Booker said. "Denzel said that someone had been putting magical bombs in all the trash receptacles. He'd taken to checking those first before hitting the beach for garbage pickup."

I raised my head. "Magical bombs?"

"Nothing major," Booker reassured me. "He said it was like magical confetti. When they exploded, little glittery bits landed on people. They were icy cold. People weren't complaining because the heat is oppressive."

"That's far from killing four men and arranging their bodies in a religious tableau," I said. "It's far different from taking on six magical beings and trying to kill them."

Galen balked. "We have no reason to believe those kids killed those men."

"Have you identified them yet?" Cole asked.

"No." Galen's eyes were dark clouds as he accepted his plate of food from Naida. "The construction crew isn't missing anyone. No tourists have been reported missing. We're going to check the cameras tomorrow. The feeds were screwed up on the local servers, but we have backups on the mainland."

Well, that was interesting. "That can't be a coincidence."

"Likely not," he agreed.

"It has to be the kids," Lilac said. "It's been a full week of youthful shenanigans and almost nobody saw the deeds carried out. The local kids aren't allowed out after dark unless for a specific event, like a festival. We're between festivals right now, so they wouldn't be out causing mischief."

"There are ways around curfews," Booker noted. He seemed much more relaxed now that he wasn't being sniffed and pawed. "Galen and I both had curfews as kids. We treated them as suggestions rather than rules."

"That's true," Galen agreed, grinning. "One time we snuck out our windows to head to the camp. We wanted to see the girls naked through the windows."

Hadley shot him a dirty look. "How old were you?"

"Twelve or so," he replied with a shrug.

"How old were the girls?"

"Sixteen." Galen's smile broadened. "It was a glorious night. I saw two more boobs than Booker."

When Booker grinned at the memory, Lilac slapped his leg. "Hey, that's not funny. You invaded those girls' privacy. That's perverted."

"We were twelve," Booker reminded her. "What sort of boy behavior at twelve isn't perverted?"

"That doesn't matter." Lilac insisted. "You shouldn't be proud of that."

"Oh, get over it." Booker made a face. "It's not as if we were peeking at you and Aurora."

"Which I would never do," Galen said solemnly. "Booker is another story. He would totally peek. I was a good boy."

"You were just afraid that Lilac would set you on fire," Booker shot back. "And Aurora always carried a spear those days. You know darned well you were terrified of both of them."

"That's neither here nor there." Galen took on an imperious tone. "I was a good boy."

"Other than peeking at sixteen-year-old girls who were minding their own business," Hadley reminded him. "You guys are gross."

"Hey!" Galen wagged a finger in her face. "I only peek at one girl now. I can't help that I was a slave to my hormones back then."

"I hate to break it to you, buddy, but you're still a slave to your hormones," Booker pointed out.

As enlightening as this conversation was — and it really did boast moments of levity — we had a problem. "We need to figure out what we're dealing with," I insisted. "I very much doubt that those two kids created all that mayhem and now they're suddenly gone. This feels … bigger."

Galen sobered as he took in my expression. "Without more information to go on, we're stuck. We have no identities for the dead guys. We have no identities for the kids. It's like strangers have somehow infiltrated our island … and that's just not possible."

"You mentioned plane doors," I insisted. "Could they have come in via that route?"

"No." Galen seemed certain. "The things crossing over from the open plane doors weren't human. They didn't look remotely human. This has to be something else."

"What?"

"I don't know." Galen leaned his cheek against Hadley's forehead as her head rested against his shoulder. She looked ready to pass out. "We have to find out. I don't want to risk my people getting attacked when their backs are turned. Kids make effective assassins because nobody suspects they can be evil. We can't let whatever this is get a foothold."

I agreed, but there was a problem with his thinking. Evil had clearly already gotten a foothold on his island. We simply didn't know how much of a foothold we were dealing with.

DINNER DIDN'T DRAG INTO THE NIGHT. ONCE we finished eating, Galen swooped Hadley up in his arms and carried her to his truck. She was down for the count, and it was obvious he wanted her to sleep off her magical hangover in her own bed. Lilac looked torn when it came time to leave, but once Kade lifted the spell protecting Booker from our lustier troupe members, they had no choice but to run.

The members of our group drifted away until only Kade and I remained. He suggested a walk on the beach before we headed back to the hotel. I was only too happy to oblige, and only partly because my mind was too jumbled to unfurl in a small hotel room.

"What are you thinking?" Kade asked, his fingers threaded with mine. The only sound on the beach was the lapping waves, the light breeze a soft caress after the heat of the day.

"I'm thinking that we're dealing with some sort of ancient creature," I replied. "Either the creature is possessing children or somehow creating the image of them."

"Which are you leaning toward?"

"I know which one I want it to be, but I'm not sure. Galen is right about us needing more information."

"Do you think we'll be able to get it?"

"We won't have a choice." We lapsed into silence, and when I slanted my eyes at him, I saw trouble in his. "What's bothering you?" I asked. "Other than the obvious, I mean."

"I ... am a little upset," he admitted. He was the epitome of "strong and silent" most of the time. Whatever was plaguing his mind must be bad for him to be willing to talk about it without stewing for hours first.

"Tell me," I prodded.

"It's Hadley."

"You're worried that you somehow changed her personality," I surmised. "I saw you looking at her over dinner. You're upset because she seems so different."

"I thought I was helping her."

"You did help her," I reassured him. "You saved her life. That's why she's acting the way she is."

"Max didn't act that way when I healed him."

"We don't know how close to death Max was. Hadley has a different personality. She was already bubbly ... and then some. I'm sure she'll be back to normal tomorrow morning."

"What if she's not? What if she's no longer the same person?"

Exasperation reared up and grabbed me by the throat. "Kade, please don't use this as an excuse to be frightened by your magic again. It's okay. She'll be fine. I promise. This is a temporary glitch ... even Galen knows that. Otherwise, he would be ranting and raving."

"Didn't you look at him during dinner?" Kade slowed his pace. "He's worried."

"He's a worrier by nature. The thing he loves most is vulnerable. That's what he's worried about. It'll be okay." I reached out to stroke his arm but missed when my gaze landed on something near the water line. "What's that?"

"What's what?" Kade sounded sullen, which meant he needed to be cajoled out of his bad mood. Unfortunately for him, I didn't have the time – or the inclination.

I left him to pout and crossed the sand, my heart pounding harder with each step as the thing that had caught my attention began to take shape.

"What are you doing?" Kade chased after me. "Poet, I'm talking to you."

"I'll listen to you whine again in a few minutes," I replied absently.

"I am not whining! I ... hey, what's that?" His tone changed in an instant, curiosity taking over.

I extended a hand to keep him outside the rock circle. Someone — and I had a sneaking suspicion whoever had done it was small — had erected a rune display on the beach. I didn't recognize the figures, but the design was clear enough even as the water encroached on the tableau.

"What is that?" Kade demanded. He might've been pouty, and sometimes lacking when it came to understanding the magic we wielded, but he recognized something was out of place. "Did those kids do this?"

"I don't know." I wet my lips and scanned the beach. It was empty except for us. "I need Raven." Even as I said it, I thought it. A year ago, I wouldn't have even considered tapping her for magical answers. Things were different between us now. I trusted her … and I definitely needed her now.

She could read my fear from wherever she was, so I sent out a mental homing beacon. By the time she arrived ten minutes later, Kade had set up a magical barrier to keep the waves from washing away the runes. The scene was preserved for Raven, who didn't look thrilled at the interruption.

"This had better be good," she grumbled as she strolled toward me, her already pale features turning white as she took in the runes. "Are you kidding?"

"Do you know what they are?" I asked. "We just stumbled across them. I think they have something to do with whatever it is we're dealing with."

Raven swallowed hard. "They do." Her eyes were wide with something I couldn't ever remember seeing reflected back at me from her face. Raven had lived so long she almost never let fear in.

"Tell me," I demanded.

Her voice was rusty. "I've seen these runes before," she said. "They're … evil."

"Where did you see them?"

"Africa, on the shores of the Indian Ocean."

"What do they mean?"

"They signify spiritual possession … and not of the horror movie variety. This is much, much worse."

She was so white I could almost see through her. "We need to call Galen."

"What do you think a shifter cop can do?" Raven's gaze darkened. "We need to get out of here."

It was unlike her to react out of fear. Running was never her first inclination. "We need to call Galen." I insisted as I pulled my phone from my pocket. "After that, you need to tell me what you know."

"I know that we shouldn't be here." Raven looked over both shoulders. "This ... evil ... isn't the sort that we can beat back with pixie magic and an ax-wielding dwarf."

"Then we'll have to go bigger," I said. "Raven, if we ever want to consider this place our home, we have to do our part to keep it safe."

"When this is over, there will be nothing left to serve as a home," Raven spat. "How can you not understand that?"

I forced myself to remain calm. "Let me get Galen out here and we'll talk."

"Talking is a waste of time. Words won't fix this."

"We have to try."

Raven's eyes flashed with bitterness. "We will fail. Remember this moment before the end comes. I'll remind you that I warned you."

CHAPTER 9

Nine

I expected Galen to park at the fairgrounds and find us by walking through the tents. Instead, he showed up ten minutes later in nothing but a pair of shorts. He'd jogged down the beach, not bothering to dress before joining us.

"Um … hello." Raven's eyes bulged at the sight of his muscles.

"He's in love with his girlfriend," I warned.

Raven shot me a dark look. "Thanks so much for the update," she grumbled. "Like I didn't figure that out myself."

Kade smirked. "Are you thinking of trading up from the clown?"

"No. Just window shopping."

He gave Galen an apologetic smile when the sheriff arrived at the runes. "Sorry to bother you. We know you wanted to be with Hadley. It's just … ." He gestured toward the runes helplessly.

Galen was grim as he planted his hands on his hips. "What in the hell?" He shook his head. "You found it like this?"

I nodded, scanning the beach behind him for his girlfriend. "Where's Hadley?" I had trouble believing he'd leave her behind given his protective nature.

"Hadley passed out like a two-year-old the second I got her home," he replied. "I didn't want to wake her in case she threw a tantrum like a two-year-old." His grin was lightning quick. "I left her grandmother to watch her, just to be on the safe side."

I was confused. "I thought her grandmother was dead. Didn't she leave the lighthouse to Hadley?"

"Yes, but May is still hanging around as a ghost. She'll alert me if anything happens." Galen's full focus was on the runes.

"It must be difficult to have a ghost living with you," Kade mused. "How hard is it to get romance in under those circumstances?"

Galen managed a chuckle. "May mostly stays at the farm with Wesley these days. They were married for years … and then got divorced. Apparently, they kept the fires alive despite the divorce. May stops in regularly during the day. She only comes at night when we call her."

"Raven recognizes the runes." I probably shouldn't have blurted it that way, but I couldn't stop myself.

Raven shot me a death glare. "Thank you so much, big mouth."

I held out my hands. "We're in this together, Raven. We need to solve it together."

"That's exactly what we need to do," Galen agreed. His gaze was speculative when it landed on Raven. "What are they?"

"Evil," Raven replied.

"I could've figured that out on my own. Nice runes don't just show up on the beach after four deaths and a magical attack."

Raven scuffed her sandal in the sand. "They're African in origin. I saw them centuries ago on a beach there. What followed was the extermination of an entire tribe."

The only sign that Galen registered what she said was a slight shift in his eyebrows. "I'm going to need more than that," he prodded.

"Back then I spent most of my time traveling between Europe and Asia," Raven explained. "My people were more prevalent then. We took a trip to Africa because none of us had ever been. We moved from tribe to tribe along the Indian Ocean. They were primitive but welcoming … something they've since learned was a mistake."

Galen nodded in understanding. "Letting others into their insular world helped wipe them out."

"It was mostly disease," Raven explained. "We brought European diseases to them … even though we didn't realize what we were doing at the time. And by 'we,' I don't mean my people. I mean Europeans in general."

"I'm not going to arrest you for genocide," Galen reassured her, earning a wan smile in return.

"We were there for two years before we talked about heading home," Raven continued. "We liked the area, we'd learned a lot, but we missed society … or what passed for society at the time. Europe simply had more to offer.

"We were heading north when it happened. We visited a tribe we'd seen about six months earlier and noticed their numbers were depleted by at least half. The language barrier wasn't easy to navigate, but we managed to figure out that they were being wiped out. They called it a scourge, and we assumed it was a sickness."

"It wasn't, though," I surmised.

"No." Raven shook her head. "We decided to delay our return to see if we could help. There was very little we had to offer other than magic. We assumed that would be enough. We were wrong." Her eyes landed on me. "On our third night there, after another two people from the village went missing, we found the runes on the beach. We couldn't read them, but it wasn't difficult to ascertain that we were dealing with something dark."

I nodded. "You thought you could fix the problem." It wasn't a question.

"It was a magical fight," Raven replied. "We assumed it was destiny that we arrived when we did. We could win a magical fight … except that we couldn't. People kept disappearing. We were directed to a shaman who lived in the jungle. He explained that the runes were a message from the gods."

"Which gods?" Galen asked, straightening.

"The gods of old." Raven said. "You have to understand, they were mixing real-world events with myth. Their take on the subject was different. They assumed it was divine intervention, that they'd somehow angered the gods, and this was their punishment. They kept making offerings to the gods — fish and pottery mostly — to appease them. That didn't work, of course."

She let loose a shaky breath and turned to face the ocean. "I don't know what it really was," she said. "I believe it was a demon because the elementals were more prevalent then, but I have no proof."

"I've dealt with demons before," Galen reassured her. "We can deal with them again."

"This demon — or demons if you choose to believe one being couldn't bring that much suffering — were possessing the children of the tribe," Raven explained. "They took over the children, who then killed the adults by draining them of life force. Blood sacrifices. They managed to wipe out the entire tribe in two months. We were the only ones left after we made our last stand.

"Even then we assumed we could fight whatever it was," she continued, her voice full of the sort of sadness that could never be reconciled. "We tried. We really did. But that last night, when the children came out of the jungle to finally show themselves, we knew we'd been beaten. We could stay and die ... or run."

"You ran," I said. There was no judgment in my tone, but Raven glared.

"We made our way up the coast. We were trying to get to Alexandria. We moved from the Indian Ocean to the Gulf of Aden, to the Red Sea. Then we cut through Cairo. We thought we were safe. The tales of dying villages followed us."

"How did that siege end?" Galen asked.

"I have no idea. We fled to Europe from there. We braced ourselves, thinking we'd eventually hear about the fall of Africa."

"Something had to stop the demon encroachment," I insisted.

"I have no idea what it was." Raven shook her head, the moonlight bouncing off her silver hair and creating a halo of beauty. "I only know that whatever it was managed to wipe out multiple tribes. This island is isolated. The people here could be considered a tribe. I would run now."

"We don't run." Galen was firm as he went back to studying the runes. "Were the runes part of it, perhaps calling more demons?"

"The runes were definitely part of it, but I don't know their function."

"Then maybe we need to get rid of the runes," Galen said, looking at me. "Did you photograph it?"

I nodded. "While we were waiting for you. We figured that was the best way to research what we're dealing with."

"I want copies of those photos." Galen dropped to his knees, wiping away the runes. "Let's see what happens when they don't have their runes leading them."

Kade and I pitched in. The rune expanse was large, and my arms were tired when we finished. Kade dropped the shield that had been holding back the water, and when the waves scoured the sand, it looked like a normal beach again.

"I'll send someone out first thing in the morning to check on them," Galen said as he dragged his hand through his hair. "I guess we'll know then if we can just screw with the runes to stop whatever this is."

Raven had moved away, standing on a small bluff watching us.

"We're really sorry for dragging you away from Hadley," Kade said as he prodded me back toward the fairgrounds. "We thought you should know."

"You did the right thing," Galen reassured him. "Listen, I know I wasn't as thankful as I should've been earlier. About what you did for Hadley, I mean. I was just thrown by what happened … and she's been acting drunk, so that added an extra layer of concern. I'm grateful you took care of her."

Kade's cheeks flushed with color. "I did what anybody would've done," he insisted.

"Not anybody," Galen countered.

"She's acting out of sorts," Kade said. "She wouldn't be doing that if I hadn't intervened."

"Something tells me she'll be fine in the morning," Galen said. "She's alive. That's the most important thing. Lilac is right about the euphoria. We've seen it before. I guarantee she'll be back to her snarky self after a solid night of sleep."

"I hope so." Kade linked his fingers with mine. "I just reacted and did what I thought was necessary."

"You saved my heart," Galen insisted. "I love her very much. Once she's back to herself tomorrow, we'll come up with a plan to deal with ... whatever it is we're dealing with. I'm hopeful the runes won't return, and we can hunt down whatever these things are and eradicate them."

Raven picked that moment to clear her throat, drawing our eyes to her. She pointed to the spot on the beach. "You were saying."

When I glanced back at the spot we'd just spent thirty minutes covering, my heart lodged in my throat. The runes were back.

"Well, crap." A muscle worked in Galen's jaw. "That is ... not good."

"They'll kill us all," Raven intoned. "I'm warning you to evacuate the island now."

Galen, annoyed, swung his eyes in her direction. "You're not familiar with Moonstone Bay so I'm going to give you a pass. I get that you're frightened. We're more than just a tribe. We're a family. We won't give up our island."

"Then you'll fall." Raven turned and headed toward the fair-grounds. "We'll all fall."

I watched her go, blowing out a sigh when Galen's eyes landed on me. "Ignore her," I said. "She's a Debbie Downer much of the time. She'll fight with us when it's time."

"How can you be sure?"

"No matter what she says, she's loyal to a fault. That won't change because she believes the odds are stacked against us."

"I hope you're right. We're going to need all hands on deck for this one I think. I'm heading back to the lighthouse. I'll be in touch with you guys tomorrow."

"Take care of Hadley," I said. "Something tells me we're going to need her at her best."

He nodded. "Something tells me you're right."

THERE WAS NOTHING MORE WE COULD DO on the beach, so we returned to the hotel. The clerk at the desk — a young man playing a video game — bobbed his head but didn't make eye contact. I was fine with that. I didn't have anything to say.

"What are you thinking?" Kade asked once we were in our room.

I started stripping — the heat of the day had caused me to sweat through my clothes multiple times — and sighed as I flopped on the bed in my underwear and shut my eyes. "I don't know," I said.

He was too quiet. When I looked up, I found him watching me with a half-smile. "What?" I demanded.

"I was just thinking that it's as if we're already married," he said, grinning. "I didn't even try to tackle you into the bed like I might have six months ago." He picked up my clothes and tossed them at my head. "Also, I'm not your maid."

I made a face as I batted the clothes away. "I was going to pick them up."

"Uh-huh." He moved to his side of the bed and tugged his shirt over his head.

"This isn't our trailer. We're allowed to be messy in hotel rooms."

"Who says?"

"I say."

"Good to know." He dropped his shorts and crawled onto the bed with me. I grinned as he elbowed his way over to me, lifting my arm as he rested his head on my chest. His skin was warm from the walk.

"Raven is afraid," I noted, my eyes drifting to the window. The shades were three-quarters drawn. I would have to finish tugging them into place before falling asleep.

"I noticed." Kade pressed a kiss to my collar bone. "I've never seen her that way."

"Me either."

"You've known her much longer." He hesitated. "Should we do what she says?"

"Are you asking me if I think we should take off in the middle of the night and not look back?"

"I'm not saying I'm for that," he cautioned. "I want your opinion."

"We can't run." It wasn't even a consideration. "Let's say we did. There's no way Cole would leave Lilac. There's no way Lilac will leave her friends. There's no way Luke will leave Cole."

"And there's no way you'll leave Luke," Kade finished. "And I won't leave you. That pretty much decides it. But what do we do?"

I didn't have an answer. "I don't know. We to have to figure something out."

"Nobody is going to abandon anyone else. We need our best fighters in place. That's the only way this will work."

"We'll talk to everybody over breakfast. We'll make them aware of what's happening, make sure nobody goes anywhere alone. And we'll get to researching those runes. The answers are out there somewhere."

"What if Raven decides she's not staying?"

"Raven won't run."

"You just said she was afraid."

"That doesn't mean she'll run." I was positive that was the case. "She's never been easy to get along with, but she's loyal. The family she was born to is gone … or at the very least scattered. We're her family now, and she'll fight with us."

"I've never seen her so rattled."

"I'll talk to her tomorrow. We'll handle this like we do anything else. We'll finish setting up, start researching, and batten down the hatches. Nobody can take us out when we work together."

Kade grinned. "It's kind of sexy when you talk like a badass."

I matched his smile. "Why don't you show me what you like about me being a badass?"

"I thought you'd never ask." He pressed his lips to mine.

CHAPTER 10

Ten

I woke to the warmth of Kade spooned behind me. The light snoring I'd become accustomed to was absent, so I knew he was awake.

"Good morning." I rolled to my back and stretched, grinning when I caught sight of his handsome face. He looked well rested despite Raven's warnings of the night before. "Are you okay?"

The question seemed to puzzle him. "I'm waking up with my future wife. Why wouldn't I be okay?"

"We have another fight on our hands." I pressed my finger into his laugh line. "The future wife stuff is cute, by the way. Are you going to refer to me as your wife constantly once we're married?"

"That's the plan. If you've got it, flaunt it."

I giggled when he tickled my ribs. "I plan to refer to you as my husband to anyone who will listen."

His gaze was soft when it locked with mine. "Why haven't we discussed details yet?"

Should I tell him the truth? I discarded the notion of lying or evading the question. That wasn't how we operated. "I want to get my meeting with Sidney out of the way first. I know that's probably not what you want to hear but … it feels like a weight settling here." I pressed my hand to the spot above my heart.

His placed his hand on mine. "I won't let him hurt you."

"I don't need you to go into Security Chief Kade mode. I'm guessing he just wants money or something. One meeting and he'll be out of our lives."

"Is that what you want?"

"What else would I want?"

"He's your uncle, Poet. He's one of the last remaining blood relatives you have. He disappeared in the wake of your parents' deaths. I assume you have questions for him."

"Questions he can't answer."

"He can tell you why he didn't save you from the system."

"Maybe, but I already know the answer to that question. My father always said he was unreliable. He didn't want to deal with raising a kid. That's all there is to it."

"It's not as if you were a toddler. You were a teenager. You could basically take care of yourself at that age."

"Well, that's not how it worked out." The conversation was making me uncomfortable. "I'm not harboring bitterness about how it played out. My time in the system wasn't great, but some of the foster homes were okay. Most of them were okay."

"You never talk about the bad ones, other than an offhand comment here and there. If you want to talk about it, I'm always here to listen."

"There's not much to say." I scrubbed my cheeks to get the blood flowing. "I took care of myself. When I sensed danger, I removed myself from the situation. There were a lot of kids who didn't have it as good as me."

"Baby, look at me."

I had to force my eyes to him.

"It's okay to have feelings about your childhood." He was earnest. "You mention your parents infrequently. You almost never want to talk about your time in the foster care system. You only get excited when you mention your time on the street, and that makes me sad."

"I was alive then." I shot him a rueful smile. "I know you can't relate because you had a mother who doted on you, but after my time in the system the freedom of being on the street was … amazing. I could breathe again."

"That freaks me out." He pressed a kiss to my forehead. "I don't like imagining you huddling around a fire to keep warm in a Detroit winter. I also don't want to think about our kids needing freedom so much they take off one day. With half your genes, the wanderlust will run deep."

I couldn't contain my laugh. "I didn't have wanderlust when I was with my parents … and they were far from perfect. I thought about traveling as a kid, but had my parents survived my life would be very different." And that, I realized, was the hardest thing to think about. "If they'd survived, I never would've ended up here. I wouldn't have known Luke. I wouldn't have found you. I believe things happen for a reason."

"So do I." He slid his arm under my waist and tugged me against his chest. His eyes were seeking when he studied my face. "We would have found one another. We're together, and nothing will ever tear us apart."

"Definitely not." I rested my head on his chest. "Do you know where you want to get married?"

The question seemed to throw him. "Are you asking if I want to wait until next year, when we're in Florida again, and get married there?"

I shrugged. "Maybe. We need to throw out some ideas and gauge which we like best."

"I don't care where we're married, Poet, but I don't want to wait a year. I would marry you today if I thought you'd agree."

"Today?" I was dumbfounded. "I don't think Luke would be on board for that. He wants to throw a bachelorette party for the ages."

Kade snorted. "I know we're not getting married today, but I'm ready whenever you are. I want you to have everything you've ever wanted. If that means heading back to Michigan … ." He trailed off. Michigan was late in our rotation. It would be more than six months before we returned there.

"How about we get through whatever we're dealing with here and then start planning?" I suggested. "We should make lists, put everything we want on paper, and then start planning. Maybe the state isn't important. Maybe it's the timing that's important."

"I can get behind that." He rested his cheek against my forehead. "We should probably get up. We need to fill in the others, and there's still work to do at the fairgrounds."

I nodded. Duty called. "Just five more minutes."

I felt his lips curve against my brow. "Let's make it an even ten."

"See, now you're thinking."

MOST OF OUR GROUP WAS ALREADY gathered around a large table in the dining room. One look at the assembled faces told me Raven had filled them in.

"Why didn't you call me?" Luke's tone was accusatory when he fixed his gaze on me.

"There was nothing you could do," I said as I sat in the open chair across from him. "They were runes. We weren't attacked or anything."

"We do have to deal with those runes today," Kade said. "I figured we could get some research in while finishing set up at the fairgrounds We open for half the day tomorrow, so we really need to get that done this afternoon."

"That's smart," Cole said. "I called Lilac this morning. She hadn't heard about the runes. She says there's a good library on the beach and promised to take me there after the afternoon rush. She also said Hadley's grandmother left her an extensive library in the lighthouse. That's a resource we might be able to tap."

"Sounds like a plan," I agreed.

We tabled the discussion until Kade and I had placed our breakfast orders and then got into the nitty-gritty of it.

"Raven thinks we should leave," Nellie said once our server disappeared into the kitchen. "What do you think?" He looked serious for a change, which did not fill me with happy thoughts.

"I'm not leaving." I opted to get that out right away. "We're considering making this island our long-term home. We can't just abandon it now … especially when we don't know what we're dealing with."

"Raven told us." Dolph, our strongman, looked frustrated as he leaned back in his chair. He was almost always ready for a fight, but today he seemed unnerved. "Possessing demons are never fun."

"They're not," I agreed. "I'm not going to force anyone to stay. I'm simply stating that I'm not leaving."

"I'm not leaving either," Cole said gravely. "Lilac is my cousin and she'll never abandon her friends. I won't abandon her."

"And Luke and I won't abandon Poet and Cole," Kade added. "If the rest of you feel you want to leave, we won't stop you."

"Oh, good grief." Raven's glare was full of bitterness when it landed on me. "You know they won't leave you. They'd die to protect you."

I didn't flinch when fixing my full attention on her. "Raven, I understand that you're frightened. Between the people who live on the island and us, we have a chance to stop these demons in their tracks. I would think you'd want that after the story you told last night."

"Don't you think I want retribution?" Raven challenged. "I do, but I'm a survivor. I don't want to die in a fight we can't win."

"We don't know that we can't win," I pointed out. "In fact, I don't believe there's a fight we can't win as a group. If the rest of you feel otherwise, you should leave. I don't want you staying out of loyalty to me."

Naida's expression was difficult to read as she focused on her sister. After a few seconds, she shook her head. "We're staying. But you already knew that."

"There's more than one type of family," Nixie agreed. "You're our family. We'll fight to the death with you."

Raven made a derisive sound. "You're all fools."

"Maybe," I said. "I guess that makes you a fool too. I know you won't pick up and leave us. You'll fight."

"Of course, I will." Raven had a surly attitude on the best of days. This was not one of those days. "We'll all join together, and probably die together. I hope that makes you happy."

"I'll be happy when we win," I said. "You'll be happy too … right up to the point I remind you that I always knew we would win, and you have a meltdown."

"Yes, we're going to learn choreography for the dance we do when we're right and you're wrong," Luke said, earning a death glare. He and Raven had a tempestuous relationship, and it didn't look to be getting better anytime soon.

"If you're not in, you should go now," I said. "We need to keep our fighting forces tight. Nobody will think badly about you if you want to go."

"Nobody's going," Dolph replied. "We're a unit. That won't change now."

"I want to behead a demon," Nellie said, his grin lightning quick. "Then I'm going to have the pixie twins turn it into a doll I can carry for all eternity."

"Well ... that sounds lovely." I forced a smile I didn't feel. "Today is for research. I have photos of the runes to disseminate to everybody. We have regular work too. Our goal is to get the circus operational and track down the origin of those runes. Any questions?"

Luke's hand shot in the air.

"Any questions from anybody who won't say something irritating?" I asked, ignoring Luke's wrinkled nose. "Okay. Everybody knows what they're doing. Let's do what we do best and defeat the enemy. The show must go on."

LUKE SAID HE FORGOT SOMETHING IN HIS room and demanded we wait for him. I rolled my eyes because one of the things we'd agreed on at breakfast was that nobody should wander alone until we knew what we were dealing with. Also, we'd decided that more than one child running around without parental supervision likely meant something bad was about to happen.

Kade and Cole spent the time in the lobby looking over brochures, some of which purported to tell the history of the island. I stood at the front doors, surveying the street. I didn't know what I was searching for — other than the obvious — but it looked like a normal day on a tropical island. There was nothing to chase. Nothing to fight. No way to protect my friends from the evil threatening the island.

"Excuse me."

The voice was small but fierce. When I glanced down, I found a blond angel watching me with expectant eyes. The girl — not even ten yet if I had to guess — clutched a doll in one hand and a lollipop in the other. Her hair, the color of wheat, was pulled back into pigtails with fuzzy ties.

"I need to get by," the girl said.

"What do you say, Ariel?" a woman prompted from behind her.

"I said 'excuse me,'" the girl, who was apparently named Ariel, insisted.

"She did," I affirmed quickly as I stepped from the door. "I was lost in thought, and it took me a few seconds to realize she was talking to me."

The mother didn't look convinced. "We've been working on manners. Some days she remembers and other days she doesn't."

"She remembered today," I reassured her. "I was the rude one." I flashed a smile for the girl's benefit. "I shouldn't stand in front of the door. That's rude."

The girl looked wary. "Do you live here?" she asked.

I shook my head. "I'm with the circus. We're here to work." *And hunt,* I silently added. I kept my smile in place for Ariel.

"You're with the circus?" Ariel brightened considerably. "I want to be with the circus one day."

"Oh, yeah?" I couldn't help myself from grinning. That was something I heard often from children. They grew out of the idea by the time they were teenagers. "What do you want to do with the circus? Do you want to be a clown?"

Ariel made a look of disgust. "Clowns are freaks."

Her mother shot me an apologetic look. "She has an older brother going to college next year and he doesn't always think before he speaks in front of her."

"That's okay," Kade said from behind me. "Clowns are definitely freaks. I'm right there with you." He held out his fist for her to bump and the girl giggled as she obliged. "You can be a member of my team," he reassured her. "I hate clowns too."

Ariel slid her eyes to me, unsure. "Does he really?"

"He does." I confirmed. "He absolutely hates clowns. He's terrified of them."

"I wouldn't go that far," Kade said.

Ariel's mother belted out a laugh as the little girl giggled. "We're looking forward to the circus, aren't we, Ariel?"

Ariel nodded. "We are." She leaned forward to grace me with a conspiratorial whisper. "My brother doesn't want to go. He only cares about looking at girls on the beach. He wants their butts to hang out of their bathing suits. I heard him telling my dad."

I pressed my lips together and shifted my eyes to the mother. I expected a look of mortification, but she looked resigned instead.

"Teenage boys are lovely," she said. "I'm almost looking forward to him going to college next year."

It was bold talk, but she wore her emotions on the outside. She would bawl her eyes out the day she dropped her son at college. She would wait until she was driving home alone, but the void she'd feel as a mother would be deep.

"Don't worry about your brother," I told Ariel, who was making eyes at Kade. She might've been young, but she was already a master at batting her eyelashes. I had a feeling her father probably encouraged that. "We'll be on the lookout for you at the circus and we'll make sure the clowns pay special attention to him. How does that sound?"

Ariel's eyes widened. "Can you really do that?"

"I'm in charge. I can do anything."

Her giggle was delightful. "Then I really can't wait to go to the circus."

I smiled as she sidled closer to her mother, and then something occurred to me. The runes signified the sort of demon who went after children. That made the younger set especially vulnerable. "Stick close to your parents on the island." I kept my smile in place. "I want you to bring the whole family to the circus when you come, okay?"

"I will." Arlie wiggled her hips and did a little dance. "Can we get ice cream now?"

"You're supposed to take a nap first," her mother replied.

"I would nap better with ice cream."

The mother sighed. "Fine, but don't tell your brother. We never let him have ice cream before his naps when he was your age."

Ariel mimed zipping her lips. "It's a secret." She waved at me before falling into step with her mother. "Can I get chocolate sprinkles as long as I don't tell Kyle?"

"I guess, but you'd really better keep your mouth shut this time."

"I will. I promise."

"You promised last time."

"I'm a whole two weeks older now."

"Right, because that makes all the difference."

Kade smiled at me when they were gone. "You're good with kids."

"So are you." I studied him. "We're not having any for a few years. We need to get settled first."

He barked out a laugh and slid his arm around my shoulders. "You're enough for me for now. Besides, we have Luke."

"That's true. We always have Luke."

"One day, though." His expression was wistful.

"One day," I agreed. "It will happen faster than you realize."

"I'm looking forward to it."

CHAPTER 11

Eleven

Apparently what Luke had to get from his room was a pair of binoculars. During the walk to the fairgrounds, he used them to scan in every direction. He tripped three times, forcing Cole to spend the entire walk making sure Luke didn't pitch face first into the pavement.

"What are you doing?" I demanded when we were across the road from the fairgrounds.

Luke's expression was droll when he lowered the binoculars. "What do you think I'm doing?"

"I don't know. That's why I asked."

"I'm looking for evil."

"You need binoculars for that?"

"We want to see it coming."

"Right." I looked to Cole and found him watching his boyfriend with abject fondness. "You don't think he's weird?"

Cole shrugged. "I think he's great … most of the time. He has a few quirks, but who doesn't?"

"I don't," Kade replied, his hand at the small of my back as he prodded me across the road. "I'm without quirks."

Now it was my turn to scoff. "Um … clowns."

"He's weird about birds getting too close to his head, too," Cole offered.

"Insecurity over your woman being stronger than you," Luke added.

"You have to eat your breakfast in order," I added. "First you dunk the toast in your egg yolks. Then you mix your hash browns and the rest of the eggs together. You eat your breakfast meat last."

"You whine because you're jealous of Poet spending time with me," Luke supplied.

Kade's eyes narrowed. "First, I'm not insecure because Poet is stronger than me. I like that she's a badass. That's why I fell in love with her. Second, it's smart to eat my breakfast that way for digestion. It works for me."

I tried to hold back my laugh … and failed. "As long as you're good with it. But you still have quirks, so don't pretend otherwise."

"Whatever." Kade's glare was dark as he moved past Luke, who was either oblivious or trying to pretend he was, and focused on me. "Let's get your tent up first. Then we can oversee the rest of the fair-grounds."

He wanted to make constant rounds in case we got another attack by children. It made sense that he would be hyper-vigilant. "Sure, but you don't have to help me with my tent. If you want to start making your rounds now, you can."

Kade vehemently shook his head. "You said we need to stick in pairs at the very least. That's the rule."

"Yeah, but … ."

He arched an eyebrow and crossed his arms over his chest.

"Fine." There was no sense arguing with him. "We'll do my tent first."

He fell into step with me, his mood heavy. Sure, we were facing another fight, but he could always find the humor in a situation … if only to make me laugh. Today, he didn't seem to want to laugh.

"Tell me what you're thinking," I asked. Searching his face, normally an open book.

"I'm annoyed that Luke thinks I don't want you to be powerful."

I waited, dumbfounded. Was he really holding onto that? "Seriously?" I asked finally. "You know I don't believe that, right?"

"I don't need to be more powerful than you," Kade insisted as we ducked into my tent. The temperature was stifling. "Oh, holy … ." He shook his head and waved his hand in front of his face. "Where is your fan?"

That was a good question. I'd left it in the middle of the tent. "One guess."

Kade's jaw turned to stone. "I'm going to kill him." He stalked to the rear of the tent and unzipped that flap. Most of the time we kept that opening closed — guests walking in from both sides would be a nightmare — but we desperately needed airflow. "I'm going to rip his head off and use it as a beach ball."

Oh, well, that was a lovely visual. "Ignore him. He's trying to get under our skin." I helped Kade tie back the flaps. Even though the heat didn't dissipate, the airflow through the tent made things ten times better. The breeze coming in off the ocean would alleviate some of the problems. It was still going to be rough going. "This won't work." I glanced around, frustration growing by the second.

"I'll get your fan back," Kade promised grimly. "I don't care if I have to pop that little maggot's head like a zit."

"I appreciate that." I flashed a smile I didn't feel. He was worked up. Part of it was the fact that he hated Mark. Nobody liked the slimy midway chief. The other part was what Luke had said. He'd taken it to heart when it was meant as a haphazard dig. I had to fix one problem before we could tackle the sweaty second. "Kade, can you look at me?"

"What?" His eyes were full of mayhem when they locked with mine.

I smiled, hoping to temper his frustration. "You know I don't believe you feel insecure about my magic."

"Of course, I do." His answer was perfunctory.

"Luke likes to bug people. He knew that would bug you."

"I just … don't want you to think that." The anger drained out of him quickly and now he looked defeated. "I love you more than anything. I'm proud of what you can do."

"I know that. You defer to me on magic every chance you get even though you're getting stronger in that department. Pretty soon, you might be stronger than me."

"I don't care about that." The fierce set of his jaw told me he meant it. "I just want you to be happy. You'll always be smarter than me. I don't care that you're also stronger. That's not who I am."

I stood in front of him and rested my hand on his chest. "You can't let Luke get to you. Once he realizes that you're irritated he'll use that to his advantage. That's who he is."

"Well … I'm wrapped a little tight these days," Kade admitted. "I want things to work out perfectly for us. I know that nothing is ever truly perfect, but I want this island to be exactly what we need so we can start planning."

And that, I realized, was the true problem. "You need a plan. I knew that when you first joined us. You don't like the traveling."

"That's not true. I don't mind the traveling, but both of us eventually want a home to call our own. I know we won't have that home this year. I'm okay with that, as long as I'm with you. It's just … ."

"You need a plan." He needed a timetable. Perhaps it was his military background. "We'll figure things out," I promised. "This possessing demons thing has thrown us all for a loop, but it doesn't change our long run."

He was morose. "I just like knowing things."

"It's one of your quirks," I said, grinning.

His eyebrows hopped. "Oh, now you think you're funny. Kade is rigid and likes things a certain way. It's shocking to nobody in particular. I'll never live this down."

"Probably not," I agreed. "But it's okay. We just have to take this one step at a time. The first and most immediate problem is the heat."

"I'll go get your fan from Mark." He started for the flap, but I shot out a hand to stop him.

"Let me deal with Mark," I insisted. "I'm his boss and we have a certain relationship. I'll handle him. I need something else from you."

"What's that?"

"Even with the fans, these tents are going to be death traps. We need to amp up the air conditioning factor."

"How do we do that when we're outside?"

"We need ice. I'm sure this island is full of Styrofoam coolers. Buy some and get your hands on as much ice as you can. Naida can use her magic to prevent the ice from melting. If we put it behind the fans, they'll blow cool air through the tents. Take Cole with you. Leave Luke with Nellie and Dolph in the main tent. You should only have to get ice once. We need enough for each tent … and if you can find a few extra fans, that wouldn't hurt."

"I can do that." Kade rubbed his chin. "But I don't want to leave you."

"I can take care of myself. I'm going to talk to Mark and reclaim my fan. Then I'm heading to the library. We can't do anything here until this tent cools off."

"How am I supposed to transport all that ice here without a vehicle?"

I could think of only one possibility. "Booker has a van. Have Cole contact Lilac. If anybody can convince him to help, she can."

He pressed a kiss to my sweaty forehead. "We're okay, right? You're not upset that I want a plan?"

"Of course not. I like that you're so prepared. You're like a Boy Scout that way."

"Ha, ha, ha." He rolled his eyes. "I don't need a plan right this second. I simply like having something to work toward."

"Well, we're going to have something relatively soon. Have faith."

"I have faith in you." He ran his hands up and down my arms. "I can't wait to marry you."

"I'm right there with you. If you can figure out the ice situation, I'll be convinced you're the perfect man."

Kade didn't look thrilled at the prospect, but he nodded. "Sure. But if he's obnoxious, don't hesitate to call me."

"He's always obnoxious. I know how to deal with him."

I FOUND MARK SITTING IN THE SMALL ticket trailer. He had two fans whirring, pointed directly at him as he sipped what appeared to be an early-morning daiquiri.

"Working hard I see," I said as I pushed open the door.

He greeted me with a sneer. "What can I do for you, Poet?"

"I believe you have my fan." I pointed toward the huge pedestal fan in question.

His expression didn't change. "You're mistaken," he hissed. "That's my fan."

"And yet it was in my tent last night."

"If your fan has gone missing, that's not on me. This is my fan."

I wanted to strangle him. "Mark, if you're struggling with something just tell me what it is. Pouting like a three-year-old who wants a lollipop won't get you anywhere."

His eyes flashed. "I don't think I like your attitude."

"Well, I know I don't like your attitude." I folded my arms across my chest. "If you have something to say, now's the time. Otherwise, shut up and stop being a pain."

"Oh, you would like that, wouldn't you?" His voice was oily, reminding me of a used car salesman in a lemon lot.

"Would I like it if you stopped pouting? Absolutely."

"No, the other part." He shook his head. "You want me to pick a fight with you so you have enough ammunition to take to Max. You think if you push your advantage, you'll be able to get me fired."

"Mark, if I wanted to get you fired, I would've already done it," I argued. "Max has argued to keep you on a time or two, but I've never really demanded that you go. If I were to really make my case to Max, you'd be gone."

"You need me," Mark fired back. "I keep this circus going. I'm the one who brings in the money. It's the games that fund this thing and you know it. All your little … *friends* … suck the money from the circus. Tickets only bring in a fraction of the money. If you think Max is going to fire me, you've got another thing coming."

I was careful when responding. "I get that you're … you, Mark. I know that you need to feel important to make it through the day. But we don't need you. You don't do anything special. Just because you're in charge of the midway doesn't make you king."

"The midway makes the money!" he exploded. "I am the midway."

"Would the midway make even more money if we didn't have a lazy jerk running it?" I mused. I'd often thought it. Mark liked to take credit for the financial success of Mystic Caravan. Most circuses had died out. We'd managed to hold on because we were magical. Mark took credit for us being able to hang on so long. "What would happen if we brought in some fresh blood to shake things up? I'm guessing it might mean more money."

Mark was haughty. "You have no idea what I do. You can't just slot someone in this position and think things will magically work out. That's not how it goes."

"Never say never," I drawled, smirking at his scowl. "I'll take my fan." I jerked the cord from the wall and grabbed the pedestal. "Have a nice day." There was a bit of extra flounce in my step as I exited the ticket booth. The sound of footsteps directly behind me deflated me a bit.

"We're not done here." Mark grabbed my arm to whip me around, but I stilled him with an icy glare. Mark wasn't magical.

Slowly, he drew back his fingers when he saw my expression. "I know what the plan is here, Poet," he said in a low voice. "I know you think you're going to be able to set up shop here permanently. I'm well aware there have been discussions behind my back."

"I have no idea what you're talking about," I lied.

"Don't even." He puffed out his chest. "I agree that we're going to have to find a permanent location … and soon. We have two years at the most of traveling before things fall apart. We need a permanent space to cut costs, but not here."

"Why would you assume we were looking at this place?" I asked blankly. I needed to know if he was fishing or had actual information.

"I'm not an idiot," Mark replied. "This island has a particular reputation in certain circles. I might not be part of your little crowd, but I know the ins and outs of Moonstone Bay. I also know I don't want to settle here. Vegas is the place for us. I've already sent out some feelers for locations."

Feelers? "Have you told Max?"

"Max may be the owner, but you're the boss. He'll defer to you because of that kid of his … and we all know Kade doesn't care about anything but you."

"Kade cares about a great many things," I replied. "You're mistaken there. You're also mistaken if you think you get a say in how we're going to do things when it does come time to pick a permanent location."

Something dangerous flashed in Mark's eyes. "Do you really want to push me on this? Without me, you'll have nothing."

"Do you really want to push me?" I fired back, loudly enough that a passing Nellie pulled up short to survey the situation.

"Is something wrong?" Nellie asked. "Do I need to get my ax?"

"Nobody's talking to you," Mark raged. "You're not part of this conversation."

"I guess we'll have to agree to disagree," Nellie said dryly. His eyes were on me. "Would you like me to hack off his head?"

I let loose a shaky laugh. "More than anything. But it's fine for today." I gripped the fan tighter and leveled my gaze on Mark. "If you have a problem with how things are playing out, take it up with Max. Otherwise shut up and get with the program. You're not king of the circus, Mark."

"And you're not queen of the castle, Poet," he grumbled. "You won't get your way on this. I won't allow it."

"I guess we'll just have to see about that."

CHAPTER 12

The woman behind the counter at the library smiled and offered help the moment I crossed the threshold. I was cagey when replying and asked where the paranormal section was located. Then, on a whim, I asked for the location of the African history section as well. She pointed me toward both and left me to research on my own.

The paranormal research section was extensive, but it didn't include dark magic. It was more a history of light magic, and I figured that had to be by design. They would want to keep the dark magic hidden from dabblers on an island where the paranormal was not only accepted but embraced. The African history section was a different story.

"Great minds think alike?" a voice asked when I was hunched over and reading through a book on coastal tribes.

I jerked up my head, frowning when I realized Hadley had managed to sneak up on me without setting off my inner alarms. I should've sensed her and yet I didn't. "Um … yeah." I offered her a smile. "Just trying to get some research in."

She sat across from me and grabbed one of the books I'd yet to look through. "Anything?"

"No. Well … maybe." I inclined my head toward the book open

before me. "There's information here about coastal tribes that have gone extinct. It's interesting … and yet there's no hard information."

"What do you have so far?" Hadley seemed much more together than she had at dinner the previous evening. The giddiness that permeated her after being healed by Kade was gone.

"You seem better," I noted. "How are you feeling?"

Her cheeks flushed. "I feel embarrassed about how I acted."

"Do you remember everything?"

"Yup. Galen gave me grief about it this morning."

I had trouble believing that. "Are you sure he wasn't just teasing? He seemed to like drunken Hadley despite his worry." I thought about how he'd looked when he joined us on the beach. "Did he tell you what we found after you fell asleep?"

"He forwarded the photos you took," she replied. "That's why I'm here. The others are busy working. I thought I would do some research. He wanted Booker to help me but apparently Booker is helping your people."

"The ice," I mused. "The tents are too hot, even with fans, so we have to jerry-rig some air conditioning or everybody will die after twenty minutes."

She smirked. "The heat takes some getting used to, but after a few months you won't even notice it. It's just part of my life now." She hesitated a beat. "I mean … if you're still planning on moving here."

"We don't know yet," I cautioned. "Moonstone Bay is a possibility. Circuses are dying for a reason. We need a permanent location to reduce costs."

"Lilac told me about it." Hadley rested her hands on the table. She looked conflicted. "Can I ask you something?"

"Of course." I liked her. She was warm and fuzzy and fit right in with our group. If we did move here, I could imagine spending a decent amount of time with her.

"What's it like always being on the road? Lilac mentioned that you fight evil. You're like the Justice League of monster hunters or something. How can you do that and run the circus at the same time?"

I laughed at her description. "Don't ever mention us being the

Justice League of monster hunters to Luke. He will totally embrace that and start wearing a cape."

"I like him. He's funny."

"He has a good heart, despite the way he was acting around Booker."

"That's not his fault." Hadley said. "That cupid magic is hard to overcome. Only other elementals are immune. Lilac told me that she and Aurora are still affected by it if their defenses are down. Kade did a good job shielding them, so it's something to consider for the future."

"Luke is a good guy. He's a bit over the top, but there are worse things. As for hunting monsters, we build a magical net around the fairgrounds. We call it the dreamcatcher. Basically, it infuses my magic with that of Raven, Naida and Nixie. It calls to evil paranormals and people, and then alerts us if the boundaries are crossed."

Hadley's eyes went wide. "Really? What do you do with the evil people?"

I wanted to kick myself for bringing it up. "Well, let's just say we take care of them and leave it at that." There was no way I could bring up the voodoo dolls now. I didn't know her well enough. "We've fought more than a few battles. I'm sure it would be the same here. It's part of our everyday life. We're used to it."

"What are we dealing with now?" Hadley asked. "Galen had his 'Don't worry because I'll die to protect you' face on this morning. He didn't want me to know, but he's worried. Something happened on the beach last night. Something more than he told me."

I held out my hands. "Raven has seen the runes before." I ran through the story and when I finished Hadley looked perplexed.

"That's a little more involved than Galen explained," she said. "I think he held back because he was worried about what happened yesterday. I've never had that reaction before — and I've been around magic nonstop since I got here."

"I think it has something to do with the healing magic," I said. I wasn't certain how far I wanted to go with the conversation but holding back seemed like a mistake. "I think you were seriously hurt. I don't know that for a fact, but head injuries can kill someone even if they're minor."

She didn't seem upset at the possibility. "I guess that makes sense. I don't remember anything. There was no white light to follow. One second things were going black and the next they were coming into view again. It was weird."

"And you felt euphoric after the fact," I said.

"Pretty much. Galen is wrecked about it, though he would never admit it. It's a balancing act for him. I'm new to the magic game and he wants me to grow into the witch I'm supposed to be. He's also the sheriff and worries."

"Worry goes with love. Don't take it personally. If he didn't worry, that would be a problem." I thought about Kade's reaction to Luke's teasing. "All relationships are a balancing act."

Hadley turned her attention back to the books. "Tell me what you've found. I figure if we all work together on this, we have a better chance of solving our mutual problem."

"That's what I figure too." I tapped the page. "There are a lot of small tribes in Africa that have gone extinct. Unfortunately, it's impossible to tell why the tribes went missing. These runes look a lot like the hieroglyphs I've seen in some of the art pieces from those extinct tribes."

"Are any of them exact?"

"No, and that's the problem." I rolled my neck until it cracked. "The other problem is that some of these tribes have been absorbed into others. One I was researching because it went extinct within a two-year period turned out to have converted to Christianity. So, the tribe disappeared, but not for magical reasons."

Realization dawned on Hadley's face. "I hadn't considered that."

"It's a lot to dig through. I'm thinking of putting Luke on it when I get back to the fairgrounds. He's good with computers, and if that information is on the internet to be collected, he can find it."

Hadley took the book from me and studied the runes. "Galen mentioned something about demons. My interaction with demons is limited. Lilac is a half-demon. I just assumed she was the norm."

"Lilac is a half-demon who is actually a fire elemental," I corrected. "The demons of old were corrupted. There are multiple factions now.

We're likely dealing with the sort of demons that mated with humans. That often destroys souls."

"Because humans are bad?"

I shook my head. "Because humans aren't equipped to deal with the magic. There's a corrupting influence on human flesh that can't be ignored. Magical lines are strengthened through centuries, growing stronger as they progress. A sudden influx of magic in an unprepared genetic line can be catastrophic. I just don't know what sort of demons we're dealing with." I flicked my eyes to the window. I could see the surf rolling on the other side of the glass. "I'm assuming the island has a unique paranormal history that explains certain things. I'm at a loss because I'm an outsider. I just … don't … know." And that was the truly frustrating thing.

Hadley closed the book with a snap and stood. "Let's take a walk. I know a bit about the history of the island, but it's probably not something we should talk about here."

I nodded. "A walk sounds good."

I followed Hadley to the beach. She stopped at one of the food vendors long enough to purchase bottles of water, handing me one before we started our walk.

"I've learned a lot since I moved here," Hadley started. "Moonstone Bay has almost every sort of paranormal known to man and they live together in harmony. That harmony doesn't always involve a sense of community, however. Some of the factions isolate themselves on other parts of the island. Like the sirens. The first siren I met was Aurora. I was here one day, and she came wandering up the beach naked, as if she didn't have a care in the world. It was very jarring."

I laughed at the image. "Is she your friend?"

"Yes, but she has an attitude. I kind of like it. She grew up with Galen, Booker and Lilac. They were a little tribe. Three of them are elementals. Galen is the only one who isn't."

Something occurred to me. "You're part elemental. I mean … you're a witch, but you're not a standard witch. When you consider your relationship with him, your small group has one representative from each elemental faction."

Hadley nodded. "That's come into play more than once. Galen says that the presence of multiple elemental factions adds balance to the island. I'm still trying to figure all that out. He's worried that the runes mean things will be thrown out of whack. Right on the tail of the plane doors opening … ." She trailed off.

"Plane doors are forbidden here, right?" I already knew the answer. "How were they being opened if they're forbidden?"

"Some creepy writer who wanted to be the top guy in his genre kept opening the doors to let creatures through to attack his competition. He had a talisman and didn't care who else got hurt in the process.

"I was trapped on another plane for a bit," she admitted, her voice low. "Galen doesn't want me to tell anyone because Lilac had to open a door and send Aurora through to rescue me. I saw another world that day. I've been thinking a lot about it ever since."

"What conclusions have you come to?"

"That I like this plane. The other one was creepy. But Moonstone Bay isn't just one thing. It's many things … and I think one of those things is a gateway." Her eyes were serious when they locked with mine. "Plane doors are forbidden but they can still be opened. Anyone who opens them and is caught is punished. What if this demon is from another plane? What if it's here because it escaped to this side when the other doors were opened?"

My mind churned. "That was two weeks ago?"

"More like two and one-half, but close enough."

"How long ago did Galen start having trouble with kids and mischief?"

"About a week ago."

"It's an interesting thought." It was so interesting, in fact, that I didn't notice a shift in the wind until it had grown silent. My instincts kicked into overdrive, and I extended a hand in front of Hadley as I looked up.

There, on the beach about two-hundred feet in front of us, stood four children, ranging in age from about nine to twelve. They stood in a line, cutting us off from moving around them, and watched our progression.

"Well, that's not good," Hadley said. She glanced to our right, her eyes busy as they roamed between the bluff and the water. "I don't think we should risk trying to pass them."

"Definitely not," I agreed. We didn't have anyone near who could heal us, and we still had no idea what the kids could do when it came to a magical showdown. We needed more information before we could take them on. "Maybe we should turn back." That idea fled as soon as it landed when I found another two kids trailing us … and they looked as if they were readying for battle. "Or maybe not."

Hadley followed my gaze, frowning. "I don't know what to do." She reached in her pocket and fumbled with her phone, frowning when she took in the screen. "There are no cell bars here. Of course."

"Calling Galen won't help," I said when one of the kids laughed. The others joined in. There was nothing delightful about the sound. "We need to figure out a way to get around them." I looked to the water. "Can you swim?"

"Yes, but I think that's a terrible idea," Hadley said. "If they trap us in the water, the undertow is strong. We could drown."

I glanced at the bluff. "This is a cave system, right?" I had no idea how I knew.

"How did you know that?" Hadley fixed me with a dumbfounded look. "I was just thinking about that. I've been in those caves. There was a sea witch trying to kill us not long ago and we ended up there. I haven't been back since."

"I likely picked it up from your head. I can read minds but getting inside your head isn't easy. I'm guessing that's the elemental thing. I can't see Cole's thoughts unless he wants me to. You likely shutter without realizing. Just now, because you were worried about the kids, you didn't shutter."

"Fascinating," Hadley said. "We should talk about it later." The kids were getting closer. "We need to get in the cave."

"Can we do it from land?"

"There's an opening on the other side of the bluff, but we can't risk it. We can get in through the water."

"You just said we shouldn't get in the water because of the undertow."

"I don't think that we have a lot of options."

She was right. "Water it is."

We took off in tandem, my hands itching to lay down some cover. Without giving it the appropriate amount of thought, I unleashed a barrage of freezing magic toward the kids on my right. Hadley picked the same moment to hit them with some of her magic, and the result was a glowing pink wall that seemed to ooze around us.

"That's weird," I said as we hit the water, taking a moment to really study the wall. I removed my sandals and waded in. "How do we get into the cave from here?"

"We have to go under, but out there." Hadley pointed. "It's going to take a few minutes. I have no idea if that wall thing will hold."

"I guess we'll see. I … ." A massive gray form sluiced through the water in front of me. I couldn't register much in those precious few seconds, but I did see a fin. And teeth … a lot of teeth. "Great White." That's all that rasped out as I turned to run back to the beach. Fighting demon kids was preferable to taking on the apex predator of the ocean.

Hadley grabbed my wrist. "It's not a shark."

Was she kidding me? "If that's not a shark, what is it?"

"A rescue." Hadley grabbed the fin when it circled around a second time. The creature was moving unnaturally slow and didn't seem interested in eating us. "I'll explain in the cave. For now, you have to trust me."

With no other real options, I grabbed the fin. "If this thing eats us, I'll never forgive you."

Hadley didn't look bothered in the least. "Hold your breath. We're going under."

I had no choice, so I did as she instructed.

CHAPTER 13
Thirteen

I held my breath for what felt like a really long time. The shark dragged us from the crystal waters of the shoreline to somewhere underground. I'd never considered myself claustrophobic, but the blackness of the water had my heart seizing. Just when I thought I couldn't take it a moment longer, we broke the surface in a large cavern.

I sucked in gaping mouthfuls of oxygen as the shark led us further into the cavern. When Hadley let go of its fin and started swimming, I followed suit.

"What in the hell?" I demanded when we climbed onto dry rock. "What was that?"

"That would be Brody," Hadley replied as she rolled to her knees. I couldn't make out her face in the darkness, but then magic sprang to life. She threw up her hand, a million sparkles coming loose. They hung in the air, offering an almost cheery ambiance.

"You named the shark?"

"I didn't name him." Hadley inclined her head toward the shelf, which was now visible. A man stood about thirty feet from where we'd exited the water. He was naked. "I'm pretty sure his mother named him."

"Yup." The man in question bobbed his head. If he was bothered about being naked in front of two women, he didn't show it. He shook his head, water flying from his dark hair, and smiled at me. "She watched *Jaws* far too many times. She thought naming me Brody was an in-joke, but everybody catches on eventually."

It took me a moment to realize what he was referring to. "Martin Brody," I said dumbly.

"Hey!" Hadley straightened, her hands landing on her hips. "I didn't even put that together."

"That's because you're so pretty." Brody tweaked her nose as he passed, his full attention on the cavern. "There's a body over there." He pointed to what I believed to be the east corner.

"That's the sea hag," Hadley replied. "Stay away from her."

"I don't suppose there are clothes in here?" Brody asked. He cast me the occasional glance but seemed much more interested in Hadley. "I could use a pair of shorts."

"It's not a walk-in closet," Hadley said. "Where are the shorts you were wearing before you shifted?"

That's when things clicked into place. "You're a shark shifter."

Brody's smile widened, but he kept his gaze on Hadley. "I shifted at the private beach. I just wanted a quick dip. I planned to shift again back there. I didn't know I would need shorts."

"Well, the best laid plans." Hadley managed a grin. "Galen is going to be really angry when he finds out you got naked in front of me again."

"Galen needs to chill," Brody groused. "Besides, I didn't intend to get naked in front of you. I saw you on the beach with those kids and … felt you somehow needed help." He cocked his head, as if trying to figure out exactly what happened. "Why were you afraid of the kids?"

"They're not really kids," I replied, pushing myself to a standing position on shaky legs. I didn't care what either of them said. If this cavern had an escape on land, that was the exit I planned to use. "They're demons."

"Possessing demons," Hadley added knowledgeably. "We're having a few problems."

"Does this have something to do with all the little things happening on the island?" Brody had clearly given up trying to cover himself because he faced us dead on, hands on hips. "Stare as long as you want, sugar," he said. "I'm here to serve you."

I realized I had indeed been staring, but not for the reasons he assumed. "I'm engaged," I said.

"Good for you. Looking is still okay."

I jerked my eyes to Hadley, glad the illumination in the cave was too dim to show my burning cheeks. "You said there's a land exit?"

She nodded. "Yeah, but is that the route you want to go?"

"I'm not going back in the water." I was adamant. "No way, no how. No offense to you." I held up my hand for Brody's benefit. "I appreciate the rescue … even if you did come at us as a shark."

"Shark shifters are rare," Hadley offered. "Like … uber rare. Most everybody thinks they're extinct, but they moved to isolated tropical waters to protect themselves."

"So you were paying attention." Brody beamed at her. "Tell me about the demons."

"We don't know anything about them," Hadley replied, turning serious. "We saw them for the first time last night. We melted two, but don't know if we killed them. Strange runes popped up on the beach, and it all might have something to do with disappearing tribes in Africa."

Brody blinked several times and then turned to me. "Do you speak English? What she said sounded like English, but it couldn't possibly be because I didn't understand a word of it."

I let loose a hollow laugh, which helped lighten the mood a bit. I laid things out for him — if Hadley trusted him, I had no reason not to — and when I finished, he seemed more perplexed than when I'd started.

"Well, that's just a kick in the pants," he muttered. I assumed he was talking about the demonic children. I was wrong. "I thought lamia were extinct."

It was only then that I remembered I'd brought up Raven's past. "Hadley said everybody thinks shark shifters are extinct, but you're more interested in meeting a lamia."

"Oh, I totally want to meet her," Brody agreed. "Is she hot?"

"Yup, but she'll eat you for lunch. Besides, she has a boyfriend. She dates a British clown."

"Obviously you don't like him if you think he's a clown."

"Oh, no." I shook my head. "He's a real clown."

"She's with the circus," Hadley explained. "They have clowns."

Brody shuddered. "Oh, gross. Clowns are the worst."

"That seems to be the consensus among adults," I agreed. I'd scanned the cavern twice and come up with nothing of use. "We can't stay here. Even now, those little demons are probably trying to figure a way to get to us. If they find the exit on the other side of the bluff ... ." I left it hanging.

"They won't come in through the water," Brody said. "They won't know about the cave. The only reason I know about it is because I've been exploring the past couple of weeks. They won't waste time doing that, especially if they don't know what happened to us. It's safer to leave through the water."

"Yeah, thank you for the offer, but I will kindly decline," I replied. "I can't swim with a shark again, even if I know you're a shifter."

Brody rolled his eyes. "Good grief. I'm perfectly harmless."

"Galen won't think that when he finds out you're naked and hanging around with me again." Hadley moved to a wall and yanked something off it. It appeared to be a tapestry of sorts. "Wrap yourself in this."

Brody made a face. "You have no idea how long that thing has been hanging there. It could be infested with black mold."

"It could be," Hadley agreed, "but Poet is right. We need to go through the tunnel and exit the other side. I should be able to use my cell phone then ... ." Something occurred to her, and her eyes went wide. She dug in her pocket and when she returned with her phone she growled. "It's dead." She tapped the screen. "Crap. I went into the water with my phone. Galen could be trying to call right now."

"Calm down." I took the phone from her and pressed it between my hands, briefly shutting my eyes. White magic closed hot around the phone, and then the screen flared to life. "All fixed." I handed it back to her.

"How did you do that?" Hadley was impressed. "I would love to learn to do that."

"I spent a few years on the streets of Detroit," I replied. "When you have magic at your disposal but limited funds, you learn tricks quickly. I fixed more than a few phones that were dumped in the trash."

"You lived on the streets?"

I blinked and then laughed. "Wow. None of us are firing on all cylinders right now, are we? Yes. I lived on the streets. I ended up with the circus when I tried to pick Max's pocket. I needed food. Instead of punishing me, he offered me a job. I've been with Mystic Caravan ever since."

"Wow," Brody said. "And I thought you were hot before. You're way hotter now. I love tough chicks."

"She's engaged," Hadley said. "Her boyfriend is magical too."

"Yes, but I'm a shark, which makes me a badass."

"I'll keep that in mind," I said dryly. "We need to get out of here and call our people."

"Yeah, I need to get Galen here." Hadley frowned at her screen. "It's working but there are no bars. You need to wrap yourself, Brody. We're sticking together, whether you like it or not."

He made a disgruntled sound but did as she ordered. "If I get black mold on my junk, I'll make you pay."

"Poet's boyfriend can heal people. He'll heal your junk if it becomes necessary."

I tried to picture Kade healing Brody in that area and choked on a laugh. "Let's get moving. If those kids figure out there's an exit on the other side of the bluff, they could be waiting for us."

THE CAVE EXIT was clear. The second we emerged, Hadley called Galen. That left Brody and me to serve as lookouts. There was no sign of the kids.

It took Galen ten minutes to find us behind the bluff, and when he arrived, he looked annoyed to find Brody with us. "Why am I not surprised?" he muttered as he pulled Hadley in for a hug. "Are you okay?"

"I'm fine," she reassured him. She was pink-faced and flushed with excitement. "Brody shifted and saved us. He took us to the sea hag cave. I had to make him wear that tapestry because nobody wants to see what's under it."

"Everybody wants to see what's under it," Brody corrected.

Hadley continued as if she hadn't heard him. "I got to swim with a shark." She bounced on the balls of her feet. "I knew it was him right away and didn't freak out even a little."

"Good job." Galen smiled at her, although there was fear in his eyes. "Are you okay?"

"I'm the one who freaked out about swimming with a shark," I replied. "Hadley seemed to think it was perfectly normal. I was more interested in fighting the demon kids."

Galen let loose a low chuckle. "I would've been right there with you." He stroked his hand down the back of Hadley's head. "I sent patrols out to check the beach on the other side of the bluff. I haven't gotten any reports back yet."

"Hadley and I managed to do something with our magic," I explained. "I'm still not quite sure what it was. I tried to freeze the kids in place — I figured I could buy us a few minutes — but Hadley did something at the same time. The magic reacted, kind of coalesced, and it made this weird pink wall."

"But it protected you guys?" Galen queried.

"It did."

"I was trying to blow them back," Hadley explained. "I was just as surprised by the pink wall as she was."

"Well, you can ask May about it." Galen forced a tight smile and pressed his lips to her forehead. He seemed to want to keep her close. "As for you ... ." His gaze was dark when it landed on Brody. "I guess I should thank you ... even though you got naked in front of my girl-friend yet again."

I had to press my lips together and look away to keep from laughing.

"I told you he'd be angry," Hadley said. "It's not Brody's fault. He stripped on the private beach and had every intention of going back the same way. If he hadn't been there ... ." She trailed off.

"That's why he gets to stay alive," Galen said, his lips curving. "Tell me about the kids. Did you recognize them?"

I couldn't answer that, so I turned to Hadley.

She shook her dark head. "No, but I don't know all the kids on the island."

"But if the lamia is right and we're dealing with a possessing demon, these kids are coming from somewhere. Lilac didn't recognize the kids that attacked you yesterday. Unfortunately, you haven't been around long enough to meet all the kids ... and that goes double for Brody."

"And I work in a bar," Brody added. "Most parents don't bring kids to a bar, well, unless they're really bad at their jobs."

Galen looked as if he was fighting a smirk. "This demon has to be getting the kids from somewhere. Lilac would recognize local kids, so the kids that attacked last night had to belong to tourists."

Hadley immediately shook her head. "Not necessarily."

Galen arched an eyebrow. "Where do you think these kids are coming from? Last time I checked, even a demon couldn't magically conjure kids."

"The kids might not be coming from town," Hadley said. "You said there are shifter factions out in the woods. The sirens too. They could be coming from some of those smaller tribes and villages."

For a moment I thought Galen would argue with her. Instead, he moved his jaw back and forth, contemplating the possibility. "Well, crap."

"Ha!" Hadley poked his stomach and wiggled her hips. "I was right for a change."

Amusement and affection warring for supremacy on his face, Galen shook his head. "I'm not saying you're right. I'm saying it's a possibility."

"I'm totally right," Hadley insisted. "At the very least, we need to head out to Cooper's Hollow and talk to Cordelia."

"What's Cooper's Hollow?" I asked.

"The siren stronghold," replied Galen, looking pained at the prospect. "That's a long drive, Hadley. If they were missing children we'd have already heard."

"They keep to themselves," Hadley insisted. "You told me they don't like outsiders mucking about their business. They might keep something like this secret ... especially if they knew about the demon and were trying to control the situation."

"Yeah, but ... Aurora would tell me." Galen looked conflicted. "If she knew there was trouble, she would come to me."

"Unless Cordelia backed her in a corner. Aurora is loyal."

"Aurora also has taken the last three days off," Brody offered. "She's been working for me. She said she had a family emergency. She's such a good worker — never late and can serve as a bouncer if needed — I didn't think anything of it."

"Well, crap." Galen rolled his neck from side to side. I could practically hear the gears of his mind working. "Okay. I don't see where we have much choice. But I need to track down Booker. I can't go to Cooper's Hollow without backup."

"You have me," Hadley reminded him.

"And me," I said. "I just need to call Kade and tell him where I'm going. Besides, Booker is helping my guys. They needed a vehicle for ice."

Galen hesitated. "Um ... ."

"I'll go too," Brody offered. "I've always wanted to see Cooper's Hollow."

"You can't go like that," Galen said, scowling and nodding to the tapestry fragment.

"We can stop at the lighthouse," Hadley suggested. "You have extra shorts and shirts."

Galen looked torn. "Hadley, I'd feel better if Booker was our fourth."

"Because he's your best friend?" she challenged.

I had no idea where she was going with this argument, but I was curious to hear his response.

"Because he's been there before." Galen growled. "Fine. We'll get the shark shifter some clothes and head out. It will be a wonderful trip. Me, my girlfriend, the shark shifter she has a crush on, and the magical circus performer who can somehow join her magic with that of my girlfriend to create big pink walls. What could possibly go wrong?"

Hadley's smile didn't diminish. "I love you too."

"Ugh." Despite his bad mood, Galen gave her a quick kiss. "You're doing the massaging later. I call dibs on being coddled."

"Yeah, we'll talk about that after Cooper's Hollow."

"I've already called dibs. That's how it works."

"We'll see."

"Man." Galen slapped a hand to his forehead. "This is going to be such a long day."

CHAPTER 14

K ade, Luke and Cole weren't happy when they learned I was heading to Cooper's Hollow without them. They all got on the call to argue that at least one of them should join the party. Explaining that I was going with Hadley and Galen did little to ease their frustration. I told them to suck it up before ending the call. I figured there would be an argument later.

Brody sat in the front of the truck with Galen. They seemed uneasy with one another, but the vantage point from the rear seat offered an interesting view of their interaction. It allowed me to monitor their relationship … and try to get inside their heads.

"What's the deal with shark shifters?" I asked once we were on the highway. Galen showed little interest in watching the road as he drove. I figured that was because he knew the route intimately.

"What's the deal with … whatever you are?" Brody shot back. He was tall, muscular, and fit, but Galen's clothes were still a size too big for him. He reminded me of a little brother dressing in his older brother's hand-me-downs.

"I don't know what I am," I replied. There was no sense in lying. Hadley and Galen already knew the truth.

"How can you not know what you are?"

I shrugged and focused out the window. "My parents were non-magical. They died when I was a teenager. After that I was in the system ... and on the street for a few years. Once I joined the circus, everyone said they could feel my power. Nobody knew where it stemmed from, so I don't know what I am."

"You were on the street?" Galen's eyes met mine in the rearview mirror. "Where?"

"Detroit."

"Seriously?" He looked horrified at the thought. "How did you survive that?"

"It wasn't as hard as you think. Winters were rough, but my magic helped. We had a small tribe. We all looked out for one another."

"Were they all teenagers?"

"Mostly. Some were in their twenties, but you wouldn't know to look at them. We were all underfed and small for our ages. There were a couple of adults who looked out for us, tried to make sure we were fed as much as possible. One of them turned out to be an undercover FBI agent, something I should've realized."

"He told you he was an FBI agent?" Galen seemed fascinated.

"No. I ran into him a few months ago. We were in Detroit for the circus and part of my old crew was drawn into a magical battle ... along with some reapers. I saw him then and that's when he told me."

"Reapers?" Hadley straightened. "The Grimlocks?"

Amusement raced through me. "You know them?"

"Aisling and Griffin came here for their honeymoon. She was pregnant and her father ended up coming down to help us with an issue."

"They had a little girl." I smiled at the memory of the dark-haired infant the Grimlocks continuously grappled over. "Lily. She's spoiled beyond belief ... and I bet she'll start crawling soon. Maybe she already has."

"Oh, that's sweet." Hadley looked genuinely happy to hear the news. "She and her brothers cracked me up. They had these long, drawn-out arguments. Apparently, it was a big deal that she got pregnant before the wedding."

"I'm pretty sure they're over that." I dragged a hand through my hair. As much as I liked meeting new magical friends, I had other things on my mind today. "So, what's the deal with shark shifters again?"

Brody made a weird noise, which earned a smirk from Galen. "I don't know what to tell you. People think we're extinct because we've largely retreated from society. I moved to Moonstone Bay because I had the opportunity to buy my own bar. That's all there is to it."

"It seems like there should be more," I said.

"There isn't."

"Are your parents still alive?" As much as I hated being grilled, I had questions.

"They are. They're … living the dream." Brody managed a small smile, which told me that was an inside joke. "I can't really talk about them. When I left, I promised not to reveal where we'd moved. It's not that I don't trust you, but … ." He trailed off, holding out his hands and shrugging.

"You don't know me," I finished. "I get it."

"You seem nice enough, your shark fear notwithstanding."

"Hey, all I knew is that there was a Great White shark swimming around and trying to gnaw on me."

"I certainly didn't try to gnaw on you," he sniffed. "Humans don't taste good."

"Do we taste like chicken?" Hadley asked.

"I'm going to refrain from answering that question," Brody said dryly. He turned to Galen. "Tell me about Cooper's Hollow. All I know are the whispers I've heard. Aurora doesn't mention her people often."

"Aurora is tight lipped for a reason," Galen replied. "She's tribe but … she's also more."

"Aurora grew up with Galen, Booker and Lilac," Hadley volunteered. "They were all really tight as kids. Her loyalties are split."

"Not really," Galen countered. "If it comes down to it, she'll always pick her people. I have no doubt about that."

A quick glance at Hadley told me she believed otherwise. I opted not to push the issue. "Do you think siren children have gone missing?"

Galen looked perplexed by the question. "They don't share information with us. When we get out there, you need to be careful. We're going to park, and you'll be able to see fragments of their village. Stay in the area where we park. They don't like outsiders."

"Even you?" I asked.

"I'm law enforcement. They definitely don't want me out there." Galen was grim. "Cordelia — she's the leader — is pragmatic. She deals with me, but only because she knows that's easier than starting a war."

"Who would win if there was a war?" I asked.

"I don't ever want to learn the answer to that question."

I slid my eyes to Hadley and found her focused on her boyfriend. Her expression was unreadable. When she finally turned to me, her smile was wan. "Have you been to Cooper's Hollow?" I asked.

"A few times," she confirmed. "It's a cool place, but they won't let me wander around. It's frustrating."

"Even with Aurora? I thought she was your friend."

"Aurora has no power out there," Galen replied. "She's not in charge. She does what she can — and the rules for her are a little different — but she's not in a position to help us. I'll do the talking when we get there."

"I assume that means you want me to be pretty but silent," I drawled.

"I'm not all that worried about you," Galen replied. "You haven't survived in this world as long as you have without learning how to read people. That's your entire job with the circus — and you're a survivor. You made it on the streets of Detroit when you were just a kid. That proves something. I was actually saying that for Brody's benefit."

"Hey!" Brody made a big show of being annoyed but I could tell he was more amused. "I'll have you know that people love me. Women especially love me, and my understanding is that the sirens are a matriarchal society. I'll have this Cordelia chick eating out of my hand within five minutes. We are both creatures of the sea, after all."

"You do what you feel is best," Galen replied. "Just FYI, though, if you incur Cordelia's wrath and she decides to take you prisoner and torture you, I won't step in and save you."

Brody swallowed hard. "Torture me?"

"Cordelia is very efficient when she wants to send a message."

Brody contorted in his seat and looked to Hadley for confirmation. "Is he messing with me?"

"I don't think so." Hadley said. "I've met Cordelia a few times and she scares the crap out of me. I would do as Galen says and let him set the tone."

"Well, awesome." Brody made a face. "I can't wait to meet this chick. There's nothing I love more than a terrifying woman."

"Then you'll love Cooper's Hollow," Galen said. "Just remember what I said. They don't mess around."

THE TRIP TOOK LONGER THAN I anticipated. The scenery was pretty, but by the time we pulled onto a two-track and headed into the woods, I was antsy.

Galen parked in the middle of a small field, admonished us one more time to let him do the talking, and then we got out. I was grateful to stretch my legs. Moving from location to location with the circus had acclimated me to long trips, but this felt different.

I scanned the surrounding trees. They were thick, giving the field a claustrophobic feeling. I felt multiple sets of eyes on us, but there was no sign of anyone coming to greet us … at least not yet.

"Look through the trees there." Hadley pointed. "You can see smoke from the fires."

"How far have you been in there?"

"I'm not allowed to wander around here." Hadley's expression told me she was bitter about that. "I keep hoping that one day Cordelia will decide she likes me and offer me the grand tour."

"Keep holding your breath," a voice said as a striking woman with auburn hair exited the trees directly next to us. Was this the famous Cordelia?

"Hey, Aurora." Brody greeted her. "Glad to see you're alive. I was starting to worry."

"I told you I needed a few days off," Aurora said. "You said you were fine with it."

"I am." Brody was the amiable sort and the smile he offered up looked legitimate. "Given recent developments, I just wanted to check on you."

Hadley seemed curious as she glanced between them. "Are you guys hanging out when you're not at work?"

Brody switched his eyes to the witch. "What do you mean?"

Aurora snorted. "She's a busybody who fancies herself a matchmaker. She wants us to get together."

"I didn't say that," Hadley protested.

"Good." Aurora's gaze was dark. "Don't even think it. I don't need you sticking your nose in my business."

"I mind my own business," Hadley sniffed.

"Tell that to Booker and Lilac." Aurora faced Galen. "What are you doing out here? Cordelia won't be happy to see you."

"Cordelia is never happy to see me," Galen replied. "We have a situation."

"What sort of situation?"

"The sort that means I have questions for Cordelia."

Aurora didn't look happy with the response, but she didn't push him. She leaned against the truck and waited. After a few minutes, the trees on the other side of the field gave way to a regal woman. She was flanked by men carrying spears. They looked aggressive, but they were clearly subservient to her.

"Cordelia?" I asked Hadley in a low voice.

She nodded and remained fixated on the woman.

"Galen," Cordelia said as she glanced between faces. "Hadley." She nodded, although there was no warmth to the greeting. "What did we talk about? Unscheduled visits aren't wanted here. And to bring strangers to our stronghold? Obviously, you've been drinking a few too many daiquiris with the demon."

Galen kept his shoulders squared and his smile friendly, but I could tell the words irritated him. "This is Poet Parker." He gestured toward me. "She's with the circus. Brody is new to the island. He took over the Beach Bungalow."

"I know who he is." Cordelia didn't bother with useless greetings. "What do you want?"

"We have a situation."

"You always do. There's a reason we don't bother ourselves with the problems of your people."

"It's an island problem," Galen countered. "We all need to deal with it. I need to know if any of your children have gone missing."

Cordelia's forehead wrinkled. "You think we can't monitor our own children?"

"We have a group of children causing trouble in town," he replied. "It started as general mischief. Now it's four murders and attacking people on the beach."

"Children?" Cordelia dropped her affected tone and seemed surprised. "Are they magical?"

"They seem to be. Two attacked a group outside the cemetery yesterday. When they fought back, the children turned into purple smoke. We don't know if that means the children are dead — or something else — but we need to know if you have children missing."

"No." Cordelia shook her head. "But we have seen some things."

"Can you tell me?"

"It's more that we've heard things," Aurora interjected, making a face when Cordelia glared at her. "If you drag this out, they'll stay longer. Tell him what he wants to know, and he'll be on his way."

"What have you heard?" Galen asked.

"Whispers," Cordelia said. "Laughter. We've had mischief problems too. A few items — mostly food — have been stolen. Even though our borders are locked down at night we've found small footprints in the center of our village. Someone managed to invade our lands."

"It's happening here too." Galen rubbed his chin. "Runes appeared on the beach last night." He started toward Cordelia with his phone in his hand, ignoring the way the men gripped their spears. "I want you to look at the photos."

Cordelia shot her men quelling looks and then stepped forward. She studied the photos. "A possessing demon."

If Galen was surprised she knew, he didn't show it. "Have any of your people been possessed?"

"No, but I've heard stories about runes like that. Some of the legends say that back when this was a pirate haven a band of children went on a killing spree. Witches stopped them."

"Witches?" Galen cocked an eyebrow.

"Every woman with magical powers was considered a witch then. I very much doubt they were actual witches."

"So what are we dealing with?"

"I don't know, but at least one of the children you chase will not be a child. It will likely be a demon in disguise. If you find that child and kill it, the other children should be freed from whatever spell they're under."

"That's great." Galen didn't look thrilled with the information. "You're suggesting I just start slaughtering children until I find a demon in disguise."

"I don't care how you do your job," Cordelia replied. "However delicate your sensibilities when dealing with children, you have very few options. The evil will grow if you don't thwart it now."

"I'm not killing children," Galen snapped. "There must be another way to deal with this threat."

"None that I'm aware of. Check with the hill packs. They breed more than they should and wouldn't make it public knowledge if their children started disappearing."

"Yeah, I'll set something up." Galen sighed. "They're shifters. They won't accept outsiders. I need to be careful how I interact with them."

"You need to be careful how you interact with us as well," Cordelia noted. "You often forget that we stay away from the rest of you for a reason. We don't want your problems foisted upon us."

"I hate to break it to you, Cordelia, but our problems are already your problems. The bodies we found were arranged in the sign of a cross. You need to be on the lookout."

"We're always on the lookout."

Galen stared at her for an extended moment and then nodded. "Keep your people safe, Cordelia. If you learn something new, I'd appreciate a call."

"I will do what I can."

Galen turned to Aurora. "You be careful too. I'm not sure what's going on with you, but make sure you stay safe."

"Aurora is one of us," Cordelia called out. "I keep my people safe."

"Aurora is one of my people too." Galen could be pushed only so far. "By the way, Cordelia, I haven't had a chance to thank you for what you did a few weeks ago."

The siren looked puzzled. "What was that?"

"You sent trackers out when we were having trouble with the plane doors. Because you did, we managed to keep the situation contained. I owe you for that."

"You owe me nothing." Cordelia was firm. "The plane doors were a threat to all of us."

"What's happening now is a threat to all of us," Galen insisted. "You need to be careful."

"I thank you for the warning. You should go now."

And just like that, we'd been dismissed. I couldn't help wondering if the long trip had been worth it.

CHAPTER 15

Fifteen

The ride back to town felt like it took even longer. I couldn't help being disappointed with the lack of information from Cordelia. I asked a few questions during the ride — mostly regarding the sirens' desire to be kept separate — but there was little to discuss.

"We'll have a barbecue at the lighthouse for everyone," Galen said when the town popped into view. "Gather your people and bring them. We'll serve food in about two hours."

I didn't find myself rankled by what clearly was an order. "What good will that do?" I asked.

"We need to start working this out. Your lamia seems to have the most information."

"You've met Raven," I reminded him. "Does she strike you as purposely helpful?"

"She strikes me as loyal. In fact, she reminds me of Aurora. In a time of crisis, she'll put herself on the line for those she cares about."

"You're assuming she cares about us."

Galen grimaced as he stopped on the road near the fairgrounds. I saw my people working. Several of them — including Kade and Luke — lifted their heads to stare at the truck. It was almost as if they sensed us. "Your lamia might be abrasive, but she's a team player. If she wasn't, given how frightened she is after seeing those runes, she'd already be gone."

"I guess you're a better judge of people than I gave you credit for." I flashed a small grin as I pushed open the door. "We'll be there for dinner. Thank you for the invitation, even though it sounded more like an order."

"He's just bossy," Hadley said. "Do you guys have any special food requests? Any vegetarians?"

"None who will be with us. I'll just bring our core group. Nixie, Naida, Nellie, Dolph, Luke, Cole, Kade, Raven and Percival should do it. I'll try to round up Max, but he's likely otherwise engaged."

"Max is the owner?" Galen asked. "I believe I saw his name on the paperwork when the request came through the DDA."

"He's the owner, but he has little to do with day-to-day operations now. That falls mainly to me."

"See if you can get him. We'll have a big spread for dinner. Then we'll talk."

I moved to shut the door and then paused, my gaze shifting to Brody. "You'll be there? I have more shark shifter questions."

"What is it with you guys and the questions?" Brody threw his hands into the air.

"He'll be there," Hadley promised. "We can double-team him with the questions."

I was still smiling when I joined my group. I was tired but rest was still hours away. "We're invited to dinner," I told Kade. "Things have changed."

"Like being attacked by a tribe of kids and hiding in a cave?" Kade demanded. "You can't just leave after announcing you've been attacked. I need to see that you're okay with my own eyes."

"I told you I was fine."

"Yes, well … seeing and hearing are two different things."

"Whatever." I wasn't in the mood to argue. "I'm fine. A shark shifter saved us. He'll be at dinner."

Luke, who had been loitering with his head down, perked up. "No way! Shark shifters are supposed to be extinct."

"Apparently they've moved their headquarters to other locations,"

I replied. "He'll be joining us for dinner, so you can pepper him with questions. He doesn't seem to like being interrogated, but he seems resigned to answering questions."

"Awesome." Luke rubbed his hands together. "I love asking invasive questions."

"I never would've guessed. They're barbecuing. We're supposed to be at the lighthouse in two hours. I need to gather the rest of the group." I hesitated. "Where's Raven?"

"In the House of Mirrors," Cole said. "I'll go with you."

I opened my mouth to argue — I didn't need a babysitter no matter what the men in my life believed — but there was something about his expression that changed my mind. "Sure." I smiled while patting Kade's shoulder. He remained tense. "If you want to argue, we can do it later in our hotel room."

"You're the boss." Kade was surly when he turned and waved his hand for Luke to follow. "Come on. Let's let her do … her thing. We need to check those ACs we set up one more time. I'm hoping they're all still operational so the tents will be cool tomorrow."

Luke gave me a saucy salute. "I'll see you in two hours to grill the shark shifter."

I managed a smile, but it only stayed in place until Kade and Luke were gone. Cole's demeanor was stiff as we crossed to the House of Mirrors. "If you have something to say, now would be the time."

"Your head doesn't seem in a good place for a lecture," he noted.

"Are you going to lecture me?"

"I'm going to remind you that you're loved. Luke loves you. I love you. Kade definitely loves you."

"I called to say I was fine."

"You also told us that you were magically attacked and were heading to a dangerous area to hang with anti-social sirens. Your only backup was people we don't know. Of course, that's going to leave us agitated."

"I can take care of myself."

"As you've proven multiple times." He bobbed his head in agreement. "We still love you. Ask yourself how you would've reacted had the tables been turned. Would you have been happy about Kade being attacked and then taking off to meet a bunch of surly sirens?"

"It was a fluid situation. The whole shark thing threw me more than I'm comfortable admitting."

Cole chuckled. "Well, lead with that when you apologize to Kade before dinner."

"What makes you think I'm going to apologize?"

"You know you were wrong. We lucked out and everything turned out fine, but I'm sure you'd handle things differently if you had them to do over again."

"You're sure of that, are you?"

"Yup."

"Well, if you're sure." I blew out a sigh. "I am sorry. Galen and Hadley are solid backup, and the shark shifter proved himself out there. He didn't have to intervene. Then he dressed in clothes that didn't fit and went with us to see the sirens. He could've avoided the whole situation."

"We still don't know him. Kade can't help being worried. He knows you're strong … and capable … and altogether terrifying when you want to be. But when you love someone, fear will always be a motivating factor."

"I'll apologize before dinner."

"I also want to know why you're hitting up Raven with the dinner invitation first. I have a feeling I know the answer, but I want you to say it."

"She's afraid."

"Kade said the same thing."

"She's never afraid."

"And?"

"And I need to know her head is in a good place. I'll invite her to dinner and make sure she understands it's important she attends. If she resists … well … at least I'll know."

"She'll complain but show up to dinner anyway," Cole said. "We both know that."

"She's important. She's one of the few people who has seen these runes before. We need her."

"She won't let you down."

"I never thought she would, but I didn't see that until recently."

"She's not an easy woman," Cole said. "She requires effort to love, but she's worth it."

"You probably shouldn't tell her that. She'll balk at being told she's loved."

"I'm not an idiot."

I laughed, and it felt good. "I don't know what we're going to accomplish with this dinner, but at least everybody will know everybody by the time we're done."

RAVEN DIDN'T PROTEST WHEN I told her about dinner. She also didn't agree to come. I left her to ponder her options, all the while knowing that she would attend. She might not be pleasant, but she would definitely make an appearance.

We returned to the hotel long enough to change clothes. I apologized to Kade. When I explained that the shark shifter threw my head into a fuzzy space, he was surprisingly understanding. Once the tiff was behind us, he returned to his normal self.

Galen and Hadley were on the patio grilling when we arrived. Booker looked leery when he caught sight of Luke, Nixie and Naida. Kade immediately used the same shield spell he had the night before to protect the cupid, and it worked even better this time, which seemed a relief to all.

Brody sat in a chair drinking a beer. He'd found some different clothes that fit better. It was obvious he was the new member of their group, however, because he seemed most comfortable sitting a few feet from the others and watching them interact.

The true surprise of the evening was Aurora. She came from the ocean. Hadley explained she kept extra clothes in a watertight compartment for her visits. Aurora didn't go out of her way to greet anybody but was instantly accepted by her friends. I found the relationships difficult to grasp but there was genuine love flowing through the group as they laughed together.

Galen waited until the food was doled out and everyone spread out at several tables. "So, I'm sure everybody has been caught up by now on what we've learned."

"You've learned almost nothing," Raven pointed out from her spot at the far table with Percival, Nellie and Dolph. She had her "I hate everybody" face on so the newcomers would know to keep their distance.

"That's not entirely true," Galen countered. "We know the sirens aren't missing any children. We also know that if we find the demon masquerading as a child, we can save the others."

"No, you *think* that," Raven stressed. "You don't know anything."

"I have no reason to doubt Cordelia."

"I've never known a siren to purposely mislead people. That doesn't mean she knows what she's talking about. Basing fact on myth is always a mistake. If I did that people would assume I turn into an actual snake when I wield my magic."

"I'm assuming you don't." Galen's expression was hard to read as he focused on Raven. It was obvious he didn't like her attitude. Given his position on the island, however, he knew how to deal with various characters. He was calm when interacting with her but showed no sign of weakness.

"Do you turn into a dog when you hump your girlfriend's leg?" Raven shot back.

Silence descended over the dinner party and a momentary bolt of panic licked through me. This was not how I wanted things to go.

"Raven … ." I wasn't certain what I was going to say.

"He's being insulting," Raven snapped. "I'm not sorry."

"I didn't mean to be insulting," Galen said. "I simply would like to know whatever information you have. You're the oldest, the most knowledgeable. You're vitally important to this group."

Raven shook her head. "Oh, it would be so much easier if you were all rude and obnoxious," she complained. "Then I could leave you to die without feeling an ounce of guilt."

"I didn't even know you could feel guilt," Luke mused.

I extended a warning finger in his direction. "Don't."

"I'm just minding my own business," Luke complained.

"Mind it with your mouth shut," Cole suggested, grabbing the ear of corn from Luke's plate and shoving it in his boyfriend's mouth. "It's quiet time."

Luke looked like he was ready to murder Cole, but he didn't say another word. He determinedly chewed on his corn, perhaps sending a message of a later argument.

"We know basics," Cole noted as he took control of the conversation. "We know that those kids tracked Hadley and Poet on the beach. That wasn't by accident."

"What do you think it means?" Galen asked.

Cole spread his hands. "It's possible these kids have been possessed for a specific reason. They might have a job to do. The problem is, we're at a loss for the type of demon we're dealing with."

"We also don't know where the demon came from," Lilac added. She was more serious than I'd witnessed so far, no hint of a smile bubbling beneath the surface like normal. "We need to give serious thought to the possibility that the demon escaped into our world through one of the open plane doors."

"Then that creates a problem," Galen said. "We were careful to keep the number of plane doors quiet. I don't relish the idea of being called before the DDA to explain how a demon got through without anyone noticing."

"You're afraid of the DDA?" Nellie was incredulous. "Why would you be afraid of a bunch of bureaucrats?"

"They're a little more than that," Galen replied. "Other towns have mayors and councils. So do we, but they're figureheads. They wield zero power. The DDA runs everything."

"That's stupid."

Galen smiled. "That's been noted on more than one occasion."

"There's nothing you can do about the DDA," Booker argued. "They're going to do what they're going to do. We have to focus on the demon. If what Cordelia said is correct, we have to figure out a way to identify which one of these kids is in charge."

"I'm willing to bet that we haven't seen the chief kid yet," I said. "I mean … why would this individual put him or herself at risk when it can use the other kids as fodder? The demon must be holed up somewhere. Do you have abandoned houses we can check?"

"No." Galen shook his head. "We rarely have open houses here. I can check the records, but if the demon is hiding, I'll bet it's farther inland. There are plenty of caves back in the mountains, even under the beaches."

"What about the dreamcatcher?" Luke asked. He'd finished his corn and was much calmer. "Can't we modify the dreamcatcher to draw in a demon specifically?"

It was an interesting question. "I don't know." I glanced at Raven. "What do you think?"

"It's possible," she said.

"What's a dreamcatcher?" Booker asked.

I explained. "We usually set it to draw in evil humans and monsters. There might be a way to modify it for demons."

"Wouldn't that draw in Lilac and Cole?" Booker looked alarmed. "You have a half-demon on your side."

Lilac shook her head. "Cole is a true elemental. Both his parents were elementals. I'm half elemental and half demon. We're different."

"I love you anyway," Cole promised.

Lilac grinned at him. "If I get called to the dreamcatcher, we'll just have to deal with it. I mean … I can just sit in a tent if I have to and wait until the other demon shows up."

"It's possible," Raven confirmed. "We can work on it tomorrow morning before the circus opens. It just might be the solution we're looking for."

"How do we kill the demon when we find it?" Aurora asked. "Can we kill it as we normally do?"

"I'm using my ax to behead it," Nellie offered. "I've yet to meet an evil-doer that doesn't work on."

Aurora shot him a genuine smile. "I kind of like that idea."

"I'm full of them," Nellie promised.

"We need to continue researching," Galen insisted. "We can't just assume this dreamcatcher thing is going to work. We need to be prepared for all possibilities."

"We can work with what we've got so far," I said. "The problem is this demon will use the children it has already enslaved as distractions. We're not going to kill them, so the demon will have the advantage."

"We'll have to deal with that as we go." Galen was grim. "I don't want to lose children — I'll fight for each and every one of them — but we might not have an option." He fell silent and then shook his head. "We'll deal with that when it becomes necessary. For now, we have a plan. Let's hope it leads us to a solution ... and fast."

CHAPTER 16
Sixteen

The barbecue lasted until almost ten o'clock. Most of us returned to the hotel — sleep, plus a full day of work at the fairgrounds, called — but I didn't miss the fact that Nellie and Aurora headed off together. I didn't want to know what they had planned.

"That's a frightening duo," Kade noted as he slung his arm around my shoulders. We were on the sidewalk preparing to cross to the hotel but could still see the two small figures on the beach.

"They're kind of funny," I said. "In a fight, I bet they could torch almost any enemy."

"Even a demon?"

"I hope so." I sent him a smile. "It would be great if Nellie could fly in and end all of this with one swing of an ax, wouldn't it?"

"It would be great. I don't know if we're going to get that lucky."

"No."

We walked the rest of the way to the hotel in silence. Once there, everybody went their separate ways. Raven headed toward the hotel bar instead of the elevator, even though Percival appeared to be going up to their room.

"Do you want to spend some time with her?" Kade asked.

"We can head upstairs."

"How about I head upstairs and get pretty for you, and you talk to Raven because that's really what you want to do?"

"Are you sure? I know you're still irritated about what happened earlier today."

"I'm fine. I was just worried. You apologized."

"Well, as long as you're fine." I kissed him. "I won't be long. She's upset and I need to talk to her about it."

"You're a good friend." He pressed a kiss to my forehead and headed toward the elevators.

I trudged toward Raven. Were we friends? How had that even happened? A year ago, I was convinced I hated her. Things had somehow shifted.

"What's up, buttercup?" Raven asked as she sipped a cocktail. She didn't bother looking in my direction as I joined her at the bar.

"How did you know it was me?"

"I can sense you."

"Have you always been able to do that?"

"It's more of a recent thing."

"Do you think it's because we somehow became friends without either of us realizing?"

She snorted. "We're not friends."

I waited.

"Well, we're not good friends," she said. "How did that happen?"

I couldn't swallow my laughter. "I was just asking myself that." I smiled when the bartender appeared in front of me. "I'll have a violet gin and tonic."

He nodded and went off to mix the drink, leaving Raven and I alone at our end of the bar. We had years of bad blood between us and only several months of tranquility. Surprisingly, it was the harmony that won out in my memories.

"I know that you're angry we stayed," I started.

"I'm not angry. I think it was a mistake. There's no point being angry when I always knew how this would play out."

"What do you mean?"

"You're a freaking hero. You can't look the other way when people are dying. Worse, you've surrounded yourself with other heroes. I think half the people we associate with would've been fine being villains until you took them under your wing and set the tone. There's no turning back now."

I didn't believe that for a second. "You're not a villain, Raven."

"You didn't think that when you believed I was interested in Kade."

"You *were* interested in Kade," I insisted. "You went after him even though you knew I was attracted to him."

"That's not how I remember it." Her lips quirked. "Perhaps I only went after him to test him. I had to make sure he was worthy of you, didn't I?"

"We both know why you went after him." I refused to rehash an old fight. "It doesn't matter now. We're engaged. You're happy with Percival. We need to focus on the demon."

"I haven't been able to focus on anything else."

"I think you're drowning in fear, something I never thought I would say about you."

"We're all afraid of something." She took a big swig of her drink.

I waited until the bartender had delivered mine and left to check on his other customers to speak again. "Today, when the kids attacked, we went into the water. I had no idea what the plan was. We just wanted to get away. The next thing I knew there was a huge Great White shark and Hadley wanted me to grab its fin so it could tug us under the water. I felt real fear in that moment, and it reminded me that it's the unknown that's scary.

"Like … the first time I fought a vampire, I was terrified," I continued. "The same with that zombie infestation in Montana. Those things don't frighten me as much any longer. I don't think I'm cavalier about the battles we fight, but some of them feel more dire than others."

"This one feels dire," Raven mused.

"It really does."

"Demons are unpredictable. If this one came from another plane, meaning it's not used to dealing with humans, we could be in for one helluva fight. Are you ready for that?"

"I'll do whatever it takes to keep the people I love safe." I drank my entire cocktail in gulps and then put the empty glass on the bar before searching in my pocket for a twenty. "That includes you, Raven. You don't have to sit here and freak out because you think I don't understand what's to come. I understand. I just can't walk away from a threat."

"This threat could kill us. I rarely say that about the enemies we face. I know that we can escape most of the things we fight. We might lose a soldier or two, but the core of our group always survives."

"You don't feel that way this time."

"That's just it. For the first time in ... well ... a very long time, I don't feel our survival is guaranteed. I know that my view is skewed because I've seen something similar in the past — and, trust me, watching an entire tribe get wiped out leaves a mark — but this feels bigger than a normal fight."

"That doesn't mean we can't win."

"Winning isn't a given this time. I always know we're going to win. The belief feels more ... fragile ... this time."

"Then we'll have to work to strengthen our position. That's the only thing we can do."

"I guess." She lifted her finger to order another drink. "You should go upstairs to your fiancé. He's likely waiting for you to soothe his ego. He was a complaining mess when you took off with the locals today."

I smirked as I hopped off my stool. "If you need to talk, you know where to find me."

"I'll be fine on my own."

"You forget, Raven, you're part of the family. You're never alone."

MOST OF OUR GROUP MET IN THE dining room for breakfast. Everyone was on edge ... and I didn't miss the fact that all eyes were on the kids as they buzzed around the room.

"I never thought I would look at kids and feel fear," Cole noted as I took the chair between him and Kade.

"I've always felt fear looking at kids," Luke said. "They're freaky little monsters when they want to be."

Curiosity lined Cole's face as he focused on his boyfriend. "Are you saying you don't want kids one day?"

"Of course not." Luke let loose a haphazard wave. "Kids are part of the package with me — at least one kid. I don't want a gaggle because that would cut into my beauty rest, but I've always fancied myself as a father. I think I'd be good at it."

"You'll be great at it," Cole confirmed. "I'm curious why you want children when you hate them."

"I didn't say I hated them. I said they were freaky little monsters sometimes."

Cole flicked his eyes to me. "Can you explain the inner workings of his mind on this subject, please?"

I laughed, as I'm sure he'd intended. Cole had Luke mostly figured out, but there were times he needed me to interpret my best friend's fevered brain. "Luke likes to be the center of attention. He doesn't want to cede his throne to anybody. It's frustrating for him because a child means he'd have to willingly abdicate his throne. For the record, he's not ready yet."

"But you'll get ready eventually?" Cole pressed. He looked legitimately worried.

"Of course," Luke replied. "I'll be more than ready for kids in three years."

"Set a timetable, have you?"

Luke shrugged. "I figure I'll reach peak maturity in three years. By then we'll know where we're settling for the long haul."

"Yeah, speaking of that … ." Nellie, who had red rings under his eyes from a late night, tapped the table to get me to look at him. "Have you talked to Mark Lane lately?"

My stomach curdled at the thought. "Twice, and both times I've regretted it. Why? What is he saying?"

"He's trying to turn everyone against you," Nellie replied. "He's working the midway people into a lather, saying that you're trying to trick everyone into relocating here."

"There wouldn't be a trick involved," I argued. "If we do end up here — and that's a big if given what we're dealing with right now — it would be voluntary. Nobody would be forced to move here."

"Well, that's not exactly true," Luke hedged, squirming on his chair. "Some of these people only know how to do one thing. It's not as if they can go to their local midway in any town in the Midwest and find another job. Mystic Caravan is their home as much as it is ours."

I was baffled. "What are you saying?"

"I'm just pointing out that we're not the only ones in the circus. I think we're the only ones that count, but others might disagree."

I turned my gaze to Cole. "Do you agree that I'm not taking the feelings of the rest of the circus workers into consideration?"

"I don't think that's exactly what he's saying," Cole said, clearly uncomfortable.

"Then what is he saying?"

"We have a lot of people who will have decisions to make," Cole replied. "We might love this island because of the paranormal aspects. That doesn't mean the others will feel the same."

"Mark is pushing for Vegas," Nellie noted. "He's pushing hard."

"I'm well aware." I'd lost my appetite.

"I love Vegas," Luke offered.

"No," Kade, Cole and I barked at the same time. Luke had a gambling problem, loath as he was to admit it. Vegas was the last place we could risk settling.

"I'm over that problem," Luke insisted. "Vegas could be fun. They make great fashion choices there."

"Even if I didn't know about your earlier problems, I wouldn't want to live in Vegas," Cole insisted. "I like a place with a view."

"Vegas has a view."

"I like a place with a non-tacky view." Cole was firm as he shook his head. "We're not moving to Vegas. I like Moonstone Bay."

I leaned back in my chair, abandoning my pancakes. "I knew we'd lose some of our workers. Island living is not for everybody."

"No decision has been made," Kade reminded me. "This is a fact-finding mission. There's a reason we kept this information to ourselves. We don't know anything yet."

"Speaking of that, how did Mark find out?" Cole demanded. "I know darned well that nobody here has been talking with him."

"He's not stupid," I replied. "He probably saw us with our heads together in the run-up to this trip. He knows life on the road isn't sustainable over the long haul. He likely just put it together."

"If he's sowing trouble with the other workers, you'll be left to clean up the mess," Kade noted. "Somebody should talk to him."

"Somebody should," I agreed.

"I can do it." Kade didn't look happy at the prospect, but he was always willing to help. "I'll talk to him as soon as we get to the fairgrounds."

I shook my head. "That's not a good idea. Let Max handle it. If you want to meet with Max, that's one thing. Max ultimately controls Mark. We need him to get more involved."

"Okay. I'll talk to Max."

This was not how I saw my day going. Adding a human demon to our problem was an unnecessary distraction. "Until we know more, we have to be careful who we talk to," I said. "The idea of moving here permanently — or anywhere, for that matter — will freak people out."

"We'll handle it," Kade promised. "You focus on the demon. We can shoulder some of the other burden."

I managed a weak smile. "Thanks for that."

He leaned in and gave me a soft kiss. "That's what I'm here for."

I FORCED DOWN HALF MY breakfast. Once talk turned to losing so many of our workers — and Mark, a man I truly hated — I didn't have much of an appetite.

Kade and Luke ran to the bathroom in the lobby before we were set to depart. That left Cole and me to loiter by the front doors.

"Don't let it get to you," Cole admonished as he watched me. "You can't fix that problem when we have a bigger one breathing down our necks. The demon has to take precedence."

"I know." I dragged a hand through my hair, frowning when the door opened and knocked me in the elbow. "I'm sorry," I offered automatically, shaking my head when I realized it was Ariel and her mother again. "I guess I need to stop standing in front of doors, huh?"

This time Ariel's mother wasn't friendly with her greeting. In fact, she looked as if she'd seen better days. She was sheet white, her hair pulled back in a messy bun, and I briefly wondered if she was going to be sick given the expression on her face.

"It's fine," she said absently. "We're just heading up to our room."

Unlike the day before, Ariel had no bright smile to offer in greeting. Her cheeks weren't pink. Her eyes were dull.

"You should get out of the way," Ariel said. Her voice sounded nothing like it had during our previous conversation.

"Excuse me?" I asked.

"Ariel, you can't talk to adults like that," her mother scolded. "I'm so sorry," she said to me. "She's been in a mood since we left the beach last night."

Something niggled in the back of my brain. "You were on the beach?" I shifted my gaze back to Ariel. Instead of a little girl, a happy one with a bright future, I saw something else this time.

"She's one of them," Cole murmured as he came up behind me, his hand wrapping tightly around my forearm.

I'd come to the same conclusion myself.

"She's going upstairs to nap," her mother informed us. "She's been up two hours and she's already thrown three tantrums."

My mouth was dry. "That's not like her, is it?"

"She's not perfect by any stretch of the imagination, but she's never been this bad. I think it's the heat. I don't do well with too much heat either."

"Yes, it's the heat," Ariel said with a loony laugh.

I was glad I hadn't eaten my full breakfast. If I had, I would be losing it right about now … all over Ariel's pink shoes. "Where were you on the beach last night?"

"Down by the fairgrounds," the mother replied. "If Ariel is good after her nap, we plan to go back and see the opening of the circus. She's not being very good."

"I'm an angel," Ariel said darkly, her eyes on me. "What do you think?"

"I think this island is full of strange things," I replied. "Some belong here, and some don't. We're going to handle the ones that don't."

"I guess we'll see." Ariel shot her mother a pretty smile. "Can I have ice cream before my nap?" The question wasn't asked with anything other than hatred this time.

"You haven't earned ice cream."

"I want it."

The mother let loose an exasperated sigh. "Fine. I don't want to hear a word out of you until after your nap, though. You're not being a very good little girl."

Ariel let loose a snort. "Yeah, get used to that."

I pressed my lips together as I watched them walk away, my heart beating a fearful rhythm.

"That's not good," Cole said when they were out of earshot.

"Not at all," I agreed.

CHAPTER 17
Seventeen

H adley and Lilac were at the fairgrounds when we arrived. I was still shaken from our interaction with Ariel, which was the perfect opening for Luke to wow his fresh audience. When he related the tale — an incident he wasn't even present for, mind you — he managed to attach a few embellishments.

"She didn't breathe fire and her eyes didn't turn black," Cole sneered when his boyfriend finished. "He's making that up."

"Hey!" Luke planted his hands on his hips, reminding me of a child playing king. "I'm a truth-teller."

"You're a tool when you want to be," Kade countered. His hand was busy on my back. He seemed to sense my unease. "What do you want to do, Poet? Head back to the hotel and see if we can somehow lure Ariel out and question her?"

It would be a lie to say I hadn't considered that. I'd almost immediately discarded the idea. "I'm pretty sure her mother wouldn't understand," I said.

"Then what do we do?" Kade didn't sound frustrated as much as ready to launch into a plan of attack.

"We modify the dreamcatcher," I replied. "We go with the original plan. That's our best shot."

Kade nodded, the grim set of his jaw telling me he was about to go into security chief mode. "I'll send my men out to surround the perimeter. You guys do what you need to do."

I flashed a smile I didn't feel. I had no idea what to do. "Has anybody seen Raven?"

"She's here," Nixie said as she joined us, looking her usual perky self. "Naida is on her way too. She's swimming naked in the ocean. I warned her to come in before dawn, but she lost track of time."

"Here's hoping she doesn't get arrested for public indecency," I groused.

"It's Moonstone Bay," Hadley said. "Odds of that happening are slim. Aurora is naked on the public beach at least once a week."

"Oh, if only I were straight," Cole drawled with a grin, trying to lighten the mood.

"How can we help?" Hadley asked.

"I'm not sure you can," I said. "We're not even sure what we're doing. This is going to be an experiment of sorts. We know what we're doing with a regular dreamcatcher. Modifying it, though ... ." I trailed off.

"I think I have us covered," Raven said as she appeared in the nearest aisle. She was dressed in her circus costume — tight leggings and a flowing shirt — but her hair was pulled back today. Most of the time she let it flow freely. Today's 'do made it obvious she was preparing for trouble.

"We've never cast a net to pinpoint a single paranormal," I said.

"We can't pinpoint a single paranormal because we don't know exactly who we expect," Raven said. "But we can pinpoint a single *type* of paranormal. In this case we're looking for a demon. If there are multiple demons on the island — or even individuals with demon blood — we'll likely call to all of them. We'll just have to deal with that."

"Okay, how do we bring in demons and nothing else?" I was ready to embrace her plan, if only because we had nothing else to work with.

"We should try blood magic first," Raven replied. "We know we have one half-demon to draw from." Her eyes went to Lilac, who looked horrified at the thought. "However, that seems too intense. If we use some of Lilac's hair, we should be fine. It will be a bonding hex, but if we capture a few extra partial demons, they'll be easy enough to cut loose once they cross."

"You need some of my hair?" Lilac's brow furrowed. "You're not going to make me look like one of those clowns?"

Raven snorted. "No. I just need to pull one out at the root … if you're game."

Lilac slid her eyes to Hadley, a silent question in the exchange. Hadley shrugged in response. This was new territory for all of us. "Knock yourself out," she said finally, tilting her head to Raven.

Raven wasted no time grabbing a strand from the top of Lilac's head and giving it a yank.

"Ow." Lilac made a face as she slapped her hand over the spot. "You could at least pretend to be gentle."

"That's not my way." Raven studied the hair and then nodded. "There's one other thing: We should add a call for possessed individuals. We've done that before and it worked fairly well. If we can call the kids here, we can lock them up to protect them … but only if we put them in the warded cages."

I realized what she was suggesting. "Wait … ."

"You're going to put kids in cages?" Hadley's eyes, which matched the ocean almost perfectly, went wide. "You can't put kids in cages."

"It's the safest place for them until we find the demon." Raven refused to back down. "They won't be able to hurt others. More than that, they won't be used as fodder in a fight with us. If we're backed in a corner where the only choice we have is to use our magic against one of those kids … well … that won't end well for the parents."

The notion made me sick to my stomach. "She's right. We already have cages warded in the animal tents. All we have to do is cage them until this is over."

"What if someone discovers them?" Hadley demanded. "They'll report it to Galen, and we'll be in a world of trouble."

"What about the animals?" Lilac added. "Won't your tiger eat the kids?"

That made me laugh. "We don't have real animals."

"You're a circus."

"We have shifters."

Realization dawned on Lilac's face, and she looked delighted. "That is absolutely brilliant. I just assumed you had real animals — I was actually going to ask to see them — but that makes so much more sense."

"Nobody knows we don't travel with animals," I explained. "We always put the animal tent in the back corner and cast a spell to keep guests from wanting to go into that area. It has worked for years."

"And it's bloody brilliant." Lilac's smile was wide. "As for putting kids in cages, I have to agree with Hadley that it's a rough idea, but I don't see that we have a choice. If we can stop the kids from getting hurt, we have to at least give it a shot."

"We're assuming we'll be able to capture them," Raven said. "Didn't you say the ones you hit with magic at the cemetery died?"

I shook my head. "Not died. They turned into purple smoke. There were no bodies. I'm not sure what happened but … I don't think we killed them."

Raven rolled her neck. "Maybe the demon possessing them allows them to teleport. If we can get them in the cages, they won't be able to do that. We've already warded the cages against that possibility."

"We need to do the dreamcatcher now," I insisted. "We open in three hours. We need our net in place in case … well, in case the demon decides to cause a scene."

Raven glanced at the hair again. "Nixie and I need twenty minutes to put together a dust with Lilac's hair and her powder. We can develop the net first and strengthen it with a directed hex."

"That sounds doable. Go make your powder." I pressed the heel of my hand to my forehead as I watched Nixie and Raven head off in the direction of Nixie's booth. "I really hope this works," I said more for myself than for Lilac and Hadley, but they bobbed their heads in twin shows of agreement.

"At least we're being proactive," Hadley said. "That's important."

It was, but it didn't feel as if it was enough. "Come on." I prodded them toward one of the food trucks. "I'll get you drinks and then you can settle in to watch the show. I'm not sure how illuminating it will be, but I'm dying to see how the dreamcatcher works on Lilac. That should be an important indicator."

"I'm ready to be your guinea pig." Lilac let loose a salute. "Let's do this."

THIRTY MINUTES LATER, OUR TEAM WAS dispersed. We each took a different direction to balance the magic.

Naida started, tossing out anchoring lines in every direction. Nixie fed into those lines with her pixie magic, allowing them to loosen and wind around one another before she snapped them taut. Normally I would add my magic to the mix last. Raven's plan gave her that position today, so I fed as much magic as I could into the dreamcatcher and waited to see how Raven would balance things.

Hadley and Lilac stayed close to me. They knew me better, but I also figured that Hadley wanted to make sure I would save Lilac if things went sideways.

"Here we go," I said as Raven's magic joined the mix. It turned the dreamcatcher lines from white to a potent red.

"Ooh, that's pretty," Hadley intoned. She seemed reverent as she watched the magic work.

"How much can you see?" I asked as I counterbalanced Raven's magic in the northern corner. It seemed to want to pool there.

Hadley shrugged. "I think I can see all of it. Why?"

"Just curious. Your powers are an enigma."

"They're an enigma to her too," Lilac said. "She's still learning. Had she been raised on the island she'd be the most powerful witch we've ever seen. She's afraid to truly let herself go."

"I'm not afraid," Hadley shot back. "I'm just ... easing into things."

Lilac smirked. "I saw you with the plane doors. The way your magic interacted with that other witch was telling. If you wanted, you could open plane doors."

"I'm pretty sure I don't want the DDA to kill me," Hadley replied. "I won't be opening plane doors anytime soon for that reason alone."

I was caught off guard. "The DDA kills people?"

"She's exaggerating," Lilac said. "Well, kind of. The DDA is a bunch of jerks. They probably wouldn't kill her for opening a plane door. They would just banish her through one of them."

"And that's better?" Hadley demanded.

Lilac shrugged. "Better than death? I think you would have to be the judge of that. I … ." She broke off, cocking her head when the dreamcatcher lines began to hum. "What is that?"

I fixed her with a curious look. "Can you see the dreamcatcher?" I was under the impression she couldn't. She might've been an elemental, a powerful half-demon, but she didn't have the sort of magic that could interact with the dreamcatcher. She wasn't like Hadley in that sense.

"I can't see it," Lilac replied, lifting her chin, nostrils flaring. "I can hear it … and I can smell it."

"Smell it?" I hadn't expected that. "What does it smell like?"

"S'mores."

"Are you yanking my chain?"

"I smell s'mores. It could be like the cupid thing with Booker. You're trying to entice demons to cross your lines. Maybe your dreamcatcher goes all out to entice demons … including using odors."

It made sense, at least in theory. "We're almost done." I locked down the magic again. "We just need to finish the anchor. That's Naida."

"She's a full pixie, right?" Hadley asked. "I did some research. There are a lot of different types of pixies."

I nodded. "Naida is a water nymph. She can control the weather. Unfortunately, when her temper is in flux, she can also cause a few problems. Nixie is more of a standard pixie. She uses dust and balances Naida's powers."

"Do they have wings?" Hadley asked. "I mean … I know I should be able to see them if they do, but the book said that some pixies have wings humans can't see."

"They have wings but they're not visible on this plane."

Hadley's disappointment was palpable. "That's a bummer."

"Totally," I agreed. "Just … one … second." I tugged with everything I had, gritting my teeth. The second the dreamcatcher snapped into place magical alarms started going off. The warnings were so loud they practically made me jump out of my skin.

"What is that?" Hadley demanded, covering her ears with her hands and glancing around.

My gaze fell on Lilac, who looked transfixed. "Lilac, is that you? She probably set off the dreamcatcher." Even as I said it, it didn't feel right. Then I heard yelling at the north end of the fairgrounds, the same place Raven's magic had been pooling earlier.

"It's the House of Mirrors," Dolph bellowed from behind the tents. "They're already here."

I cast one more worried look to Lilac before jabbing a finger at her and bellowing at Cole. "Protect her," I ordered as I put my head down and raced in the direction of the House of Mirrors.

I wasn't surprised that Hadley followed me. Her features were a study of concentration as we bolted through the House of Mirrors main door ... and pulled up short.

Raven and Naida were already inside, their hands raised for battle. Unfortunately, the sight that greeted us indicated we had more enemies than should be possible. In every mirror, every reflective surface, laughing children pointed and sniggered. Not a single reflection belonged to us, which shouldn't have been possible.

"What the ... ?" I was flabbergasted.

"Are those demons?" Hadley asked, her voice higher than I'd ever heard it. She sounded as if she was preparing for a meltdown.

"They're possessed kids," Raven replied grimly, her eyes narrow slits of disgust as the laughter grew. "They had to have already been here when we cast the spell."

"Does that mean they're trapped?" Hadley asked. Her expression told me she wasn't certain which answer to wish for.

"I ... don't ... know." Raven looked as baffled as I felt. "There must be at least ten of them."

"There are hundreds," Hadley said.

I shook my head. "The reflections are repeated. There's ten or so." I pressed my lips together. "Where are they?"

"Where are they?" one of the children repeated in an impressive mimic of my voice.

"Where are they?" The others joined in, the question echoing, hundreds of voices asking the same question.

"They're messing with us," Raven groused. "They're trying to freak us out."

"It's working," Hadley hissed. "I've never been this freaked out. Also, my ovaries are threatening a boycott. I think this just turned me off ever having kids."

Under normal circumstances I would've laughed. "We have to do something." I raised my hands and pointed them toward the second floor. I couldn't find a single kid to aim at on the first. They had to be hiding in plain sight.

"Don't blow up my attraction," Raven warned.

"I'll do my best." I tossed out the magic, this time trying a freezing spell. I figured if we could stop them in their tracks, we could collect them one by one and throw them in a cage for their protection.

"Oh, no, little Romani," an eerie voice called out. A hint of movement drew my eyes to the second floor. A boy who looked about twelve stood with hate pouring from his eyes. "You can't stop us with parlor tricks."

"We have much more than parlor tricks," Raven warned.

"You really don't." The kid let loose a menacing laugh. "You think you can control this situation. You think you can beat us. You can't. The sooner you realize that and give us what we want, the sooner you'll find peace."

"What is it you want?" I demanded.

"Everything." The boy extended his hands, a wave of magic spurting out in an arc.

My first instinct was to duck, but the magic was too fast, and it rolled through me without knocking me back. I believed it was a misfire until it hit the mirrors. The sound that followed was that of a million glass panes breaking. Shards of glass flew at us from every direction.

I reacted without thinking, freezing the glass in place. The pressure coming at me from every direction — something external trying to break down my magic — was massive as I fought to maintain the spell and keep my people safe.

"I can't hold it," I gritted out.

Raven's eyes were wide. "If we run, we'll die. That glass will cut us to ribbons."

"I don't know what to do."

Before she could respond, help arrived through the front door of the House of Mirrors in the form of Kade and Max.

"Shield them," Max ordered his son as he strode to the middle of the room. He paid little heed to the glass, as if it wasn't a consideration at all.

Kade followed his father's orders and moved toward us. In a split-second he erected a protective dome around us. The second it was up my magic faltered and the glass fragments pelted into the shield.

"Max!" Fear coursed through me as I turned to the man who had saved me from the street. I thought for sure we would see him fall. Instead, the glass avoided him and flew in every other direction.

"*Non Nunc*," he intoned, raising his hands in the air.

"Who are you?" the boy demanded from his perch on the second floor. Another look at his expression told me he was afraid. Max's magic gave him pause.

"I'm the one who is going to give you a firm spanking if you don't leave my kingdom," Max replied. He began whirling his hands, drawing all the glass into a huge ball. "It's time you learned a lesson in manners, boy." He released his magic, the ball exploding outward.

Kade instinctively covered my head even though his shield spell already protected us.

The glass fragments flew back to their source, back to the mirrors where they'd originated, and slowly the sheets were restored. When they were whole, only ten reflections remained.

"Tell your demon friend I'm coming for him," Max warned. "You can go now. When you return, know it will be the last time."

The boy in charge — the other kids moved to flank him — let loose a growling laugh utterly lacking in humor. "You can't win."

Max didn't as much as blink. "We'll see about that." He raised his hand again. This time the kids poofed into the purple smoke before he had a chance to unleash his magic. When he turned to look at us, Max appeared exhilarated. "Well, that was fun, wasn't it?"

CHAPTER 18
Eighteen

"**I**s everyone all right?" Max was his usual calm self as he regarded us. He acted as if he hadn't put on a magical show and was simply the guy who had broken up squabbling toddlers by offering them ice cream.

"We're fine," Raven replied as she batted at Kade's shield, which was still in place. "Hey, big guy, want to unclench?"

Kade dropped the shield. His hands busily moved over my back and arms. "Were you cut?"

I shook my head. "No, but my magic didn't work as I expected." I flicked my eyes to Max. "They crushed my attempt to stop them within seconds."

"They're getting stronger," Raven mused. "The attack you fought off at the cemetery was child's play — pun intended — compared to what we just saw."

"Speak for yourself," Hadley countered. "I almost died that day."

"You almost died because of a fluke," I corrected. "You hit your head."

"If you say so." Hadley blew out a sigh and then turned quickly, as if remembering a burning cake in the stove. "Lilac!"

It was only then that I remembered the half-demon. I took off after

Hadley, the rest of the team following. Cole was a pacing mess when we arrived.

"She's not speaking," he hissed. "She just sits there and stares."

"Calm down, Esmerelda," Raven drawled as she moved in front of Lilac. "Can you hear me?"

Lilac, staring at nothing in particular, didn't respond.

"Hey!" Raven snapped her fingers next to Lilac's ear, drawing her attention. "Hi. How are things?"

Lilac opened her mouth, but no sound came out.

"Fix her," Cole growled.

"Chill out," Raven warned, slapping her hand against Cole's chest when he intruded on her space. "You're being a freak."

"She's my cousin."

"She's in no danger right this second," Max said. He studied Lilac. "How did you build the dreamcatcher?"

Raven explained the process, though she didn't look thrilled about laying it out yet again.

"I think Lilac is being affected more strongly because you used her hair." Max rested his hand on her forehead, pursing his lips. "Kade, come here."

Kade seemed surprised to be addressed but moved to his father's side.

"Put your hand next to mine." Max smiled encouragingly. "There you go. Now, close your eyes."

Kade darted his eyes to me.

"I think your dad wants to show you a trick," I said. "It might be helpful."

"It will definitely be helpful," Max promised. "Now, close your eyes."

Kade squeezed his eyes shut.

"Look inside her head," Max prodded. "You don't have really strong mind magic like Poet, but you're part mage. You should be able to see the basics. You'll see what looks like a small red spiderweb."

Kade gasped. "Holy … there it is! I can see it."

I grinned as I watched father and son work. This was the sort of relationship I always wanted them to have. Kade was reticent when first learning Max was his father. Several months later, they were making great strides.

"You need to smash the web," Max said. "That's what's freezing her in place. She'll become immune to the dreamcatcher."

"But … how?"

"Just reach in with your mind and squeeze it to dust."

"But … ."

"Try," Max ordered. "I know you're nervous, but there's no reason to be. You're strong enough to do this."

After a few seconds, Kade exhaled heavily. He stepped back and studied Lilac's face. "I did it," he said.

"You did indeed." Max nodded proudly. "Now, let's see if it worked." He kept his smile in place as Lilac's vision slowly came into focus. "How do you feel, young lady?"

Confusion washed over Lilac as her eyes bounced from face to face. Cole and Hadley were her touchstones, and she appeared happy to see them. When she finally focused on Max, however, her confusion returned.

"Who are you?" she asked around a thick tongue.

"Max Anderson." His grin widened. "This is my circus."

"He just saved our bacon in the House of Mirrors," Hadley said. "The possessed kids were there and they totally kicked the crap out of us. We were almost shredded by glass shards. It was wicked freaky, but he made it as if it didn't happen at all."

"Not quite," Max replied. "I merely set the timetable of their spell into motion from the reverse. It was not all that impressive."

"It impressed the heck out of me," Hadley insisted.

Max shot her an adoring smile. "You're quite cute, aren't you?" He shook his head. "If you weren't crawling with the scent of a wolf shifter, I might ask you out. That's how cute you are."

Kade made a strangled sound in his throat. "She lives with the sheriff."

Max pressed his hand to Lilac's forehead. "I didn't say I was going to pursue her. I said she was cute."

"She's the same age as your son," I pointed out.

"I happen to like people with energy." Max winked at Hadley before holding out his hands to Lilac to help her from the picnic table. "Can you walk for me? I want to test the dreamcatcher's hold on you."

"Is that what happened?" Lilac readily took his hands and let him lead her from the table. I had no idea if she was so trusting on a normal basis, but she appeared to have faith that Max was trying to help. "All I remember is watching Poet work with the others. The next thing I knew, it was as if a dark veil had been dropped over me. I was not inclined to move … or think. I definitely didn't want to use my magic. It was very strange."

"I believe that indicates the dreamcatcher modification worked as intended," Max noted.

"Except we have no demon," Raven pointed out. "And we also got our asses handed to us by kids."

"Possessed children," Max corrected. "They're wielding magic that doesn't belong to them."

"They're getting stronger," I noted. "Somehow the demon is funneling more power to them."

"I can't comment on that because I didn't witness the earlier attacks," Max said. "That seems to make sense, though."

"It's frustrating. We don't want to hurt the kids. They can freaking teleport. I mean … they were here, and we didn't even know it."

"The second you enacted the dreamcatcher you were alerted to their presence," Max said pragmatically. "They're gone now. If they should return, which I think is likely, they'll trip over the dreamcatcher again."

"We still don't have a demon," I argued. "We have to take out the demon if we want to save the kids."

"The demon is likely taking refuge outside the city." Max led Lilac to the dreamcatcher line and prodded her to step over it. "I want to test something, my dear. If Kade's magic worked, you'll no longer be attracted to the fairgrounds."

"How do we find the demon?" I asked. "Even though we're on an island, there's still too much ground to cover in a search." I watched with more than a little curiosity as Lilac crossed the line.

"I don't know yet," Max replied. "Despite what you may think, I don't have all the answers. I can only tackle one problem at a time." He offered Lilac a small smile. "How do you feel?"

Lilac tilted her head, considering, and then grinned. "I feel fine. In fact, I feel pretty good. I think you fixed the problem."

"It wasn't difficult. You were caught in the middle of a magical trap. I removed the lure from your mind."

"Well, it's fancy." Lilac grinned at me. "I like that I can come and go from the fairgrounds without turning into a zombie."

"We're glad for you," I said. "That doesn't change the fact that there's still a demon out there possessing children. We don't even know where he's getting the children. I know that Ariel was somehow taken over. She's a tourist, but nobody has recognized the other kids."

"Galen is tackling that today," Hadley said. "He's hitting the shifter compounds outside the city. He thinks they're the obvious answer."

"What if they're not?"

Hadley's shoulders hopped. "I guess we'll have to wait and see what he comes up with."

"What do we do until then?" Kade asked.

"We have a circus to run." Max was firm. "The show must go on. The other things will work themselves out."

I wished for his faith, which I was severely lacking these days thanks to the demon threat, but nodded. "The show must go on." There was nothing else to focus on but that. "Let's get to it. We don't have much time before the gates open."

WE WERE READY WITH THIRTY MINUTES TO spare. Even though we'd been riding an emotional roller coaster for days, our team knew what had to be done to provide a successful opening.

Kade stopped at my tent ten minutes before the first guests arrived and gave me a huge kiss. He seemed exhilarated after what he'd managed to pull off with Lilac. I wanted to ask him about the process, but that would have to wait.

"I'll make regular stops by your tent," he promised as he stroked my hair, his eyes drifting to the fan. Thanks to the cooler of ice and

Naida's magical enhancements, the tent was not only tolerable, it was almost comfortable.

"Don't worry about me," I said. "The dreamcatcher will alert if the kids come back."

"We hope. For all we know, the demon has already found a way around that little hurdle. He's figured out how to make those kids more powerful with each visit."

"I'll be fine. There's no way the demon is going to send a bunch of kids to throw down in the middle of the day at the circus. He wants to fly under the radar … at least for now."

"He wants to capture as many people as he can," Kade confirmed. "I need you to be hyper-vigilant."

"Aren't I always?"

"No."

I laughed. "I'll do my best." I rolled up to the balls of my feet and gave him a firm kiss. "I was really turned on watching you embrace your magic earlier," I purred. "I look forward to talking about that later."

"Oh, yeah?" He puffed out his chest. "What kind of conversation are we talking about?"

"You're going to have to wait to find out." I gave him another kiss and then pulled away. "Have your men on the lookout for gangs of kids. Text me if they find anything."

Kade nodded, his smile fading. "I'm going to pay you back for torturing me about the 'conversation' later," he warned as he headed for the tent flap. He paused before ducking outside. "Have I mentioned I love you?"

"Not today."

"Well, I do."

"I love you too." I beamed at him until he was gone. Even after he'd disappeared, I kept my smile in place. Yes, we had an enemy to fight. That didn't mean there wasn't joy to be found in our everyday lives. We would figure it out. Somehow. We had no other choice.

• • •

TWO HOURS INTO MY READINGS AND I'D practically forgotten the threat breathing down our necks. I'd had a steady stream of nincompoops — seriously, that was the best way I could describe them — and the woman I was dealing with now was no exception.

"Yeah, I don't think I want to go that route," Emma Silver said as she stared at the tarot cards I'd dealt. "I was thinking there might be an easier way."

They always thought there was an easier way. "You just said you want to be the top health and fitness influencer on TikTok," I said. "You have no choice but to work out."

"But I want the position without having to do the work," Emma insisted.

It was unusual for my customers to come right out and state the obvious. Usually they had excuses, or even justification, for why they didn't want to do the work. Emma was embracing her laziness.

"Well, that's … one way to approach achieving a dream," I said after a few seconds. "Just out of curiosity, how are you going to pull that off?"

"That's why I came to see you."

I should've seen that coming. "Unfortunately, the cards say there is no way to become a fitness icon without actually being fit."

"There has to be something. Keep looking."

"If you want to be taken seriously in the fitness world, you're going to have to work out." I didn't mean to snap at her — that rarely worked in my favor — but I couldn't help myself.

"Well, we'll just have to agree to disagree," she huffed as she got to her feet. "Good day, *madam*."

Rather than welcome my next guest, I put my "back in fifteen minutes" sign on the tent flap and slipped out through the back. I liked reading fortunes. Most of the people who ended up in front of me were harmless. Every once in a while, I crossed paths with a true sociopath, or someone who needed a swift kick in the behind. Today, however, I'd had a nonstop string of jerks. I needed some fresh air, which is why I headed to the outskirts of the fairgrounds.

I was lost in thought, scuffing my shoes against the ground with each step, my mind on missing children and dark demons. I was almost to the dreamcatcher before I noticed it, and when I lifted my head, I caught sight of a woman and child standing on the other side of the magical boundary.

My heart lodged in my throat. The demon had indeed figured out the dreamcatcher, at least enough to decide he wanted to avoid it for now.

"What do you want?" I asked, risking a glance at the woman with the child. She looked dazed. She was also unbelievably pale, making me wonder if the kids were somehow a bridge to the parents … and thus weakening them. The woman looked drained, as if she shouldn't be able to stand.

"Is that any way to treat a paying customer?" the girl asked with an impish grin.

"If you were a paying customer, you would be here." I pointed to a stop across the dreamcatcher line, one close to me. "Come on over."

The girl laughed. "I'll pass."

"Somehow I knew you would say that."

"I'm here to deliver a message," she said.

"To me specifically, or will any member of our group do?"

"You're the leader."

"What's the message?"

The girl bared her teeth. "You can't win this fight. Your only hope of survival is escaping. This one time, we'll let you go. If you stay, we will destroy you."

The words were chilling coming from what was likely a seven-year-old. "Well, if we're sending messages, I guess I should send mine. We're going to stop your demon and save all the children. We know what we're dealing with and we're not afraid. We know how to fight back."

The girl blinked once. Twice. Then her feral smile returned. "You don't realize what you're up against. You're doomed to failure."

"We'll have to see about that."

"We'll only make this offer once."

"We'll turn it down each and every time." I flicked my eyes to the mother, who had started swaying. "Are you feeding on her, or is it the demon?"

The child snapped to attention. "You're going to regret this decision."

"No, you'll be the one regretting things. I'll see you soon."

"Count on it."

CHAPTER 19
Nineteen

The interaction with the kid rattled me, but that didn't stop me from tracking her movements.

At first, she treated it like a game, making a big show of lifting one foot and dangling it tantalizingly close to the line. She grew tired of her own antics quickly, however, and drifted toward the beach side of the fairgrounds.

I followed.

"What are you doing?" Kade asked when he stumbled across me almost an hour after I'd left my tent. "People are lined up outside your tent and complaining. You've been gone a lot longer than fifteen minutes."

"We have a visitor," I replied, my eyes dark as they pinned the girl. "See if Galen is around."

"I saw him a little bit ago. He was with Hadley on the midway. There was some bold talk of winning her a stuffed animal, but he refuses to win her a shark. They're arguing as foreplay."

"I would like him to come here." I never moved my eyes from the girl, who was starting to glare at me whenever she turned and found me still following. "I want to see if he knows this kid."

"Okay." Kade took one step away from me and then stilled. "Don't cross the line and pick a fight with her."

"That's not my plan."

"Keep it that way."

I didn't watch him as he left. I continued my staring game with the girl.

"Are you going to follow me everywhere?" she asked.

"I'm considering it."

"Why?"

"I'm invested now."

The kid's lips twitched. "I can fly. I have the power."

"If you do, you'll have to leave her behind." I inclined my head to the dazed mother. As the minutes ticked by, she became increasingly unsteady. I was convinced that the child had cast a spell on her. If she passed out, the kid wouldn't be able to carry her. At the very least, I could save the mother … and maybe get a little insight into the child.

The girl snapped her eyes to the woman, as if remembering that she wasn't alone. "She's not important," she said finally.

"See, that's where you're wrong." I relished the idea of irritating the girl, but only because the thing conversing with me wasn't really a child. Whatever had taken root inside of her belonged to the demon. The longer we were in proximity, the easier it would be to get inside that head. Her thoughts were shuttered, but there were gaps. If I wanted, I could push inside. That wasn't a viable option without backup, so I was forced to wait. "I think she's more important than you want to let on. Why else would you bring her?"

"She's an adornment, nothing more."

"She's a shield," I said. "You want her close because you can't wander around freely without her. It's not like before, back when you were running the people ragged in Africa. Back then children matured faster. They had jobs to do, tasks that needed to be carried out. They weren't constantly watched by helicopter parents."

"I don't believe I understood a single word you said," she drawled.

"That's fine. I know I'm on to something. You might have a gaggle of kids at your command, but you're not the power you once were."

"You wish that were true," she hissed, her eyes snapping to the right at the sound of footsteps. Kade had found Galen and Hadley, and now multiple eyes were on my possessed friend.

"Amelia Fields," Galen said as he joined me. "Her mother is Greta Fields ... and she's seen better days."

"Ah, the sheriff," the thing with Amelia's face trilled. "Are you here to arrest me, sheriff?"

"I'm kind of wishing I could gag you," Galen replied, "but that probably wouldn't go over well with the tourists."

"Probably not," Amelia agreed. She lifted her hand to study her fingernails, as if bored. "Don't you think you should move on me? I've been waiting for what feels like forever. You don't do anything but stand there like idiots. I'm starting to think you don't care."

"Who is she?" I asked Galen.

"Greta was ahead of us in school," Galen replied. He looked torn between racing across the dreamcatcher to snatch the woman and lobbing the ball he still carried from the midway games at the girl's head. "She was always quiet. She runs the maid staff at the hotel."

"The hotel we're staying at?"

He shook his head. "The big hotel. She's a nice woman. She tried forever to get pregnant. Her first husband left her because she couldn't. He blamed her and married some young thing from the field shifter tribe by Wesley's farm. They don't have any kids yet. Greta married Trent Fields. He's about ten years older than us, has a heart as big as the moon. He fell head-over-heels for Greta and said it didn't matter if she couldn't have kids. They were looking into adoption when she became pregnant."

"That means her first husband was the problem."

"Yeah. I'm sure he'll divorce that girl he married when she doesn't provide him with an heir. It won't ever occur to him that he could be the problem."

"And I'm sure Greta considers the kid her little miracle," I mused.

Amelia beamed at me as if she didn't have a care in the world.

"Yeah." Galen looked tortured. "What are we going to do?"

I didn't have an answer, but I did have an idea. "Amelia, you wanted to offer me a deal. That's why you stopped by."

The girl's eyes lit with a glint of mistrust. "You said you would never deal."

"We're not willing to give you what you want," I reiterated. "We won't leave so your demon friend can wipe out the population. But we will offer you something you need."

"What's that?"

"An escape." I smiled. "You want to take off, make sure that I can't follow you. That's why you're still hanging around even though your mother is flagging and your powers are weakening. You can go. We won't follow."

Galen growled. He wanted to argue. Instead, he monitored the girl for her reaction.

"You can't follow me," Amelia replied. "I told you, I can fly."

"You can turn into smoke," I said. "That's a neat trick, by the way. I'm curious how you manage to do that."

"I'm awesome. That's how I manage it."

"Or the demon is doling out power he probably can't recoup fast enough," I said. "Here's the deal: If you leave now and leave Greta behind, we won't follow you. If you try to hurt Greta, or force her to march away with you, then we're going to give chase."

Galen's eyes lit with understanding. "That's the deal," he agreed, his voice stronger this time. "We won't agree to anything else."

Amelia's scowl was petulant. She might have a demon taking up residence inside her, but she was still a child. "You can't take her. I won't allow it."

"You said she wasn't important," I argued. "You said she was nothing to you."

There was hesitation in Amelia's eyes, enough that I had to wonder if the child trapped inside was aware enough to register what was happening.

"If you're in there, Amelia, you can be assured we're going to get you back," I said softly, keeping my expression level even as the demon regained control and narrowed the girl's eyes. "You're a big talker. You like to throw around your strength. If you're truly as strong as you say, then keeping the woman is unnecessary."

Amelia worked her lips. Ultimately, she threw up her hands. "Fine. If you want her so much, you may have her." She made a sweeping motion with her hand. Greta followed and tipped forward, whatever strength she had left waning.

Galen lunged forward to catch her. Amelia expected the move, because her eyes lit with delight the second Galen stepped over the dreamcatcher.

Unfortunately for her, I knew she wouldn't follow through on the agreement. As Galen caught Greta, Amelia started in his direction, magic sparking from her fingers.

I slid in front of Galen right before Amelia made contact and grabbed her wrists, grinning when the girl's eyes went wide. "That would be cheating," I tsked. "We can't have that."

Amelia's mouth dropped open as Kade moved beside me. I placed the girl's wrists in his hands and engaged his magic, slamming one of the domes he was getting good at erecting around her to trap her in place. We were inside the dome with her, not exactly safe from the things she could do, but she was cut off from the outside world.

"What ... ?" Amelia's eyes were so wide I thought they might pop out of her head. Before she could utter a single word, I moved my hands to the sides of her head and engaged my magic.

"*Dormio,*" I intoned, grinding my teeth as the girl went rigid.

"Knock her out," Galen growled as he dragged Greta to the safe side of the dreamcatcher. "Don't let her get away. I cannot explain to Greta that her precious daughter is missing when she wakes up. I won't tell her that."

"*Dormio,*" I repeated, keeping my eyes on Amelia's slack-jawed face. I leaned close, the girl's eyes tracking me. "Just think, if you'd stuck to the agreement, you wouldn't be in this predicament."

She made a mewling sound, but the magic wouldn't allow her mouth to open.

"We'll talk soon," I promised as I wiped my hands over her eyes and muttered a curse. The girl pitched forward and Kade caught her.

"We have to move fast," I insisted as we crossed the dreamcatcher. It alerted almost instantly. Only our paranormal team members could register the alert. "We have to get to the animal tent right now."

Kade stepped to the front of the group. We stayed on the outskirts of the circus, doing our best not to draw too much attention. When several sets of eyes did fall on us, I whipped out a convincing lie ... and reinforced it with magic.

"It's very hot," I said in a dull voice, allowing the magic to weave the words through our guests' brains. "They need water and some shade."

"That's horrible," one of the women clucked. "I hope they'll be okay."

"They'll be absolutely fine," I replied, my tone never changing. "There's nothing to worry about. In fact, you should have a slushie to make sure you're not dehydrated."

"What a good idea." The woman beamed as we disappeared behind another tent.

"That's an interesting sales technique you've got," Galen noted on a grimace. He showed no signs of faltering under Greta's weight. "Do you use it often?"

"Almost never," I replied as we reached the animal tent, and I drew back the flap. "I only whip that trick out when we need cover. Believe it or not, that rarely happens. Most of the attacks play out at night."

Galen scanned the empty cages. Thankfully we'd thought to cool the tent like the others. "Where?"

"Put her over there," I instructed, pointing to the wolf cage. "All of them are warded, but we want our prisoners separated."

"Greta isn't to blame for any of this," Galen argued.

"No, but we don't know if she's under a spell." I pulled open the tiger cage door so Kade could carry Amelia inside. "She might just be drained because of what they've done to her mind. She could also freak out when she sees her kid in a cage."

"She'll freak out over that regardless," Kade said as Hadley pulled open the door for him. "I don't want to have to explain this."

"It's the best option," I insisted.

Kade carefully lowered Amelia to the ground. He ran his fingers through the girl's hair, shook his head, and then joined me on the other side of the cage door. Rather than focus on Amelia, who I knew was neutralized by the cage wards, I moved closer to Greta. I stopped Hadley from shutting the door, and instead crawled into the cage with the woman.

I rested my hand on her forehead, infiltrating her mind. "They're feeding off the parents," I said as I waded through the tangled web of

Greta Fields' mind. "Deep down, she knew something was wrong with Amelia before the attack. The father hasn't been touched. All the attention is directed at Greta."

"Can that be the case with all the kids?" Galen asked.

"I ... don't ... know." I had a lot of questions. "Did you check with the shifter tribes? Hadley said you were going to this morning."

He nodded. "They're missing kids, but they won't admit it. I didn't see a single kid there."

"Now we know where this started," I mused, darting my eyes to Amelia. She looked like a little girl sleeping in a cage. I wasn't filled with joy at the sight. "Okay, we need to keep Greta sleeping. As long as she's not aware of her surroundings, that benefits us. But she's dehydrated and needs water. She also needs to be bolstered magically."

Kade nodded. "I'll get Nixie for the bolstering and Luke for the water. What about her?" He tipped his head to Amelia. "Are you going to keep her unconscious?"

"I'm going to keep her down until we're done for the day. After that, I'll wake her."

"And then what?" Galen demanded.

"Then I'm going to find out what she knows."

"What if she refuses to cooperate?"

"She won't."

"How can you be sure?"

Now it was my turn to unleash a feral smile. "I won't give her a choice." I was firm. "Now, come on. We have things to do. We need to make sure Greta is okay, make her as comfortable as possible, and keep Amelia cut off from her magical friends. They might come looking for her after dark."

Realization dawned on Galen's face. "You want to sucker them in. You can't kill the kids the demon sends."

"I have no intention of killing the kids," I promised. "There's no reason we can't lock them up with Amelia, though. That cage is big enough for more than one ankle-biter. That's the safest place for them. Not only can they not use magic on us from in there, they can't use it on each other."

Galen hesitated and then nodded. "Okay, that sounds like a plan.

How do we find the infected kids? I know some of them, but not all of them."

"The kids are being swept up fast. There may be more infected than not now."

"How do we keep the uninfected ones safe?"

That was a good question. "I don't know. Can you fake a lockdown for any reason?"

If Galen was surprised by the question, he didn't show it. "That's a really good idea. I'll make some inquiries."

"I'm full of them." I was grim as I pulled away from Greta and shot a dark look toward a prone Amelia. "We don't have all the answers yet, but this is a start."

CHAPTER 20

Twenty

Returning to work when we finally had a tangible lead was torture, but I had no choice. I sleepwalked through most of my readings, telling customers what they wanted to hear, and then closed up my tent just as the show was kicking off in the big top.

I poked my head inside long enough to see that things were going well and then returned to the animal tent.

"What are you two doing here?" I demanded of Dolph and Nellie. "You're supposed to be performing."

"Slow your roll, girlfriend," Nellie drawled. "We had our performances moved to the middle. We wanted to stick close until you got here."

"They didn't think I could handle sitting in a tent alone," Galen said. He looked more tired than upset, but the smile he shot Nellie showed plenty of teeth.

"I don't know you, man," Nellie argued. "You might be sympathetic to the enemy."

"I've got it from here," I said. "You two need to get to the big top. Keep your eyes open for a gaggle of kids without parents." Something occurred to me. "Also, make sure you scan the parents. If any of them look zoned, call me."

"You're so bossy," Nellie groused as he moved around me. "Have I mentioned how bossy you are? I don't like being told what to do."

"You'll live." I rubbed my forehead and took a moment to calm myself before drifting closer to Galen. "Anything?" I asked as my eyes fell on Amelia. She was awake, her back resting against the cage bars. The looks she shot us promised mayhem were she to get out.

"She's not talking," Galen replied. "Her first move when waking was to pretend to be a helpless little girl who wanted her mom. I knew better than falling for that."

"That's probably why the demon decided on kids," I said as I approached the cage. Amelia continued to glare. "Even though kids back in the day would've had more autonomy, it's human nature to protect those smaller than you. Even if the parents in those villages had known their kids were acting out of sorts, they wouldn't have wanted to hurt them ... even to protect themselves."

Galen's arms were folded across his chest. "By the time the parents realized something was truly amiss, it was too late. Some of the tribes would've embraced the idea of possession rather than discard it."

I pursed my lips as I moved to one of the chairs facing Amelia's cage. "Do you have anything to say?" I asked the possessed girl. "We're all ears."

"You're all going to die," Amelia hissed.

"Oh, you can do better than that. Now do 'You should've listened to me if you wanted to live.' That's always a favorite."

"It's going to be painful ... and bloody ... and this island will be a wasteland when we're done."

"This island has survived worse than you," Galen said as he grabbed a chair and placed it beside mine before sitting. "How are things out there?"

"Everybody is watching the big show," I replied. "The dream-catcher hasn't alerted since we brought her over the line. I have no idea if that's a good or bad thing."

"Why wouldn't it be a good thing?"

"I don't know." I had a sense of dread that had been settling in my chest for hours and I couldn't shake it. "They've adapted several times.

This demon hasn't survived for centuries without being able to think on his feet. They'll adapt again."

Galen extended his long legs in front of him. "How do you know we're dealing with the same demon? Isn't it possible that more than one demon operates this way?"

"It's just a feeling. When I brought up the African coast, she reacted as if she'd been slapped. She was surprised I knew about those instances."

"We could be dealing with more than one demon. It could be a pack. Maybe they move from location to location."

I'd considered that, but it didn't seem likely. "Or maybe our demon shows up when it's been summoned."

Galen stilled. "Wait … you think someone deliberately set this in motion?"

"There are a lot of demons out there," I replied. "A lot would have to line up perfectly for this one to have magically managed to slide through randomly opening plane doors a few weeks ago."

"Stranger things have happened."

"I don't think we can close the door on any possibilities." I rested my elbows on my knees and planted my chin in my palm as I glared into Amelia's hate-filled eyes. "What's the plan here? Are you working on a timetable?"

"I'm not talking to you," Amelia hissed.

"That's quite a change. You wanted to brag earlier. I'm guessing that your demon is figuring out that we're going to be a little harder to dismiss than he thought."

"You only want to believe that," Amelia shot back. "There's nothing you can do to stop this. Things have already been set in motion. There's no turning back the clock."

"But we don't have to turn back the clock to end this, do we? We just have to find one little demon."

Amelia let loose a disdainful snort. "Good luck with that."

"We have an army. We don't need luck." I turned to Galen and gave him a "come hither" motion with my fingers. He followed me out of the tent without a word, waiting until we were out of earshot to speak.

"You have a plan," he noted as he studied my face.

"How do you know?" I was honestly curious.

"Because Hadley always gets the same look on her face when she has a plan. You have a lot of similarities."

I smirked. "You guys are good together. You get her."

"I love her," he said, "but I don't know that I always get her. We're going to have a lifetime together to figure each other out."

"That's sweet." I didn't have much energy for pleasantries, so I decided to push forward. "We need to tweak the dreamcatcher again. They're going to come from a different angle tomorrow. We've used the magic at our disposal. We might need your team's magic to strengthen the lines protecting us."

His expression didn't change. "How so?"

"You have representation from all four elemental groups. That's pretty much the most powerful magic there is. We need to fortify the dreamcatcher with that magic."

Galen rubbed his chin, his eyes going to the big top.

"Is Hadley in there?" I asked when he didn't speak for a full minute.

"She's with Lilac. She wanted to see the performances."

"I know you want to keep her safe, which often means keeping her out of the line of fire, but it's too late for that."

"I don't want to diminish who she is," he said. "She's so … strong, but she's still learning. She has a tendency to get hurt because she rushes in headlong without thinking."

"And she almost died the other day."

He closed his eyes, a muscle working in his jaw, and then opened them again. "I don't know if she realizes that."

"She does. She just doesn't want you to dwell on it."

"I can't lose her."

"Then we have to keep the island safe. The best tool we have in our arsenal is the dreamcatcher. We have to fortify it, but we don't have enough magic. We need your people to help."

"You need one of each." He blew out a sigh. "Lilac, Hadley and Booker will be easy enough. I have to get on the phone with Aurora. The sirens aren't always team players."

"I'm not sure that's true. I heard some of what you and Cordelia said to one another. You thanked her for helping with the plane doors. It seems that's something she didn't need to do. Just because they like their privacy doesn't mean they're not part of the team."

He nodded. "You have a point. I'll call Aurora and get her here. Is tomorrow morning soon enough, or should we do things after everybody clears out tonight?"

"It has to be tomorrow. I need to think about what we need for the spell."

He gestured to the tent. "What about them?"

"Greta will sleep until the end of this. I'm not sure what the deal is with her husband. He hasn't been affected by the magic Amelia wields, but he might start worrying about his wife."

"I'll handle that."

"How?"

"This is a magical island, Poet. When magical things pop up, they need to be explained. I'll tell him what's going on. He'll play nice because he'll want to protect his family."

"That's good, but every night more people are taken over. We have to be very careful tomorrow … and we also have to go on the offensive. At a certain point, if Amelia doesn't start playing nice, we might have to go into her head to get the information we need. That could be traumatizing to the girl trapped inside."

"You're saying we might not have a choice."

"I hope we do, but we have to prepare for all contingencies."

He sighed. "Okay. I'll have my team ready in the morning. Come to the lighthouse for breakfast so we can talk things out."

He started toward the big top and then stilled. "Are you going to keep guards on the tent all night?"

"We're going to lock down that tent. Nobody will be able to go in or out. Our guards will take up position on the exits, but it won't matter. Nobody will be able to get inside until we drop the wards."

His eyes were haunted when they met mine. "This is my home. I grew up here. I know that it might seem weird at times, and you might not fully understand the magic of this place yet, but we need to save it."

"That's the plan," I said. "It's not our home, but you're our people. We'll fight to keep it safe."

"It might not be your home yet, but I can see how it will become your home." He shot me a rueful smile. "I can already picture you running around with Lilac and Hadley. The trouble the three of you will drum up … ." He chuckled. "I'm going to develop an ulcer before it's all said and done."

"Here's hoping, right? There are worse things than an ulcer."

WE SHUT DOWN THE CIRCUS WITHOUT a problem, erected wards on the animal tent, and put guards at both entrances. Then we retired to the hotel. Normally I might like a drink on opening night. That wasn't the case this evening. I tumbled into troubled sleep the moment I climbed into bed.

The next morning, we showered quickly and gathered our troops. I had a plan for the dreamcatcher. The walk to the lighthouse took less than ten minutes and Galen's team was already assembled when we arrived. One member of that team — the obvious one — didn't look happy.

"I can't just agree to lend my magic to strangers," Aurora snapped, hands on hips. Galen towered over her, but she didn't seem to care. Their past — a friendship built on loyalty and platonic love — made them comfortable with one another, even if the interaction involved a fight. "Cordelia will melt down."

"You're not lending your magic to strangers," Galen replied, offering up a haphazard wave for our benefit even as he kept his gaze on her. "You're joining with people we trust and building a trap to catch a demon. How is that not a good thing?"

"I have no idea, but I guarantee Cordelia won't like it. She's already on my case enough as it is."

"About what?" Galen demanded. "You're her most loyal solider."

"Not always." Aurora shook her head. "She won't like it. I should just bow out now. It's probably for the best."

"What I have planned won't work without you," I interjected, drawing the siren's eyes to me. "I'm sorry this will cause problems with your boss, but we need a representative from each elemental team."

"She's not my boss," Aurora snorted. "I don't have a boss."

"Then why are you so worried about what she'll say?"

"Because she's a pain. I don't like dealing with pains."

"And yet you deal with us," Lilac said. Her smile disappeared in an instant when Aurora swung her laser eyes to the half-demon. Lilac drifted closer to Booker to partially hide behind him. "Just pretend I didn't say anything."

Aurora waved her hand dismissively. "How can you trust these people, Galen? You don't even know them."

"I know enough," Galen replied. "They have a stellar reputation in our world. They've saved a lot of people, fought a lot of battles. They're the good guys."

"They have a dude in a dress," Aurora growled. "What monster-fighting team totes around a little dude in a dress?"

"Only the very best kind," Nellie replied. If he was bothered by the statement, he didn't show it. Apparently, their mischief session from the night before wasn't enough to keep him from being called on the carpet by the fiery siren. "Are you grilling sausage? It's a sausage type of morning."

"We have a little of everything," Galen promised. He seemed at his wit's end with Aurora. "I know you're worried about Cordelia, but if she gives you grief direct her to me. I'll ... take the blame."

"Oh, right." Aurora rolled her eyes to the sky, as if silently communicating with a deity only she could see. "She has no jurisdiction over you. She'll do that thing where she says she's really disappointed, warn you not to tap her people again, and then keep the peace. That's what she does with outsiders. My punishment will be different."

Galen worked his jaw. "You could leave the tribe," he said finally. "We could set you up in town."

"So now you want me to be ostracized by my own people. That's just great." Aurora threw her hands up and turned her back to him. I thought she might stomp away.

"Aurora, I'm sorry if this will be difficult for you." Galen was choosing his words carefully. "We have to work together on this. If we don't, the island will be lost. Your people might be safe now, but there's nothing that will stop this demon once the rest of us are gone. He'll have an army to go after your people."

Aurora was silent a long time before turning back to him. "Well, aren't you just a regular ray of sunshine?"

Galen smiled. "You know me." He rested his hand on her shoulder and leaned closer, lowering his voice. "We always said there was something magical about our group. Four different species and yet we were all drawn together as kids.

"I know it seems easy to tell you what to do because I'm not the one providing the magic," he continued. "It feels somehow kismet that Hadley came into our lives the way she did. She's with me … and she's the final piece you need to build the four elements at the same time.

"I don't know Poet well, but she seems to be on top of her game. She says she needs you guys to bolster the magic. If it's possible to end this — and soon — can you really risk not helping?"

Aurora smirked. "Oh, that was just manipulative," she said. "I can't believe you actually said something so ridiculous with a straight face. Love has made you soft."

"Love has made me determined," he corrected. "We need you. We may have only one shot at this. If we lose control, the island will be lost forever."

Aurora licked her lips, her gaze slowly tracking to me. After a few seconds of staring, she nodded. "Fine. But if I get in trouble, I'm taking it out on all of you."

Galen's shoulders relaxed. "I would expect nothing less." He turned to me. "We have our team."

"Great." I bobbed my head. "Let's get some food and then I'll lay things out."

CHAPTER 21

Twenty~One

"How is this going to work?" Kade asked when we arrived at the fairgrounds. The others were still making their way to the circus — Galen's group opting to remain at the lighthouse for another twenty minutes to plan further — and that gave me time to check on Amelia and Greta.

"We're going to separate them," I replied. "There are four of them and four of us. I want to make the pairings as strong as possible."

"Then what?"

"Then we tweak the dreamcatcher. The elemental magic will strengthen it to the point the kids should be drawn to us even if the demon wants otherwise."

"So … we want to be attacked by a group of kids?" Kade's expression was dubious. "I thought it would make more sense to keep the kids away."

"Then they'd wreak havoc on the town. The hope is to bring them here in small waves. Then we'll lock them up, keep them safe, and force the demon to come for us if he wants to reclaim his acolytes."

"Right." Kade was alert as we cut through the fairgrounds. "What if we don't have enough room for the kids?"

"We have three cages."

"But we have no idea how many kids we're talking about."

"We're just going to have to play it by ear. If we need more room, we can take over my tent."

"Max won't like that."

"What won't Max like?" a voice asked as a figure stepped out from between two tents and fixed us with a curious look.

I pulled up short when I realized Max had heard part of the conversation. "Thanks for coming." I hugged him. "I wasn't sure you'd gotten my message. You really need to learn to text back."

Max smiled. "I'll keep that in mind. I did get your message. That's why I'm here. I have questions about what's going on inside the animal tent."

"Well, you're in luck." I gave him a solid clap on the shoulder. "That's where we're heading right now."

"We have two people in cages," Kade explained. "One is a possessed child."

"I figured. I couldn't get inside. Kudos on erecting a very good spell, young lady." Max beamed at me. "I have no doubt that spell will keep out a demon, on top of whatever else might be in the area."

"That's the plan." I rested my hands on the side of the animal tent when we arrived and flooded the barrier with magic. "*Aperio*."

Max's expression didn't change as he watched the wall fall. "The normal wards are still in place?"

I nodded as we ducked inside the tent. "They're probably strong enough on their own to keep our precious cargo safe, but I wanted to be sure."

"Well, you definitely ensured that. I couldn't push my way through — and I tried — so, well done."

I grinned as I took in the scene inside. Greta was still asleep. Amelia, however, clearly had some sort of meltdown during the night. Her hair was as wild as her eyes, and the blanket and pillow we'd left her had been shredded.

"I don't know why you insist on being uncomfortable," I offered blithely. "All you're doing is making things worse for yourself."

"You're going to die in a river of blood!" Amelia screeched.

"Oh, you're delightful." I inclined my head toward Greta. "Kade, can you get some water in her? We don't want her to dehydrate."

"Sure. What are you going to do?"

"Have a conversation with our friend."

"Just a conversation?"

"Yup." I bobbed my head. "We don't have time for anything else. The rest of our team will be here in twenty. We need to get our house in order before the circus opens for the day."

Max stuck with me as I approached Amelia. He seemed content to let me headline the intimidation.

"It's a fresh day, Amelia," I sang out in my sunniest voice. "Would you like to rethink your position on the deal I offered you yesterday?"

"I have nothing to say to you." Amelia folded her arms across her chest, looking very much the petulant child who had been told she couldn't have dessert before finishing her broccoli. "You're going to die so hard."

"You keep saying that." I purposely kept my voice light because I knew it irritated her. "So you don't want to help us?"

"I'll never help you."

"I'll sit here for five minutes and let you think some more," I said, lowering myself into one of the chairs.

"Her mind is interesting," Max noted as he sat next to me. "There's a dark shadow around it — clearly that signifies the possession — but there's a white ball inside. I can't penetrate that ball."

"I think that's the real Amelia," I said. "She's still in there. I've seen … glimpses … of the real girl. I'm not sure how much she's aware of."

"It would be best she didn't remember any of this."

"It would," I agreed, "but there's nothing we can do to guarantee that outcome. Maybe … I don't know, maybe we can tap into Booker's cupid power and somehow modify their memories after the fact."

"There will be no after," Amelia growled. "You'll be gone long before you have to worry about something like that."

"Hmm." Max angled his head, as if studying Amelia in a new light. "The demon is clearly frightened. It seems an alien emotion. He's used to being in charge. There's too much uncertainty on the island for him to feel like he's winning."

"I'll kill you first!" Amelia screamed, hopping to her feet and racing toward the cage bars. The magic had her bouncing back the instant she made contact.

"That's a bit of rage, huh?" Max looked more amused than worried. "She doesn't seem like she's having a good time."

"Not at all," I said. "I think the demon is outside of town. He started out there, in the shifter communities that live off the grid. That's how he built his original army. Then he sent them into town so he didn't have to do the heavy lifting."

"That makes sense. There's more than one community out there, however. I was under the impression that the sirens had a stronghold on the far side of the island as well."

"They do, and they've been seeing mischief in their village. Cordelia — their leader — said none of their children have gone missing. If they haven't, it's only a matter of time."

"Your tone suggests you don't believe her."

I hesitated and then held out my hands. "She's a strong leader, not the type to admit weakness. I'm guessing she wouldn't admit to losing one of her own unless backed into a corner."

"By hiding that fact, she's putting others in danger."

"I think that's a risk she's willing to take. She walks a fine line out there. Her people are strong, and she wants to keep them separate. That's not always feasible."

Max nodded in understanding. "You seem to be learning the quirks of Moonstone Bay pretty quickly. You always were a quick study. Do you think this is the place for us?"

I wasn't expecting him to ask the question, especially not now. "I like it here. I'd be lying if I said otherwise."

"But?"

"But should we really settle on a place when there are other options to consider? The island will be great for us, serve as an added layer of protection for those of us who have magic. But what about the others?"

"The clowns ... and the midway workers ... and the janitorial staff."

"They might not like island living as much as us."

"I don't think there's an answer that will make everybody happy. We need to focus on our family, the needs that must be met for them.

188 AMANDA M. LEE

You can't worry yourself sick about the others. Once a decision has been made, we'll pick a date. We'll give the workers plenty of time to figure things out."

It made sense. "It's a big decision."

"And yet it feels as if it's already been made. You've already formed friendships with some of the islanders. If I understand your plan correctly, you trust them enough to mix magic."

"They're strong magic-wielders."

"As are you."

I pressed my lips together, debating. "I think this place can work for us. The question is, will they want us here? The DDA is supposedly formidable and wields all the power."

"You let me worry about the DDA. If you think the island works, that's good enough for me."

"What about you?" I studied his strong profile. "Could you be happy here?"

"Yes. I would consider this a good home base, but I'll continue to travel. You're more than capable of running the circus. I'll come in and out, visit my son and grandchildren every few months. I think it could be a grand place to settle." His eyes twinkled when he mentioned "grandchildren" and it caused me to squirm.

"You know grandchildren are still a few years off?" I asked.

"I'm well aware. We still have at least a year on the road."

I rolled my neck. "I think it could work, Max. But if you agree we can make this our home base, there are other problems to consider."

"You mean Mark."

"He's going to rile everybody up. He's unhinged." I paused, debating, and then went for it. "Cole wants Mark's job. He would be good at it. His cooperation would definitely be better for Kade and me."

Max's lips twitched. "Are you asking me to oust Mark?"

"I'm asking you to consider what's best for our people."

"And you think that's Cole?"

"Don't you?" I legitimately wanted to hear his opinion. "Cole fits in. He's smart. He'll break from the mold and make the midway even better."

"I happen to agree. Cole and I have had two talks in as many days on this subject and I like where his head is at."

"So?"

"I haven't yet decided how to deal with Mark. It's not as easy as you would like for me to simply fire him. He's been a regular fixture with Mystic Caravan for a very long time."

"But he's dragging us down."

"Yes, and there will be a reckoning because of that."

"When?"

"I haven't decided yet."

I let loose an exasperated sigh. "Could you be any vaguer?"

"I could." His grin widened. "Let me handle Mark. You focus on this. Once we solve this problem, we can start planning for the future."

I wanted to press him now. I felt as if I had the advantage. But it wasn't the time. "Fine." I flicked my eyes back to the demon-possessed child. "We'll deal with this first. Still not talking, Amelia?"

"I'm going to rip your guts out and wear them as a hat," the child seethed.

"Nice conversation." I pushed myself to a standing position. "I'll be back to check on you in a few hours. Think hard because I will have only one question when I get back. There will be no escape until you agree to my terms."

"I'm not afraid of you."

"Then you're dumber than you look."

I SPLIT THE ELEMENTALS AND PAIRED them with our dreamcatcher magic-wielders according to strength, Aurora with Naida, Hadley with Raven, Lilac with Nixie, and Booker with me.

"Are you sure this will work?" Booker asked as Raven laid out the first threads. "You thought it would work last time. What makes you think this time will be any different?"

"Technically, the previous dreamcatcher did exactly what we wanted it to do," I replied.

"Then why don't we have our demon?"

"Because he's hiding. He's in your hills somewhere. He doesn't need to be here to see his plan come to fruition. He has soldiers."

"You mean children." Booker made a face. "What kind of demon uses children?"

"The absolute worst kind." Naida and Nixie added their magic to the mix. "Okay, I'm going to anchor the first layer of magic. Then your people will add their magic. That's going to exponentially increase the power. I need you to anchor them — just follow my lead — once their magic joins what we've already laid down."

"Yeah, yeah, yeah." Booker waved his hand. "I get it."

I nodded, hoping he really did understand, and then collected the ends of the magic my people had placed. The dreamcatcher lines hummed with a bright blue, and I pulled tight on the ends as more magic joined.

"That's Aurora," I said as the blue grew stronger. "Her magic is water magic and melds with Naida's magic."

"Awesome." Booker shot me a sarcastic thumbs-up.

The magic Hadley added was pink. "That's earth witch magic." I tilted my head. "It's not very stable."

"She's new," Booker replied. "Don't worry. She always figures things out. Her instincts are top notch. She's a doer, not a studier."

I smiled when the pink magic melded with the blue and solidified, making a pretty purple color. "Here comes Lilac."

The magical strings flooded red and burned so hot I had to suck in a breath. "She is powerful," I muttered, trying to ignore the fact that my hands were burning.

"She's … everything," Booker replied in a low voice, his hand landing on mine. His eyes were fierce as our gazes locked. The white magic he let loose was soothing. It didn't counteract Lilac's magic. It did mold it, however, and enhance it.

"You guys have been working together for a long time," I noted when he'd quickly tamped down the temperature.

"We've been friends forever," he said as he started tugging on magical strands to smooth them. "Even when we were kids, I gravitated toward her. My relationship with Galen was always full of static. Lilac eased the static."

"So she's like a dryer sheet," I teased.

"She has the best heart." Booker grunted as he tugged, his eyes zipping from one end of the dreamcatcher to another. "Look at that. It's working."

I nodded. "Okay. We need to pull. It's like a rubber band. We take it to the breaking point and then let it snap into place."

"I've got it. I see what you're doing."

"Do you think it will work?" Why I needed his approval was beyond me. I did, though.

"Does it matter at this point?" He pulled with everything he had, growling as dreamcatcher edges snapped out. When they ricocheted back in, they made it only so far before the barriers caught. For one brief moment, the dreamcatcher bounced vertically. Then the magical trap settled to the ground and disappeared.

We'd done it.

"Well, that was interesting." Booker swiped the back of his hand across his forehead. "I can't believe that worked. I thought you were blowing smoke."

"Now we just need it to trap something," I said. "I ... ." The dreamcatcher sounded almost immediately.

"There's already someone here," Max said as he pushed past me and headed into the fairgrounds.

Everybody knew what they had to do. We followed the sound — it grew louder as we approached the midway — and converged as a group. We were ready. Some of us were champing at the bit. We saw a lone figure standing in the middle of the midway aisle ... and everything changed.

"Mark?" I was dumbfounded as the man snarled, his eyes glowing red.

"Is he the demon?" Galen demanded, his fingers elongating into claws.

That was a very good question. "I ... don't ... know."

"Let's kill him," Booker suggested. "Even if he's not the demon, he's a threat."

I couldn't disagree. Still, killing Mark felt like going too far.

"I think a conversation is in order," Max said to the thing with

Mark's face, ignoring the possessed man's spitting and growling. "We promise not to kill you if you answer our questions."

When the creature laughed, it was with Mark's voice. "What makes you think I'll agree to your terms?"

"You have no choice. We can end you right here. You either work with us, or we'll treat you as the enemy you clearly are. Those are your only options."

Mark's eyes filled with fire, but he nodded. "Ask your questions."

CHAPTER 22
Twenty-Two

I wanted to grab Mark and shake him until answers fell out of that smarmy mouth. Instead, I slid to Max's left and fixed the midway chief with my sternest look.

"Perhaps we should take this indoors," I said.

"I'm good here." He talked like Mark. He looked like Mark. Was he possessed? Was he the demon?

"Who are you?" Max demanded, arms folded across his chest.

"Don't pretend you don't know me," Mark drawled. "We've been friends for years."

"Mark would never say that." Max kept his voice even. "In fact, Mark would say the opposite. He's a businessman. He doesn't believe in friendships."

"You have no idea the things that go through this head," Mark cackled. "You're not smart enough to understand what I have to offer."

I rolled my neck. Under different circumstances, he would already be dead. His relationships with the members of our group, however fraught, made killing him impossible. "How long have you been inside Mark?" I asked.

"I am Mark."

"No, you're not. You're … something else."

"You would like to think that." Mark scuffed his foot and edged to his left. For a moment, I thought he might bolt in that direction, but Nellie and Dolph had him cut off.

"If you have demands, now is the time to share them," Max said.

"I want you dead." Mark's teeth gleamed as he bared them in something akin to a smile. "Can you make that happen?"

"I don't understand this," Galen said from his spot on the other side of Max. He studied Mark as if he were a bug he wanted to pull the wings off and leave for dead. "Has he been this way the entire time?"

That was the question. After a few seconds, I shook my head. "No. Mark has been focused on the possibility of us moving here. He's been fighting the effort ever since we landed … though I still don't know how he figured out what we were planning."

"You always underestimate Mark," Max chided. "You look at him as a slimy worm with no ability to think for himself. That's not who he is."

"See?" Mark puffed out his chest. "Someone finally gets me."

"You're not Mark," Max pointed out. "I am curious how you managed to get inside of him. He's not the type to simply invite you in."

"I don't think you know me as well as you think," Mark drawled, his fingers rubbing over one of the anchor lines of the tent. "I also don't think you understand the gravity of this situation."

"Then why don't you tell us what we're dealing with?" Galen suggested. "If you have something to say, say it."

I took advantage of Mark's distraction — he seemed to greatly dislike Galen — and shifted my eyes to Kade. It was as if he sensed me watching him because his gaze immediately moved to me. Then, no words spoken, I tried to convey what I needed from him with my magic. He didn't move for a long time, and then finally nodded.

"Did you come in last night?" I asked, drawing Mark's attention back to me. I needed him focused in this direction so he wouldn't notice Kade. "Or did Mark leave himself open when he left the fair-grounds last night?" That seemed like a more viable option.

"I am Mark. Why are you talking about me as if I'm not here?"

"I've seen inside the head of one of those children. You take them over, change who they are, but you can't eradicate what's really inside. While they do your dirty work, you hide and talk through them."

"Just like a coward," Nellie growled as he gripped his ax. I hadn't even seen him retrieve it. "I know what to do with cowards."

I shot him a quelling look.

"He's one of us, Nellie," Max said.

"Oh, please." Nellie made an exaggerated face. "He's never been one of us. You're the only one here who regards that guy with anything other than disdain."

"It's true," Raven noted. She stood to Mark's left, looking at him as if he were a pile of dog crap she'd inadvertently stepped in. "We don't feel loyalty to him, Max. He's a threat. We should end the threat. It's not like he's an innocent child who can be saved. He was lost long ago."

"Raven … ." Max trailed off, his eyes drifting to me. There was a plea there.

"We don't want Mark dead," I said, even though I wasn't certain I believed it. "He's traveled with us a very long time. He might not be a friend, but he is a colleague … and he didn't ask for this."

"You'd like to believe that, wouldn't you?" Mark let loose another cackle and wiggled his hips, doing a little dance. "You just don't understand what you're dealing with. You people are blessed with more magic than brains. That's why you'll never win this war."

"Fortunately for you, our hearts are bigger than our brains, too," Max noted.

"Says the feeble old man who lets the children run the asylum," Mark drawled. "Why are you even here? You don't care about the circus. You were supposed to retire two years ago and leave me in charge. Instead, you hang around, draining the life out of everybody and propping this little girl in my place." Hatred hung like a cloud over the words.

I snapped my eyes to Max. "Is that true?"

"Don't worry about it, Poet," Max said. "Don't listen to him."

"Were you going to retire two years ago and leave Mark in charge?" I found the notion appalling.

"You should probably tell her the truth, Max," Raven said in her coolest voice. "I know things have changed, but she has a right to know." She waited a beat. "I'll save you the trouble." The smile she fixed on me was tight. "What Mark says is true. Max told me. He wanted to make sure I was ready to fall into a leadership position — second in command behind Mark — if you decided to leave the circus."

I couldn't believe the words spilling out of her mouth. "Wow."

"Why would you do that?" Luke demanded. His eyes were fire. "You've been grooming Poet to take over for years. You told us as much."

"Poet wasn't ready two years ago," Max argued. "I was tired, needed a break, but she was still living in the past. She wasn't ready, and I had no idea if she would ever be ready."

The words hurt. "Something must've changed between now and then," I murmured.

"Things did change," Max confirmed. "You grew up. On top of that, I learned that Kade's mother died. I want to get to know my son. I thought the only way to do that was to bring him to us."

And that's when I realized what he wasn't saying. "And you needed me to serve as an enticement for Kade."

"Please don't say it like that." Max grimaced. "I've always loved you, Poet. I knew from the day I met you that you were destined for greatness. But you were emotionally stunted. You didn't want to open yourself to certain things. I needed you to do that if you were going to be in charge."

I let loose a hollow laugh. "You were going to hand over the reins to Mark, even though you always told me otherwise. He's far more emotionally stunted than I ever was."

"She has a point." Mark looked as if he was enjoying himself far too much. He was effortlessly sowing the seeds of discontent in our group, putting our team in danger of cracking. That was exactly what he needed to happen.

"Poet, Mark was never going to be in charge over the long haul," Max insisted. "He's telling half-truths, which is the norm for a demon. I thought that learning Mark was going to be in charge for a year — and it was only for a year — would be enough to get you in gear. But you did that yourself. You stopped being a girl and grew into a woman … a fabulous woman.

"As for enticing Kade," he continued, "I had no idea you two would hit it off the way you did. When I saw the chemistry you both tried to deny that first day, I knew things would work out. I didn't use you to lure Kade. I won't deny being happy about the fact that his love for you anchored him with our group as he worked through his anger with me. That would be a lie … and you know I don't lie to you."

I did know. I was still rocked by the realization that Mark could've been my boss. "I don't know what to say."

"Don't believe him," Mark hissed, his insidious voice taking up residence in the back of my brain. "He's lying. He wanted you subservient to me."

I reacted without thinking, not waiting for Kade to carry out his part of our plan. I couldn't help myself. I had to know.

I took two long strides forward, slapped my hands on either side of Mark's head, and plunged inside his mind. "*Declaro*," I intoned.

Almost immediately, I felt as if I'd been dragged under water. Thankfully there was no Great White there to greet me this time. It was like swimming through sludge to peel back the layers of Mark's mind, but I forced myself to look. I had to see.

Unlike with Amelia, I wasn't afraid to hurt Mark in the process of seeing his memories.

I had no idea how long I peeled through the layers. I finally emerged breathless. My hands dropped and Mark's body rocked back, forcing Luke to catch him before he slammed to the ground.

"What did you see?" Max demanded.

I kept sucking in huge mouthfuls of oxygen, my hands planted against my knees. "We need to lock him up," I said when I could finally talk. "We'll throw him in one of the animal cages, the open one. He'll be safe there."

"What did you see?" Max repeated.

I ignored him and moved to grab Mark's feet as Luke grappled with his weight. "We have to get him to the tent now," I snapped. "The gates open in twenty minutes. We don't have time to screw around."

"I've got this, baby," Kade said in a soft voice as he nudged me out of the way and took over lifting Mark's feet. "It's okay." He looked grim, but there was only love reflected in his eyes.

"Move him now," I insisted.

"We've got it." Luke grunted as he hefted Mark's weight.

The trip to the animal tent was made largely in silence. The look on Amelia's face when we dragged Mark inside and dumped him in the third cage would've been funny under different circumstances. Nothing was funny about what we were dealing with, however. Things kept spiraling with no end in sight.

"What are you doing?" Amelia asked. "Now you're out of cages. That means you're out of options."

"Shut up." I waved my hand at her and focused on Mark as Luke and Kade placed him in the cage. I motioned for them to hurry, which turned out to be a good thing, because by the time they were outside the cage, Mark was awake ... and he wasn't happy.

"You lied!" He threw himself at the bars, fruitlessly tugging against them, raging. "We had an agreement!"

"Not really," I said. "We vaguely agreed to talk. There was no discussion about what would happen when the talk ended."

"You lied!" he shrieked.

I remained calm as I dragged a hand through my hair. I was in my fortune-telling uniform — long skirt, over-sized peasant blouse — but this was hardly a normal day at the circus. "You should let him go," I gritted out. There was no question that I was talking to the demon controlling Mark.

"I'll kill him first," Mark seethed as he glared at me. "You're in over your head, little girl. You're not smart enough to stop me. You're not strong enough to stop me. Daddy dearest knew that. Why do you think he refused to give you control of his kingdom?"

"Stop," Max ordered. He looked wretched when I risked a glance at him. "You're like any other demon. You lie to prove your worth. Well, your lies have no effect on my family. There's nothing you can do to break us apart ... including this." He moved closer to the cage. "We're going to end your reign of terror."

"You've already lost," Mark insisted. "You're just too stupid to know it."

"If that were true, you wouldn't be so desperate to get us to turn on one another," I fired back. "Either way, that's your new home until this is over." I headed for the exit. "Raven, we need to silence any noise coming from this tent. We can't risky curious looky-loos trying to get inside."

She nodded. "No problem."

"The rest of you, treat it like a normal work day," I ordered. "The show must go on. That's the one rule we abide by. We'll deal with the rest of this ... after." After what? I didn't know the answer. I had no other choice but to force myself to grapple with what was right in front of me.

When I stepped outside the tent, that happened to be Max.

"We need to talk." He caught my arm before I got too far away.

"Max, I have work to do," I argued. "That's the responsible thing, right?"

He made a face. "Back to work, everybody. This is between Poet and me."

Kade looked torn. That's when Max softened his voice. "It's okay, son," he said. "I promise. Poet and I just need a moment in private."

Kade pressed his lips together, looked left and right, and then nodded. "You have ten minutes. I'll come looking for her after that, and there will be no getting rid of me a second time."

"I only need five minutes," Max reassured him. He kept a firm grip on my arm until everybody was gone and then released me with an apologetic smile. "I don't like manhandling people. I was afraid you would run, and I don't want this to fester."

"There's nothing to say." I hated — absolutely *hated* — how petulant I sounded. "You don't trust me."

"That is not true." His tone was grave. "Poet, I knew that day you tried to pick my pocket that you were a force to be reckoned with."

"So you've said."

"I've never once deviated from that assessment. But you needed time to mature. You might've had to take care of yourself at a young age, but you weren't prepared to run the circus two years ago. Now you are."

"Because I've matured so much in two years?"

"Yes." He nodded. "You have no idea the adult you've grown to be. It's been a privilege to watch the transformation. You have to know, even when I considered leaving Mark in charge, it wasn't for the long haul. I always meant for this circus to become yours."

"And Kade's," I added.

"No. You're the heart of this circus. You, more than I ever could, have inspired loyalty in this group. Kade is part of the group, but the circus is yours."

"Do I make the decisions going forward?"

He hesitated and then nodded. "That's the plan. I was going to tell you once we made a decision on Moonstone Bay. I want you to make all the decisions this year. I'll still be around, but only as backup. The circus will be yours in a year."

I should've been excited — and part of me was — but the other part was still bitter about information on Mark. "Well, since I'm in charge, I want Mark gone. I want Cole put in charge of the midway. I want peace our final year on the road."

A muscle worked in Max's jaw, but he ultimately nodded. "We'll make it happen."

"Great." I moved to walk away but he stopped me.

"Poet, we still have to do our level best to save Mark," he said in a quiet voice. "He might not be a good man, but he should not be sacrificed."

"Oh, I have no intention of sacrificing him." I meant it. "I do look forward to firing him, though. When he comes to you, crying and carrying on, I expect you to tell him my decision stands."

"You're in charge," Max promised. "You make the decisions."

This time the smile I mustered was real as I took off in the direction of my tent. I stopped after about ten feet. "One of my decisions is, no matter how much you want to travel after your retirement, you have to be around for at least one group dinner a month. Your son deserves your time and attention."

Max smiled. "I think that can be arranged."

"Good. That's what I wanted to hear."

"You're going to make an excellent boss, Poet," Max called out.

"I already do."

CHAPTER 23
Twenty-Three

"Are you okay?" Kade found me in my tent. He looked concerned. "If you need me to talk to Max … ." He trailed off, uncertainty clouding his handsome features.

"I'm fine," I reassured him. "Max and I already talked."

"And? He can't put Mark in charge."

"Mark isn't going to be in charge," I reassured him. "In fact, I'm in charge now."

Kade's eyebrows migrated up his forehead. "Did you fire Max from his own circus?"

I let loose a hollow laugh. "Max is planning to step down, so I guess he's technically still in charge. But this year I'll be making the rules. It's basically our last year on the road — or close to it — and he wants to retire when we pick our permanent location."

"And then what?" I didn't miss the lick of panic rolling through Kade. "Is he leaving?"

I realized then I should've phrased things differently. "Not leaving. He'll be stopping in to spend time with us at least once a month. I'll be running the circus."

"I'm confused." Kade planted himself in my chair.

I laid it all out for him. When I finished, he looked relieved … and maybe a little impressed.

"So, you're the boss." He gave me a smile that lit up his entire face. "Are you going to make me call you ma'am?"

"It depends on how much lip you give me."

He caught me around the waist and tugged me between his legs and tilted up his chin. "I want to give you some lip right now."

I pressed a soft kiss to his mouth and ran my fingers through his hair. The relief rolling through him was palpable. I knew why he was feeling the way he was, what had triggered the panic. I could've let things go, at least for now, but I felt the need to comment. "Max is your father, and he wants to spend time with you. If that's what you're worried about, don't. It's not as if he's abandoning you."

Kade's smile was sheepish. "You know me so well. How did you figure out that's what I was thinking?"

"He's the only blood tie you have left. You were angry when you found out he was your father and hadn't bothered to tell you. Now, you've bonded in a new way. He's been teaching you to use your magic. He's an integral part of your life."

"You're the most integral part of my life," he countered. "But you're right. I would miss him if he suddenly picked up and took off."

"That's not going to happen. He doesn't want to leave you. He just doesn't want to be in charge anymore."

Kade rested his chin on my stomach and kept his eyes on mine. "I guess it's good that you do want to be in charge, huh?"

"I don't necessarily *want* to be in charge," I hedged.

He snorted. "Please, baby, you love being the boss."

"It's going to be good," I promised. "Once we deal with this demon, we'll be able to sit down with the others and work out some enhancements. I want to get feedback from the others."

"I think they'll all like it. What about Mark, though?"

"Mark will no longer be a concern after this trip. I'm firing him and putting Cole in that position."

Kade's eyes looked as if they might pop out of his head. "Are you kidding me?"

"Nope. He's gone, no matter what happens here."

"Well, that will be fun. Have you told Cole yet?"

"I haven't had time. We need to focus on today. The rest will have to wait until we have this settled."

"But you're the boss."

I smirked. "I am. I think that means you're going to have a list of things to do on a daily basis to keep the boss happy."

His eyes lit with wicked intent. "Can I have input with this list?"

"Maybe."

"Well, things are definitely looking up." He swooped upward, catching my mouth with his and cupping my chin for a kiss potent enough to rock me back on my heels. "I love you." The declaration was fervent. "So much."

"I love you too." I patted his chest to get him to back up. "We'll play a few games regarding your daily to-do lists later. For now, we need to focus on work."

He nodded, his eyes sobering. "I'll keep an eye on the animal tent. I'll also be on the lookout for potential problems with kids."

"The dreamcatcher should bring them in," I reminded him. "The goal is to lock the kids in the cages and deplete the demon's army. We don't want to hurt the kids."

"I've got it." He leaned in to give me one more kiss, this one more chaste. "I'll stop in to check on you, too."

"That's not necessary. I'll be fine."

"I have to protect the boss. That's part of my job."

I grinned. "Well, I wouldn't want you falling down on the job."

"Not even a little," he agreed.

I WAS ANTSY AS THE GATES OPENED AND the guests flooded the fairgrounds. It felt like something was going to happen. What that something would entail was anybody's guess. After twenty minutes of constantly checking the tent opening, I settled back into my normal routine. That meant readings, and apparently people were in a finicky mood today.

"I want to know the truth," Meghan Lassiter insisted. Her hair was so blond it was almost silver, pulled back in a severe bun. "My husband denies it, but I know it's true."

"Your husband denies what?" I shuffled the tarot cards and handed the deck to her to cut.

"Shouldn't you already know?" Her eyes lit with suspicion.

Well, great. She was one of *those*. Since her mind had no locks, I had no trouble sliding inside to see what had her worked up. "You think your husband is having an affair," I said.

"Not just an affair. I think he's doing … you know … with my sister."

I had to stop myself from laughing, not because the possibility was funny, but because she couldn't even utter the words. "You think your husband is having an affair with your sister?"

"My twin sister."

I frowned. "Are you identical twins?"

"What does that matter?"

I shrugged. "I'm just guessing that personality must come into play if you look exactly alike."

She scowled. "People call her the 'fun' twin." She used air quotes. "I'll have you know that I'm fun too. Just not in an obvious way."

I saw a flash of something in her head. "Needlepoint is totally fun," I agreed.

"Right?" She was incredulous. "One of the women in my needlepoint circle saw Jeremy at a restaurant one town over the day before we left for vacation. He was supposed to be working, but Marian — that's her name — said that she saw me coming out of the restaurant with him. I wasn't there, so there's only one thing that could mean."

Despite Meghan's high-strung nature, something about the story didn't sit right. I started laying out the cards, but everything I needed to know was in her head. "How old are you?"

Meghan straightened. "What does that matter?"

"I'm just curious."

"I'm thirty-four."

"You're about to turn thirty-five, right?"

"I guess." She clearly wasn't thrilled about being reminded of her birthday. "My sister will be the same age, so I don't think that has anything to do with it."

"I think it has everything to do with it." I wasn't in the mood to drag things out. "Your husband and sister are planning a birthday party for you. They were meeting at the restaurant to split up tasks."

Meghan froze. "Are you kidding?"

"Your sister wants a joint birthday party. You shot her down because you figured you would end up doing all the work. I'm guessing you always end up doing the heavy-lifting for these things. They wanted to do something nice for you."

Meghan looked caught between excitement and disbelief. "How do I know you're telling me the truth?"

"Why would I lie?"

"Maybe they got to you first and paid you off."

"You think they somehow knew you would come to a fortune teller on your vacation? By the way, this trip is part of your birthday present. Your husband has big plans for you back in Florida. I'm not going to tell you, because that would ruin his surprise."

"But … ." Meghan worked her mouth like a guppy. I decided to take advantage of her silence.

"You're insecure," I said. "That's okay. Everybody has some level of insecurity. The trick is not to let your insecurity take over. You love your sister. You love your husband. That's why you're freaking out. The idea of losing your husband terrifies you. The notion that your sister would hurt you freaks you out even more.

"Here's the thing," I continued, gathering steam. "People aren't built for betrayal. That's something they slide into after the fact. Most people never slide into that mode. You need to let go of your suspicions and embrace the loyalty." Even as I said it, I knew it applied to me. That's what had changed me, caused me to mature enough for Max to feel comfortable leaving the circus in my hands. Two years ago, I was still living with the mindset that people would hurt me if they could. I'd been wrong and loosening the reins on my fear had been the best thing I'd ever done. It had given me a family … and brought Kade into my life.

"So, you need to unclench." I reached over and patted her hand. "Nobody in this scenario wants to hurt you. They love you."

Meghan seemed baffled by the realization that she'd created all the drama in her head. "Does flipping out over something that wasn't really happening make me the bad guy?"

"It makes you human."

"I should probably stop being mean to them." Meghan turned sheepish. "I've been pouty two days straight."

"Now would be the time to get over yourself," I agreed.

The sigh she let loose was gusty. "I feel stupid."

"It's okay to feel stupid. That feeling is just a reminder that nobody is perfect. Not you. Not your husband. Not your sister." *Not me*, I silently added. "Everybody has faults."

"Thank you so much." Meghan was on her feet and reaching for me. I wasn't much of a hugger, especially with strangers, but I didn't pull away. "I don't feel like crying any longer. You're a miracle worker."

I awkwardly patted her shoulder. "I'm just a fortune teller." Just as the words slipped out, the dreamcatcher alerted. Meghan didn't hear it, so she didn't react. I immediately tensed. "You should find your husband and sister," I insisted, gritting my teeth in an attempt to keep her from suddenly turning suspicious following her breakthrough. "I'm sure they will be happy to see you."

"Thank you so much."

I remained frozen to my spot until she disappeared through the flap, and then I took off in the opposite direction. I knew the customers would be confused, but one of the kids had crossed the dreamcatcher. We had to find that child and remove him or her from the chessboard.

"Where?" Nellie asked, appearing at my side. He was surprisingly quiet on his feet despite his bulky frame.

"I'm not sure." I narrowed my eyes and cocked my head before pointing to the left. "There. We need to move slowly."

"Yeah, yeah, yeah."

I took the lead, carefully picking my way through the tents. The guests were cut off from this area thanks to signs and wards. We'd barely made it past two tents when we stumbled upon a dark-haired girl standing with a woman who was likely her mother.

"Who ... ?" The question died on her lips as the girl fixed her angry eyes on me. "I'll scream if you touch me."

I wasn't all that worried about her screaming. Children screamed at the circus all the time. It turned into background noise, people assuming the screams were from delight rather than terror. Instead of focusing on the girl, I flicked my eyes to the mother. She had the same glazed look as Greta.

"Why do you guys go after the mothers?" I asked. "Is it because they're more likely to question bad behavior from their children?"

"It could be an accessibility thing," Nellie noted. "Mothers are often more present in their children's lives. Fathers work and whatnot."

"Mothers work too."

"Oh, don't turn this into a war of the sexes. I was just making an observation."

"I'll scream," the child warned a second time. "I'll yell that you're a pervert."

"Go ahead," I prodded, unbothered. "Go ahead and scream."

The girl's eyes filled with suspicion, but she opened her mouth, as if testing me. I waited, practically daring her to do it. I saw the moment she made up her mind to push me and took one stride forward and slapped my hand over her mouth. Instead of muffling her scream, I shoved a cloud of sleeping magic down her throat.

The girl's eyes went wide when she realized she'd fallen victim to a trap. It was already too late for her to do anything about it, though, because her eyes were drifting shut. "You tricked me," she lamented as I lowered her to the ground.

"Trick is an ugly word," I said, my eyes following a small trail of magic that was suddenly visible thanks to the angle of the sun. It led to the girl's mother. "Call Galen," I instructed Nellie as I focused on the magic. It seemed to be a tether of sorts, anchoring the mother to the girl. I hadn't seen anything like it when dealing with Amelia and Greta, but it was dark in the animal tent.

"This is … very odd." I rested my finger on the thread. It felt tenuous. "The mother is feeding the girl," I noted as Nellie texted for the sheriff. "I thought it was the demon, but I was wrong. The mother's energy is bolstering the girl."

"How much do you want to bet the kids are bolstering the

demon?" Nellie asked as he finished sending the text. "He's on his way."

I nodded and went back to studying the tether. "I think I can sever this. The question is, should I do it?"

"If it saves the mother, how can you not do it? The kid is going to need someone to raise her when this is all over. A dead mother isn't going to help anybody."

I licked my lips and ignited my fingers in red flames. "I guess we won't know what will happen until we try." I touched the flame to the tether, my eyes going wide when the magic burst forth in either direction. It ran the length of the thread, burning bright, and then dissipated into nothing when the tether had been eradicated.

"What was that?" Galen demanded as he arrived, Hadley behind him. He reached out and caught the woman as she toppled, the severing of the tether causing her to lose consciousness.

"I separated the mother from the daughter," I said, rolling back on my haunches to look between the unconscious parties. "We need to test it when they both wake up to see if the mother is back to normal, but I'm almost positive that's what I did."

"We should check Greta and Amelia too," Nellie suggested.

"Yes. We need to monitor the situation before I do it again, just to be on the safe side."

"Do you recognize her?" Nellie asked of the woman Galen had scooped up into his arms.

Galen shook his head. "She must be a tourist."

"Which means there's likely a husband out there who will make a stink if she doesn't show up at the hotel this afternoon," I mused.

"We need to test your theory quickly," Galen said.

"We do, because if the tether between child and mother can be severed there's a good chance the tethers between the children and the demon can be too."

"Which will weaken the demon." Galen nodded in agreement. "This is good. We need to get this kid and her mother out of here before anybody sees them."

"Get Nixie," I said to Nellie. "She has that cart. You can hide them in there and transport them to the animal tent."

Nellie was all business. "Should I put the kid in with the other kid?"

"Yes, but make sure Kade is there when you do it. Cole wouldn't hurt either. They have enough magic to fight off Amelia if she tries to attack."

"I can take a kid."

"Not these kids," I countered. "Do what I say. Safety has to be our first priority."

"Ugh. Is this how it's going to be now that you're the boss?" Nellie didn't look thrilled at the prospect. "You were already intolerable."

"You'll get used to it," I reassured him. "Do as I say. If I'm right about this, the playing field just tilted in our direction. That's what we've been waiting for."

"I'll do it, but only because I want to do it. You're not the boss of me."

"If you say so."

CHAPTER 24
Twenty~Four

The dreamcatcher didn't alert again, and I pushed through fifty readings. By the time I closed my tent, the fairgrounds were mostly empty. Those who remained were watching the big show.

"There's nothing out of the ordinary," Galen said as I ducked into the animal tent. He sat on the floor, his back to one of the chairs, rubbing Hadley's back as she reclined between his legs. "They're not doing anything but staring."

I turned to the cage containing the children. Amelia and the new girl were huddled together. An outsider would assume they were afraid given the slope of their shoulders, but the looks they shot me were full of murderous intent.

"Where's the mother?" I asked, glancing around.

"I put her in with Greta," Galen replied. "She's still asleep. That can't be healthy. She hasn't eaten in at least twenty-four hours."

"I think we'll be able to fix that soon." I moved closer to the other woman, the one whose tether I'd severed. Her eyes were closed, her face pale, but she looked better than she had. "Has she said anything?"

"Her name is Tina Donovan," Hadley volunteered. "The daughter is Annie. Galen checked her identification and tracked her to the resort hotel. They're from Indiana. She's here with her husband and son, too."

"Have they come looking for her?"

Galen shook his head. "No, and that's suspicious."

"Unless the son has been infected too," I mused, rubbing the back of my neck. "Maybe he's tethered to the father."

"I have my men running interference for any calls that come in. If someone is reported missing, I've told them I want to be the first to know."

"Well, let's see what we've got." I opened the door to the cage holding the mothers and slipped inside. I didn't bother locking myself in. If I was right — and I had to believe I was — Tina was no longer a threat.

"Ma'am." I kept my voice soft. "Ma'am, can you hear me?"

The woman slowly opened her eyes.

"Hi. My name is Poet."

"She doesn't care what your name is," Amelia hissed.

I ignored her. "Can you tell me your name?"

Confusion shone in the woman's eyes and my heart went out to her as she turned to study her surroundings.

"Has she been out this entire time?" I asked.

"She's been awake but not exactly present," Galen replied. "It's more like she's been sleepwalking."

Well, that was interesting. I sat on the cage floor next to her. "Can you tell me what you remember?"

"I … ." The woman's voice was raspy when she tried to speak, and she broke off to lick her lips.

"Here." Galen cracked a water bottle and slid it through the bars to me. I took it and handed it to Tina.

"I know this is probably confusing for you," I said, "but we're here to help. Tell us what you remember."

"Don't talk to her," Annie demanded in a shrill voice. "Don't you dare."

When I risked a glance at the new girl, I found her enraged. Her eyes were wide as she searched the ground for something that didn't appear to be there.

"You're no longer tethered," I offered, curious to see how Annie would respond. "That bond you were using to suck her dry, it's gone."

"I'm going to kill you," Annie growled. "You'll wish you'd never met me."

"You'd be surprised how many times I've heard that threat," I replied. "It no longer has any meaning to me." I turned back to Tina, who was watching her daughter with wide-eyed terror. "Please tell me what you remember. We can't help until we know exactly what we're dealing with."

"I don't know what happened," she said. "She just … wasn't my daughter. I don't even know how I came to that realization. When I looked at her, it was like looking at a stranger." A small sob escaped as Tina closed her eyes. "You must think I'm the worst mother in the world."

"On the contrary. I know you're right," I replied. "She's not your daughter right now. She's … been possessed." That wasn't the word I wanted, but we were on a timetable. "How long ago did you notice the changes in her demeanor?"

"I don't know." Tina rubbed her cheek. "What day is it?"

"Thursday."

"I guess it started Monday night, but she wasn't that bad. My husband noticed. She'd been hanging around with a group of kids on the beach, having a good time. She was surlier than usual, more demanding. I thought she was just tired."

I nodded in understanding. "I'm guessing you put her to bed and figured she would be back to her normal self in the morning."

"That's exactly what I did. But she was horrible when she woke up Tuesday morning. She kept trying to pick a fight with her brother, and then she tried to pick a fight with me when I separated them."

"Was her brother acting out of sorts as well?"

Tina shook her head. "No, he was normal Monday night and most of the day Tuesday. Then we went to the luau on the beach. He hung around with a few of the boys running around there. He had the same attitude problems when he came back, but I'm not sure they registered because we spent the entire evening fighting with Annie."

My heart went out to her. "Something else changed Tuesday night, didn't it?" I prodded.

"I … don't know how to explain it. We put the kids to bed and went out to the balcony to have a glass of wine. We were talking about their bad attitudes and then … I don't know, it was like a cloud descended over us. I was aware of what was happening, knew it was bad, and yet I couldn't struggle. That must sound crazy to you."

"I'm not surprised."

"Everything remained cloudy until a few hours ago. I swear it was like I was crawling through pea soup. I was awake again, but now I'm here." Her eyes were plaintive when they locked with mine. "Is this a nightmare? Am I trapped in a dream?"

"It's a nightmare," I confirmed. I reached over to grip her hand. I was careful when I tiptoed into her mind, but I needn't have worried. "You're not tethered to Annie any longer."

"She's my daughter," Tina blurted. "She's tethered to my heart."

"We're going to fix that," I promised, giving her hand a tug as I brought her to her feet. "Come with me." I led her out of the cage and toward Galen. "She's back to normal but we can't let her run wild. The kids will try to tether her again."

"We'll put her at June's place," Galen replied. "She still has some rooms open."

"There are kids staying at that hotel," I pointed out, thinking of Ariel. "There are possessed kids there."

"Actually, there aren't," he replied. "I've got men there. None of the kids returned to June's hotel this afternoon. They're all holed up at the main resort, whether they're staying there or not."

"They're closing ranks."

"It would seem so."

I pursed my lips, several scenarios playing through my mind. "Okay, let's keep the kids segregated. We'll use June's hotel as our home base. I'm guessing the demon pulled his troops out of there because we're staying there."

"I would assume that's the case," Kade confirmed. "We can put the uninfected parents there, but I have trouble believing parents will willingly be separated from their children."

"It won't be easy," I said, "but I think some of them understand the children aren't behaving normally right now."

"I want them back," Tina whispered. "My children. I want them back."

"We're working on that," I promised. I handed her off to Galen. "Have your men transport her to the hotel. She needs to steer clear from the rest of her family until we've figured this out. We didn't capture nearly as many kids today as I hoped."

"That's because we're not idiots." Amelia said. "We're on to you."

"Obviously you two are idiots because you're in cages," I shot back, smirking at the way she glared at me. "Now be quiet. The adults are talking. If you don't have anything good to contribute to the conversation, play with a teddy bear or something."

"That's bold talk for a woman who is losing," Amelia growled.

"If you believed that you wouldn't be so worried."

Galen arched an eyebrow as I turned back to him. "Is taunting the possessed kids the right way to go?"

I shrugged. "I can't seem to help myself. I think it's because I spend so much time with Luke."

Galen smirked. "What's the plan here? How are we going to beat this demon when we can't make a dent in his army?"

"We can make a dent," I countered. "We just have to go about it a different way."

"Do you have ideas on that?"

I shook my head. "Not yet." I wished I had a different answer. "I need to make sure that the tether thing isn't a fluke."

"You're going to separate Greta and Amelia." It wasn't a question.

"If it works, Greta will have to go to the hotel too."

"At least we can get her in some fresh clothes there," Galen noted. "She needs food and liquids."

"That's why I'm going after her next."

"You're not going after anyone," Amelia howled. "You're going to leave her alone."

I slid my eyes to the girl, not surprised to find that she appeared to be bordering on some sort of mental breakdown. "Severing the tethers leaves the kids adrift," I noted. "I'm guessing that there's supposed to be a symbiotic relationship here, the demon feeding on the kids and the kids doing the same with the parents, but there's a possibility that removing a link in the chain puts another link in danger."

"You mean the kids," Galen surmised. "Without an energy source to boost her, Annie will be drained by the demon faster."

My stomach constricted as I nodded.

"What about the tether between the kids and the demon?"

"I haven't found a tether yet," I reminded him. "The fact that I found the tether between Annie and Tina feels like a small miracle. There's no visible tether between Greta and Amelia. I just feel that one is there because I found the other one. It's the only thing that makes sense."

Galen swallowed hard. "Free Greta. If you do that, we'll know we're on the right track."

"With still miles to go," I said as I turned back to the furious girls in the cage. "We need to speed things up."

"I'm all for suggestions."

"I don't have any."

"Then you've got to do what you've got to do. We have to take this one step at a time. We have no choice."

"Yeah. One step at a time." I blew out a heavy sigh. "Greta first and we'll go from there."

"Sounds like a great plan," Hadley said.

"Unfortunately, it's our only option. It's all we have, so it's what we're going with."

SEVERING THE TETHER between Greta and Amelia turned out to be easier than I thought. I'd done it once, so I was reasonably assured I could do it again. After a few seconds of tracking, I burned the tether until it was nothing but dust. Unfortunately for us, Greta was in worse shape than Tina. She didn't wake when freed, so Galen decided to transport her to the hospital rather than the hotel.

"She needs fluids and care," he said as we slipped out of the animal tent, leaving a raving Amelia and Annie behind. Mark hadn't said a word during our stay in the tent, opting to watch and glower.

The night breeze was a welcome relief from the stilted air inside the tent. The big show had let out fifteen minutes earlier and the guests were gone. The only people who remained were our workers, who were steadily searching to make sure no stragglers had been left behind. "I hope she's safe at the hospital."

"I'm guessing it's not a priority to take over the hospital," Galen replied. "At least not yet."

We rounded the corner to the picnic table area — where we'd agreed to meet the other members of our group — and I abruptly stopped when I saw the line of bodies on the other side of the dreamcatcher. There had to be at least fifty children — adults interspersed between them — standing on the outskirts of our stronghold, watching us.

"Look at that," Galen intoned in a breathy whisper. He started in their direction, but I grabbed his arm to stop him.

"Don't." I shook my head. "That's what they want."

"Do you see what's happening out there?" Luke demanded as he approached from the east. He had a bewildered look on his face. "Wait … it's happening here too."

The declaration had the hair on the back of my neck standing on end. "This is happening on the ocean side?"

He nodded. "Yeah. Almost as many people."

"Are they doing anything?"

"They just appear to be watching."

"They're showing us that they're aware of where the dreamcatcher lines are," Raven added as she appeared between two tents. She looked furious. "It's an intimidation tactic."

"Well, it seems to be working," Galen said. "I'm intimidated."

I would never say it out loud, but so was I. "Is there a leader?"

"There is no leader," a small voice called out from my left. When I turned, I found a towhead boy who couldn't be older than five watching me from the safety afforded him outside the trap we'd set. "When you talk to one of us, you talk to all of us."

"If you have something to say, say it," a dark-haired girl said from several feet away. "We're dying to know your opinion."

I narrowed my eyes. "They're playing with us," I muttered. "This is a show of force."

"Well, their army is twice as big as ours, so I can see why they're flexing," Luke said.

"Their army isn't stronger than ours," I insisted. "We can take them."

"How many of them can we take without killing them?" Raven demanded. "That's the difference. This demon utilizes a child army knowing that the adults will be reticent to take them out. That's how he does what he does with little resistance."

"He hasn't faced off with the likes of us before." I refused to cede defeat. We were close to figuring this out. I could feel it in the very marrow of my bones. "He's afraid. He wants to throw us off our game."

"It appears to be working," Luke said. "I can't even work up some decent spit in my mouth I'm so weirded out."

"We can't give in to the fear." I was adamant. "We know they're utilizing magical tethers. The key is to figure out how to sever the tethers all at once."

"That sounds great in theory," Galen said. "How do we make it a reality?"

"I'm still figuring that out."

"You'd better figure it out faster. We're running out of time."

CHAPTER 25

Twenty~Five

I circled the fairgrounds twice, kids calling out to taunt me from all sides. When I returned to the front of the fairgrounds, helplessness was starting to creep in.

"What should we do?" Kade asked. He stood with Galen, their heads bent together.

"I … don't … know." I pressed the heel of my hand to my forehead and looked to Raven. "Now would be a good time to say, 'I told you so.'"

"Believe it or not, I take no joy in what's happening here," Raven replied.

"We have to do something," Luke insisted. "We can't just let them bully us into staying here. I mean … they're smaller than us."

"They also outnumber us quite a bit," Cole noted as he slid between Luke and me. "Luke is right. We have to do something."

"The only thing I can think of involves hurting little kids," I argued. "That can't be part of the plan."

"Well, maybe." Cole folded his arms across his chest. "Tell me what you imagine us doing."

That felt like a trap. "I just told you we can't kill a bunch of kids."

"But is there a reason we can't take your ideas that would result in killing them and scale them back?"

Realization dawned and I bobbed my head. "I get it."

"Good. What do you have?"

"Naida can create tornadoes," I replied, warming to Cole's idea. "We're talking a lot of wind. We can use the wind to dole out your fire."

"That sounds horrifying," Galen drawled.

"But what if we use the wind to dole out something kid-sized?" Now my mind was working as it should've been all along.

"Like plastic knives," Luke offered. "We can't stab them with real ones, but plastic knives will leave little indentations instead of stab wounds."

I made a face. "I would rather not do that," I said. "What if ... what if we use Naida's magic to upset the balance inside the kids?" An idea was beginning to form. "Like ... what if we could confuse the demon's tethers with an actual storm?" My eyes slowly drifted to the water side.

Raven bobbed her head in excitement. "That's a smart idea. We create a mean storm to make the kids take cover."

"Wouldn't we have to take cover too?" Galen challenged.

"I have a man who can shroud us in a shield." I slid my eyes to Kade. "He can protect us long enough for a storm to send the kids running."

Hadley looked nervous. "What if the demon decides that it doesn't matter if the kids are sacrificed to the storm gods?"

"I don't think that will happen," I replied. "He needs an army."

"The demon's whole reason for using children is that he assumes we won't move on them," Raven pointed out. "If we actually do put the children in danger — or at least he believes we will — we might be able to propel him to do what we want."

"We'd have to be willing to follow through on it." I licked my lips, my agitation threatening to ramp up. "We can't break formation once under the shield and run out to save the kids if things look hairy."

"I have trouble believing we're going to amp this up enough to put the kids in even a little danger," Kade argued. "I don't think we can do this. You know darned well that the first kid who goes down will result in someone running to the rescue. That will make us vulnerable."

I pressed my lips together, debating. Slowly, I tracked my eyes to Nixie. "Wait … ."

"The dust," Raven said. "Nixie can make human voodoo dolls. We just won't shrink these voodoo dolls to size. If she only uses a small dose and Naida doles it out with her storm we should be able to walk right through the horde and they won't be able to do a thing about it."

It made sense, and it was a lot better than dropping a tsunami on kids and hoping they would survive. "We can direct the magic to freeze them," I said. "The demon might control their minds, but he can't do anything if we freeze their bodies." Something else occurred to me. "What if we just go after one side — the beach side? We can attack the tethers once they're frozen. That might be enough to have the demon calling his army back to him. He'll want to protect the troops he has left."

Raven snapped her fingers and jabbed a finger at me. "When the demon calls the others to retreat, we can use Kade's shield to follow. A small group of us can learn where this demon has set up shop. Once we have that location, we're golden."

The hope I thought gone returned with a vengeance. "We can save some of the kids here tonight and get the information to save the rest of them tomorrow. This is going to work." I turned my smile toward Galen and Hadley and was disappointed to find they weren't returning it. "What?"

"I'm glad that you're happy." Galen held up his hands in a placating manner. "I truly am. I just … don't understand what it is you're planning."

I laid it out for him, keeping my voice low so the kids on the other side of the dreamcatcher couldn't hear. He started nodding his head. I would've preferred if he would've jumped up and down, clapped his hands, and told me I was a genius, but his agreement was enough to bolster my spirits.

"Okay, this is a decent plan," Galen said. "Who are you sending out under the shield? We need at least one of our people included. We know the geography."

I rubbed my cheek and glanced at Kade. "How about Booker? Kade is immune to his charms. They're both strong and fast. They can follow the kids. With only two of them, Kade won't have to expend much magic to keep them covered."

Galen bobbed his head. "I can deal with that."

"Can you?" I asked Kade.

"Of course." He rubbed his hands up and down my shoulders. "But I don't like the idea of being separated from you."

"We don't have much choice. I need to be here to handle the tethers. There are only a few of us who can wield that magic. You need to be with the group that follows the kids to the lair." I hesitated before pushing forward. "I wish I could go with you. We haven't really had to separate for big fights."

Amusement flooded his features. "Are you worried I can't handle myself without you there to back me up?"

"No." I didn't want him to think that. "It's just ... ."

"We're a little co-dependent," he finished when I didn't. "It's okay. I promise to come back."

That was what I needed to hear. "Go to the hotel. I'll meet you there."

"You'll probably beat me back. Try not to worry too much until I'm there."

That was a tall order. "Try not to worry too much about what's going on here," I said. "Focus on what you need to do." I slid my eyes to Booker. "You'll be careful."

"I'm always careful," Booker replied. If he was bothered about being sent on a mission with Kade, a man he barely knew, he didn't show it. "I have people I want to get back to just like he does."

I nodded. "I expect them to run fairly quickly. You should stick toward the front of the fairgrounds, get under the shield early, and go as soon as you have an opening. Don't worry about the rest of us."

"I'm not worried." Booker always had an air of slacker about him. It was part of his charm. "I know this island better than almost anybody. If you're right about the demon being close, I'm guessing he's holed up in the hills on the west side of town. I just need a location and then we'll come back."

I nodded. "Okay." I rolled up to the balls of my feet and gave Kade an extended hug. "I'll see you soon."

He pressed a kiss to my temple. "I want to hear all about your heroic exploits when you get back."

I held on a beat too long and then pulled back. "I'll see you soon."

"Of course, you will. There's no way I won't make it back for the wedding. Are you kidding me? You in a white dress and cake? That's pretty much the best thing ever."

I laughed, as I'm sure he'd intended. "I'll see you soon."

KADE AND COLE TOOK UP POSITION BETWEEN the tents so the possessed army couldn't see them erect the shield. The rest of us headed toward the beach, a wall of magic wielders facing off with pint-sized terrors we were determined not to hurt.

"Oh, this looks fun," said one of the kids, a boy about twelve years old in a muscle shirt.

"Caleb," Galen said as we drew close. "I guess you're the answer to that question."

"What question is that?" Raven asked. "You obviously know him."

"He's the son of one of the hill shifters, a shirttail cousin of mine."

Caleb, his teeth gleaming, smirked. "My father says that you're so big because you're full of hot air. I kind of want to stick a sword in you to see if he's telling the truth."

"Your father once hit on his first cousin and wasn't even embarrassed about it," Galen shot back. "He was more upset that she said no. I think that says all that needs to be said about him."

Rather than react with anger, Caleb let loose a chilling laugh. "Have you always been so funny? You missed your calling. You shouldn't have gone into law enforcement."

Galen was stoic as he sent his gaze to me. "There's nothing of the real Caleb in there. I've had more than a few run-ins with that kid. In fact, he was my first thought when all the vandalism began."

"It makes sense that the demon went after the kids living in the fringe groups first," I noted. "The takeover wouldn't have been as noticeable out there."

"No. Ten kids and it would basically be over with," Galen agreed. "Still … this kid is a pain and I have no doubt he'll end up doing hard time."

I slid my eyes to Raven. "I told you what to do with the tethers?"

She nodded. "I've got it. There are only four of us. A few other magic wielders would be helpful."

I turned to Hadley and Lilac. "You guys might be able to help. You'll have to use your magic to make the tethers visible, but once you see them it shouldn't be that hard to sever them."

"Or you could use your magic to make all the tethers visible and let me go to town," Lilac countered, her expression grim.

I was taken aback. "What do you mean?"

"Why only show one tether?" Lilac demanded. "Can't you expand your spell to show all of them? That would be a big help."

"A big help for what?" I was beyond confused.

"I'm not just a normal fire elemental," she said as she placed her hands on her stomach. Her grimace was dark. "I'm … more." As the second word escaped, her hair caught fire. It turned from blond to red, and her hands began glowing.

It wasn't the first time I'd seen hellfire weapons, but the ones Lilac conjured were a thing of beauty. They were swords, small enough to be used in close quarters. Their blades were of a fiery metal, not so broad they couldn't be used in tight quarters.

"Now those look fun," Raven purred, her eyes lighting. "Poet, she can burn through a lot of tethers with those swords. I think we can do more damage than you thought."

I nodded in agreement. "Okay, new plan." I extended my hand toward Raven. "We're going to expose all the tethers and Lilac will go to town."

"I can help too," Hadley said. "I don't want to be left out."

Galen chuckled. "You're a total badass, baby," he reassured her. "You can definitely help."

"Listen," I said, "since we're going to be cutting a bunch of tethers, most of the parents on this side are going to drop. We need you guys who aren't involved in the initial assault to collect them."

"You want us to do grunt work," Nellie whined.

"If the grunt fits," Raven said.

Nellie's only response was to give her the finger. He kept his gaze on me. "We all know what we need to do." He was serious for a change. He hadn't even bothered to grab his ax. "You have nothing to worry about. That includes Kade. He's turned into a badass in his own right and knows what he's doing."

"I'm not worried about Kade," I lied.

Nellie snorted. "Okay, you keep telling yourself that. We've got this. There's no reason to get worked up. We have a plan. We all know what we're doing, but you need to start things off. So … you do you. We'll handle the rest."

I sucked in a breath and nodded, my eyes drifting to Raven. She'd linked her fingers with mine and was ready. "Okay, here we go."

Magic flared to life between Raven and me. She provided most of the power and I directed it so it would do what needed to be done. I kept my eyes on her but didn't miss the ripple of worry that went through the children as they watched the ball of magic grow.

"Ready?" she asked when the ball was so big it covered our entire group.

I nodded without hesitation. "Let's do this."

We released our hold on the magic. It spun three times in place and then barreled outward, toward the beach. The kids who were gathered could do nothing but stare as the magic slammed into them. They weren't bowled over — that wasn't the purpose of the spell — and initially Caleb looked smug when he raised his head and realized he hadn't been damaged in the assault.

Then Lilac crossed the dreamcatcher line, her swords drawn. She began touching the freshly-illuminated tethers, her fire magic burning through them quickly. She looked like a badass superhero in cutoffs and a tank top. I stood there for a moment, rooted to my spot, and watched her work with awe.

"If I rolled that way, I would be totally turned on right about now," Raven said.

I laughed and then reminded myself that Lilac wasn't the only one who could sever tethers. "We need to help," I said as I started after her. Galen and Cole were already catching falling women as Lilac's magic laid waste to the only thing keeping them on their feet. "We need to cut as many of those tethers as possible."

"I'm on it." Raven motioned for Dolph and Nellie to move with her. "We'll cut into that side as much as possible," she instructed. "I'll have to go fast. You guys do the catching."

"You're so bossy," Nellie complained. "I don't need you to tell me what to do. I've got this."

"I'm right behind you," Percival called out in his fake British accent. His hips wiggled as he gave chase. "Don't worry about me, my love, I can take care of myself."

I shook my head as I watched them go and then focused on the kids retreating toward the water line, Caleb among them. When I saw him, I put my head down and broke into a run. He might know things that could help us.

Caleb was already knee deep in the ocean when I caught up with him. It was fascinating to watch as his body pitched forward. It was almost as if part of him wanted to keep going but the other part wouldn't let him. Then the reason occurred to me.

"You can't swim."

There was a snarl on Caleb's lips when he turned to glare at me. "Don't be ridiculous. I ... ." For a moment, just a brief split-second really, I saw the fear of the child underneath. It was shuttered quickly.

"*Intra me,*" I intoned as I took two large steps and slapped my hands to either side of his head. This time I didn't hesitate. I knew exactly what I wanted to see. "Here I come," I said as Caleb gasped. He couldn't pull away from me despite his best efforts.

I plunged into his mind ... and headed straight for the ball of light that constituted the child. The dark cloud was the monster. Inside that, the real child remained. That's who I wanted to talk to, and I wouldn't leave without the answers I so desperately needed.

CHAPTER 26

Twenty-Six

Caleb's head was cluttered, but he was a twelve, so that was to be expected. The first room I found inside the protective bubble that encompassed his mind was full of girls.

"Well, this is about what you would expect, huh?"

I jolted at the voice, my eyes sliding to the left to take in Hadley's amused countenance. "You're here?"

She nodded. "I figured you might need some help."

"I didn't know you had mind magic."

"I don't even know all the magic that I have. I keep thinking I should take lessons, but then it all falls by the wayside when we have a catastrophe. Galen is convinced I should just embrace my instincts, but that doesn't always feel smart."

"Have your instincts led you astray?"

"No."

"Then I'm with Galen." I shot her an easy smile. "Just out of curiosity, how did you know you could follow me in?"

"I've done it before … kind of. Once I went into the past to see how the elementals split. This seemed like it would be a similar experience, so I decided to give it a try. By the way, Cole is standing guard over us. He's like a big, fiery sentry."

"Cole is a good guy." I went back to studying the room. There had to be at least five young teenagers, all female, sitting around brushing their hair. Some were applying makeup at the same time, which shouldn't have been possible, but this was Caleb's mind. Clearly he didn't understand the logistics of a beauty regimen. "Caleb seems confused about girls."

"He's almost a teenager," Hadley noted as she moved closer to a pretty brunette. The girl was wearing way too much makeup. She tilted her head. "This is Cassie Bateman. She works two days a week at the taco place — you should go there for the scallop tacos if you like that sort of thing. She doesn't wear nearly this much makeup. And she's way older than him."

"His perception is skewed," I mused. "We have to keep that in mind as we pick our way through his memories. We're looking for the demon, but he might not understand what happened to him. We have to be careful."

"I'm always careful."

I swallowed a snort. "Yeah, I'm betting you're careful like I'm careful."

"Have you been talking to Galen behind my back?"

I barked out a laugh. "He seems like a good guy. I'm always leery around law enforcement, but I like the idea of having someone like him in charge when we finally pick our final location."

"Does that mean you've decided on Moonstone Bay?" She looked hopeful.

I hesitated. "The decision can't be just mine. We all have to talk it over, but there's a distinct possibility we could end up here. We still have at least a year on the road. We have contracts to fulfill, and some of us aren't quite ready to settle down."

"Are you ready?"

"Two years ago, I would've laughed at the notion," I admitted. "When I left Detroit, I couldn't see beyond the idea of freedom. Now ... ." I trailed off. "I want different things than I did when I was a kid. Survival seemed like the most important thing. Somehow — and this is hard to admit — but somehow, I've grown up without realizing it. Or I guess it's more apt to say that I didn't realize how immature I was before I finally embraced growing up."

"I'm still immature." Hadley bobbed her dark head. "It's okay to embrace the immaturity sometimes. It's good that you know what you want. Did Kade change things for you?"

"No. I love him, and I never considered pledging myself to one person for the long haul or having a family, but it's more than that. It's Luke … and Cole … and Max. It's Raven." And that realization was the hardest to swallow. "They're my family. I never wanted another family after I lost the first one, but here I am. I can't imagine my life without them."

"I get it." Her expression was serious. "When I moved here, all I could think about was living in paradise. I didn't have much going on for me financially, and it was like this opportunity dropped into my lap. I had no idea what else I would find when I got here."

I smiled. "Galen?"

"Yeah, but like you, it's not just a man who fuels my happiness. Lilac, Booker and Aurora have given me more than I ever thought possible. I also found my grandfather, and my grandmother is still running around as a ghost. I'm happy here. It feels like I'm home."

"That's good." I moved out of the room with the preening girls. "I can see it being my home too. Eventually. We have to keep it safe."

"Then let's find the demon." Hadley gave a tense smile. "I'm ready."

We moved into the next room, the interior of some sort of house. Whoever lived here either didn't own a vacuum … or didn't care to use it.

"I wonder if this is his house." I glanced around, my eyebrows drawing together.

"Galen says the hill tribes live rustic," Hadley offered. "That was his word. I know those guys are shirttail relatives of his, but he doesn't talk about them much. They're like an open secret — but nobody openly spills the secret."

"I'm guessing they live off the grid for a reason," I said, my eyes drifting through the filthy living room to the adjacent kitchen. A woman in ill-fitting yoga pants, her hair pulled in a messy bun, waved a spatula as she yelled at a shirtless man sitting at the kitchen table.

The words didn't make sense, a hodgepodge of angry declarations, but I understood what the memory was showing me.

"Caleb lives a rough life," I mused. "He might live in paradise, but that doesn't mean his life is ideal. I'm guessing Moonstone Bay life is different for the haves and the have-nots."

A muscle worked in Hadley's jaw as she nodded. "I've never really thought about it. Galen has never taken me there to see how they live. I thought the sirens were as bohemian as it gets, but Galen didn't want me to see that Moonstone Bay has a dark side."

"This isn't Moonstone Bay's dark side." I shook my head. "This island has secrets, but this isn't one of them. These people just have a harder life than those who have made their lives in the town."

"It makes sense when you think about it, though," Hadley said. "This demon, he's been doing this for a long time. If he came through one of the plane doors that were opened a few weeks ago, he could've been dropped in the middle of the woods. He might've needed a bit of time to get the lay of the land. Going after the hill people first was smart. Outside of their own tribes, nobody pays them any attention."

"And the demon has survived a long time," I said. "He was in Africa hundreds of years ago."

"How can you be sure it's the same demon? I know I've asked before, but it could just as easily be another demon."

She wasn't the first one to ask me that question. "It's a feeling I get. The runes weren't the start of a spell. They were a warning. This creature likes ritual. That's why he dropped the bodies by the fairgrounds. He enjoys playing games."

"He's not the one putting himself at risk to win the games. He exploits others to get what he wants."

"That's why we have to end this here." I pressed my lips together and moved on from the kitchen. I opened what I thought was a bedroom door, but it led me outside. The yard I found myself standing in was overgrown, garbage strewn about. To my left, men sat on lawn chairs drinking beer and having a good time. To my right, women were canning in the front yard of another ramshackle home. It was what was in front of me that caught my attention.

"The kids are in that field." I inclined my chin. "Let's see what they're doing. I think we're being shown this for a reason. Caleb wants us to see the moment things shifted for them."

We weren't physically exerting ourselves despite the climb up the steep hill. When we reached the field, I realized the kids were playing a game, a form of stick ball — something I'd seen on the streets of Detroit.

"There's Caleb." Hadley pointed to where the posturing boy was holding court as he prepared to throw a ball. "I don't think he's been taken over yet."

"Look toward the forest wall." I pointed. There, a younger boy stood. His shirt was filthy, as was his face, and he wasn't engaged in the game. Behind him, the darkness had come alive and was advancing. It wasn't a shadow as much as a figure wrapped in robes. The shadow was small, child-sized, and there was no hesitation as it approached. "That's our demon."

We ran toward the boy. The boy and the shadow were engaged in conversation, which seemed odd because we were in Caleb's mind. How could he know what the shadow had said to this boy? Then it occurred to me.

"Caleb is extrapolating," I said. "He's assuming this is what happened when it started. He wasn't the first one enticed by the demon."

Hadley nodded.

"You don't want to stay here forever, do you?" the demon asked in an oily voice that reminded me a bit too much of Mark. "The others, those in the city, live so much better than you. Don't you want to take that from them? I can help you."

I frowned. "He's like a used car salesman."

"Or the snake in the garden of Eden," Hadley said.

I snapped my eyes to her.

"I was just joking," she said hurriedly.

"Some of the biblical stories weren't parables at all. They likely happened to people in the real world and became fanciful stories, just like Caleb is extrapolating now."

"You think the Eden story is true?"

"I think there's more than one place that can be called paradise," I replied. "This place, for example, is another form of paradise." I looked down the hill, where the adults ignored their children. "I'm betting those tribes that were taken out in Africa lived in beautiful locations."

Hadley's gaze was on me. "I don't understand what you're getting at."

"It's the ritual," I replied. "This demon keeps coming in to corrupt paradise."

"Okay, but how do we stop him?"

"I think he was stopped by being pushed through a plane door," I replied. "You said you crossed over to another world. What did you see?"

"I'm not supposed to talk about it," Hadley hedged. "Lilac had to open a door and send Aurora through to save me because I had no idea how to get back. Lilac and Galen believe I can open plane doors. I think that's true, after fusing magic with another witch and seeing a hint of what's possible. But I have no idea how to do it. I haven't even tried, and because plane doors are forbidden on Moonstone Bay, I don't expect I'll be trying anytime soon."

"I don't want you to open a door," I reassured her. "I want to know about the other plane."

"Oh, um … it was weird. It was like being in our world, but different. It was all wilderness. The colors were wrong. Like … there was this woman who had been banished there. She was a snake shifter or something. She was sitting on a yellow tree."

I jolted. "Snake shifter?"

"Yeah. She had really weird eyes and she creeped me out."

"Is it possible she was a lamia?"

"I don't know what that is."

"Raven is a lamia."

"Raven doesn't have those weird eyes."

"Her blood lines are pure. She said her people mated with humans at some point. Maybe the woman you saw is a result of that."

"Belinda," Hadley volunteered. "That was her name."

"Belinda means bright serpent in Old High German," I said. "Did she rule the plane?"

"She was banished there as a kid," Hadley explained. "Her mother did it, and then sealed her there with a blood ritual. Belinda was the same age as Galen. He knew her in school. She's trapped there now. She can't return. Of course, she didn't realize that. She thought her mother was still alive and wanted to dish out some payback."

"The mother probably picked a dark plane to banish her to." My mind was churning. "What if she wasn't the only creature to ever be banished to that plane?"

Hadley's face screwed up in concentration. "You're talking about the demon."

"From what we know, it was taking over the African continent, focusing on the ocean villages while building an army. Somehow his forward momentum was stalled. We have no idea what happened, but somewhere he ran into a problem he didn't foresee. I'm willing to bet a shaman — or maybe a group of shamans — joined together to banish him to a different plane, much like the snake shifter girl. They essentially made their problem someone else's problem."

Hadley wet her lips. "And then what? He was stuck there until the plane doors opened here? I thought you were leaning toward someone using a talisman."

"Now I think the plane door coincidence makes more sense. He took advantage of the doors opening and popped across. He took some time, got the lay of the land, and then started his infiltration."

Hadley's expression didn't change. "That doesn't help us figure out a way to end the threat."

"He's a demon. We end the threat by killing him. He's here because of the plane doors. Unlike the individuals who stopped him before, we're not going to make him someone else's problem. We're going to end him here."

"We need to figure out where to find him," Hadley said.

"If we kill the demon, the kids should be freed. The parents should follow suit. The demon has to be our focus. We can't keep messing around with the kids. He wants to keep us distracted."

Hadley rubbed her forehead, as if warding off a headache. "We can end all this tonight if everything goes as planned."

"*If*," I agreed, turning. A small gasp escaped when I realized we were no longer alone. Caleb had crept up behind us. "Hello." I studied his pale face. He looked to be struggling. "Can we help you?"

"It's too late for that," Caleb rasped out. "He's getting stronger." He looked pained as he uttered the words. He didn't in the least resemble the smug possessed child we'd caged. "He's going to kill us all."

"No." I shook my head, firm. "He won't. We're going to take care of this. You have my word."

"It's already too late." Caleb's eyes glistened with tears. "You have to run. There's no saving us."

"Nobody is running," I replied. "We're going to end this … and we're doing it tonight." With those words, I grabbed Hadley's hand. "Just hold it together for a bit longer, Caleb. We're coming for you."

We'd learned all we could from his memories. We had no choice but to leave him trapped for now. He would be safe, and that was important, because we were about to go to war to reclaim his soul.

I was ready. This time I knew what to do.

CHAPTER 27
Twenty-Seven

The beach looked like a war zone when we left Caleb's head. Adult bodies lined the safe side of the dreamcatcher, but there was not a child in sight.

"We didn't catch any of them?" I asked, my heart dropping.

Cole looked so relieved to find me conscious that I was blown back by his hug. "We captured twenty of them," he replied. "They're in the cages."

That was more than I hoped for. "How did you manage that?"

"Nellie is better at herding little monsters than you might think." Cole's smile was broad when he pulled back. "Dolph, Galen and Luke carried them two at a time. I left you for a little bit — even though I didn't want to — and helped. I figured catching as many kids as possible was important."

"You figured right." I beamed at him before focusing on Hadley. She seemed a little slow as she emerged from the mindscape. Galen was on his knees next to her, the lines in his forehead telling me he was worried. "Are you okay, Hadley?"

"I'm fine," she whispered. "Just give me a second."

Galen pulled her in for a hug. "Just sit here for a few minutes." He smiled at her and then turned to me. "What did you see?"

"Nothing we didn't know," I replied. "How long were we gone?"

"Almost two hours," Cole replied.

My hand shot out and gripped his wrist. "That can't be right."

"It is."

I looked to Galen for confirmation and he nodded.

"How long was it for you?" Galen asked.

"Twenty minutes tops," I replied, rolling my neck. No wonder my back felt stiff. I'd been frozen in the same position for two hours. "We blew through the scenes in his mind. The demon approached in shadows when it hit the village. Caleb wasn't the first. He was obviously confused when it happened to him, and he's afraid that his future is already lost."

"Well, he's a pain in the ass, but we're still going to get him out of there," Galen said. "None of the kids are talking."

"That's probably because the demon is reeling," I said, grimacing when my neck cracked. It was only then that I realized something was wrong. "Where's Kade?"

"They're not back yet," Cole replied in a soft voice. "Luke and Nellie have moved to the front of the fairgrounds to watch for them. Luke knew you would ask. That's why he's not waiting with you. Well, that and he was bothered by the fact that you wouldn't respond when he was talking to you. He wouldn't admit it, but he was shaken."

He wasn't the only one. "They should be back by now." I stood, but my legs still felt wobbly. "We have to go after them."

"No, we have to wait here." Galen was firm. He'd situated Hadley so her back was to his chest. "You came up with the plan. We have to see it through."

"They've been gone too long." I insisted. "They might need help."

"We don't know where to look for them."

"But … ."

"We have to wait." Galen kept his voice soft even though his gaze was hard. "Your plan was the right one. We don't know how far they had to go. Just … hold it together."

I didn't like being upbraided by anyone. "I'm supposed to be the boss," I lamented. "I feel helpless without doing something."

"Sometimes being in charge involves waiting and trusting others to do the tasks you've delegated," Galen said pointedly. "Just hold it together. They'll be back soon enough."

"They'd better." I flicked my eyes to the fairgrounds and forced myself to focus. "As soon as they're back, we need to head out. We can't give the demon time to replenish his army. We have to go tonight."

"I agree." Galen moved his hands to Hadley's shoulders and rubbed. "Tell me what you saw in Caleb's head."

I laid it out for him, and he started nodding.

"I think you're spot on," he said. "It makes sense that he came over when the plane doors were open. It also makes sense that the shamans in Africa would've done the only thing they could to protect their people by pushing him through a plane door."

"That Belinda woman Hadley mentioned," I prodded. "Do you think she would've aligned herself with him?"

Galen shrugged. "Possibly, but Belinda wasn't a team player. She's not our concern. The blood ritual her mother performed means she can never cross over again. We explained that to her weeks ago. I don't think she has anything to do with this."

"If only the shamans had sealed in the demon with a blood ritual," Cole said.

"We're not going to make the same mistake," I said. "We're killing the demon. We're not banishing it."

"How?" Galen looked more curious that doubtful. "I'm willing to go with whatever plan you come up with, but I would like a plan before we go in there."

"We have options," I said. "We've got fire elementals. Lilac is a total badass with those swords. Where is she, by the way?"

"Waiting for Booker," Galen replied. "Her hair is still on fire. She needs to vent. It's normal for her when she embraces the magic too hard. She'll be fine. She decided to take a breather away from the rest of us, just to be on the safe side."

"If she can't go with us, Cole has fire power. He can amplify it with my help. We're good."

"What if the demon is impervious to fire magic?" Galen asked.

"Naida can drown him. We have Nixie. Her dust can shrink him to pocket size, and we'll turn the demon into a doll and destroy him."

Galen's nose wrinkled. "Doll? Those voodoo dolls you sell used to be monsters?"

"Or sociopathic killers," I confirmed.

"Oh, geez." Galen squeezed his eyes shut. "I did not need to know that."

"We all fight evil in our own way. Between your group and mine, we have a lot of firepower. It might be as simple as freezing the demon and letting Nellie hack off his head."

"Well, that's a delightful picture," Galen drawled. "But you're right. We have plenty of magic at our disposal. What about the kids? The second that demon realizes we're coming for him, he'll put a hundred kids between us and him. He'll use the distraction to run."

I'd already thought of that. "We'll surround him so he can't run. We'll box him in."

Galen pressed his lips together, debating, and then nodded. "We can do that."

"Just as soon as we have a location." I turned back to the fair-grounds. "They've been gone too long. Maybe I should call Max. He shares Kade's blood. He can use his magic to track him."

"If it comes to it, Hadley can track Booker," Galen said.

"Let's give them a little more time," Cole insisted. "They'll come back as soon as they can. There's no reason to panic yet."

I wanted to believe him, but it was difficult to tamp down my fear.

And then I felt him.

His presence was like a whisper on the wind, a warm breeze on a cold night ... or in Moonstone Bay's case, a cool breeze on an oppressively humid night. I took off toward the fairgrounds without uttering a single word, following my heart as it led me along a path between the tents. When I emerged at the far end, I let out the breath I'd been holding. Kade was back.

His smile was the first thing I saw when he lifted his head. Other than being sweaty, he looked none the worse for wear. I launched myself at him, biting back tears when he wrapped his arms around me.

"There she is." His lips brushed my cheek. "I take it things went okay here."

"You've been gone two hours," I snapped, my gaze accusatory when I pulled my head back. "What were you thinking?"

"We had to get the lay of the land," Booker replied for him, extending a finger when Luke closed in. "Don't make me beat you. I can't deal with the red velvet cake discussion again. We have other things to worry about."

To my surprise, Luke ignored him and approached Kade. "I was worried." He gave Kade a stiff bro-dude side hug. "Don't scare us like that again."

Kade arched an eyebrow. "Did something happen here that I should be aware of?"

"We're fine," Galen replied. He had his arm wrapped around Hadley's waist when they emerged from between the tents. "Lilac is fired up and needs you to help her vent, Book. She's by Poet's tent. She can wait for a few minutes, though. We need to know what you found."

Booker's expression told me he would rather go to Lilac, but he stayed. "They're behind the new resort, which makes sense because you identified those bodies as belonging to the new construction crew that arrived on the island a few days before they were found in the ditch. You remember that spot in the woods where the guy running the high school janitorial staff dumped all that stuff that one time? That's where they are. They've turned the old junkyard into their base of operations."

"They're in a junkyard?" Now it was my turn to make a face. "I wouldn't think you would have one on an island this small. I thought it would be like Malta and you would ship your garbage elsewhere."

"That's how it is," Galen said. "There was a time when Milton Slade did otherwise. He pocketed the money he was supposed to spend on garbage disposal. Then he dumped the refuse in the woods there. Most of it is gone now. Nature reclaimed it. The hills it formed are … odd. It's a weird little area."

"Which is why I think the demon picked that location to hide," Booker said. "There's more. We followed the kids, kept a discreet distance so we could listen. The demon looks like you'd expect ... except he's about four feet tall. His face is hidden and occasionally glows green under his hood. His eyes glow. He mentioned a transformation. I'm pretty sure he's transforming himself into a human. Or something that can pass for a human."

"How?" I demanded. "How can he do that?"

Booker held out his hands. "I think he plans to take over an existing human body. I'm not sure how all that works." He took a step to the right. "I'll let Kade tell you the rest. I'm going to Lilac. I don't want her anger getting a foothold before we head out. We're going to need her out there."

Galen nodded. "We'll give you as much time as we can, but we have to go there tonight. We can't wait."

"Definitely not," Booker agreed. "He has at least a hundred of our kids out there. We have to get them back or this island will never recover."

"Oh, we're getting them back." Galen was grave as he turned his attention to Kade. "That shield thing you do, how many of us can you take there under it?"

"I don't know. I feel okay after the last one, but it's draining. If I put too many people under the shield, I won't be able to help with the fight."

"Maybe that's okay," I said. "Maybe we only need Kade to get us close to the demon. Once we're there, we can take control. If you know that area, you'll know how to get in close and surround him."

"I have a few ideas," Galen confirmed, "but we need more people." He turned to Aurora. "Will Cordelia help?"

Aurora looked caught off guard by the question. "Probably. You're racking up quite a bill with her."

"I don't have a choice," Galen replied. "You guys can handle the west side, hide in the water in case they run in that direction. We can spread out and handle the other directions. We need as many bodies as we can muster."

"We should bring Brody in," Hadley suggested. "He can help with the water side."

Galen nodded. "I don't like him, but we need him."

"You only dislike him because Hadley has a shark fetish," Aurora countered. "He's not a bad guy. We should tap Jareth too. He might be helpful if we need to perform a blood ritual to kill the demon. Capturing shouldn't be all that hard, but killing him … well, that won't be easy."

"Who is Jareth?" I asked.

"He's a vampire," Galen replied. "He was born, not bitten. He's a decent guy. He runs the funeral home."

"Your mortician is a vampire? That's a little spot-on, isn't it?"

Galen shrugged. "I'm used to it." He turned back to Aurora. "Get your people in the water by the resort. Lay low until you see us move in."

Aurora nodded. "Do you want me to notify Jareth on my way out?"

"If you could." Galen looked resigned. "I can have my men serve as an outer layer of protection when the kids run — and they will run — so hopefully we'll be able to collect as many of them as possible. We're going to conduct searches all day tomorrow to track all of them down, but that's future Galen's problem. For now, we have to focus on the demon."

"We have to box the demon in and then get him talking," I said. "Kade can get us close, but he won't be able to help with the fight."

"It will be okay," Hadley reassured me. "We have a lot of people to help."

"That doesn't necessarily mean we'll save all the kids. It's going to be a free-for-all in there." I turned to Raven, who was unnaturally quiet. "What do you think?"

"We have no choice." She was resigned. "The most vulnerable people on this island are going to be used as fodder against us no matter what we do. Waiting only makes our position more precarious. We have to protect them to the best of our ability. We don't want to lose any of them, but if we don't finish this tonight, we could lose all of them."

My heart heaved at her words. "Does everyone understand what we have planned? If you have to take on a kid, try to knock them out. Don't do more than that unless you absolutely have no choice."

"We'll get it done," Dolph promised. "We've faced worse. You can count on us."

I hoped he was right, for all our sakes. If we had to fight children, possessed or not, it would leave a stain on our group.

"Let's just get it done." I was tired, but there was no turning back. "That demon needs to be taught a lesson. Let's make sure he learns it this time."

CHAPTER 28
Twenty~Eight

"The sirens will be there in fifteen minutes," Galen announced as he joined the group at the edge of the fairgrounds. "Let's use this shield to walk the beach until we get to the woods."

I nodded in agreement. "Will the sirens text when they're in position?"

Galen shot me an amused look. "How many cell phones work underwater?"

I cocked my head. "Good point. Are you ready?"

He nodded. "Just one thing." His hand was light when it landed on my arm, and he leaned in close. "If there comes a time when it appears Lilac is going off the rails, stay away from her. Let Booker handle it."

I studied his face for signs of what really worried him. "She won't hurt us, will she?"

"Never on purpose. It's just … when her demon side takes over, sometimes she sees red. Booker can funnel her magic. It will be fine."

For a moment I considered suggesting we leave Lilac behind. Then I thought better of it. She was a complete and total badass, and we would need her. "Maybe, when it's time, we'll set her on the demon and let her have her way with him."

"I don't have a problem with that. I want to make sure it's understood that Booker needs to stay close to her."

"We can manage that."

"Good."

Nobody spoke as Kade erected the shield. We kept our formation tight so he wouldn't expel too much energy. I had no doubt that once we reached our destination, he would have little to offer in the way of magic. That would have to be okay.

I held his hand for the walk. His palm was sweaty, his concentration tight, and I sent him a series of reassuring smiles. He didn't return any of them. He was wound too tight.

Galen took the lead as we closed in on our destination. He pointed at the woods when it was time to veer from the beach. I released my hold on Kade and pressed a kiss to his cheek.

It was time to focus.

Galen and Booker were at the front of the group as we picked our way through the trees. They knew the area best. It wasn't hard to imagine them running through the woods as kids, playing war games and whooping it up. Now they looked ready for war.

The silence of the forest was overpowering. No birds chirped from their nests to warn others that we were encroaching on their territory. There was no rustling of scampering animals. Our footsteps were light in the darkness but even the limited noise sounded deafening thanks to the feeling of dread.

I was about to whisper to my team when a new sound engaged with the night. It was someone speaking. We slowed our pace in unison and I hurried forward for a better look.

Galen had explained that we would see a reclaimed garbage dump. The hills were bigger than I anticipated.

His eyes keen when they locked with mine, Galen lifted a finger to his lips. "I'm going to take my team to the far side," he said. "You split your group to take the west hill and this side."

I nodded. The shield would be dropping soon. I turned and caught Cole's eye. He didn't need me to tell him what to do. He winked before grabbing Luke's arm and peeling off. Raven and Naida went with them. The rest of us remained under Kade's shield.

My heart hammered as I waited for the others to get in position. From this vantage point, the demon — wrapped in robes and pacing relentlessly between the hills — looked deranged. He raved as he moved back and forth, his child army remaining immobile as they watched him fall apart.

"One-third of our army lost," he hissed. "It was over in a matter of minutes. They haven't returned. How is that possible?"

I licked my lips, rolling my neck to alleviate some of the tension, and then lifted a finger toward Kade. "Let me talk to him before all the others are in place," I insisted. "He won't attack at the start. He'll want to talk. Wait until I give the signal."

Kade hesitated and then nodded. It was clear he didn't like the idea of me being exposed, but that was part of the plan.

I slipped from beneath the shield and moved to the edge of the hill. From where I stood, I looked down on the demon. Before I could speak, several of the children registered my presence. A ripple went through them as they turned in unison — a visual that would make any horror movie director proud — and fixed their eyes on me.

"I can answer that question for you," I called out, grim satisfaction running through me when the demon jolted and glared in my direction.

"What question is that?" he hissed, doing his best to pretend that he wasn't caught off guard.

"You wanted to know how it was possible." I remained on top of the hill, drifting to the right to put myself between my group and Cole's. "You're a demon who has a knowledge base that revolves around how the world used to be. You haven't adjusted to the way things are."

"Is that a fact?" The demon planted his hands on his hips, and when he tilted his head so I could get a look under his hood I found green and cracked skin. His size made him a child. The rest of his appearance signified exactly how dangerous he was.

I nodded. "That's a fact. When you were running rampant through Africa all those years ago, things were easier. There were no warnings that could be sent out via technology. You could creep in under the cover of darkness and wipe out entire villages within weeks. That must've been gratifying."

"I've been around long enough to know that the world always changes," the demon drawled. "This is just another change."

"Yes, but you've been living on another plane." I wanted him to know that we'd put the entire story together. I wanted him to be thrown off guard. "Did you meet Belinda there?" I didn't know the woman who had been banished, but I figured any knowledge — especially things he believed I couldn't possibly know — would be a benefit when it came to rattling him.

"You know the Dark Queen?" he demanded.

The Dark Queen? I was momentarily thrown. "Not personally. I've heard stories. I know she's trapped on that plane forever."

The demon made an odd noise, almost a snort. "She doesn't believe that. Her delusions are legendary. She's not my concern, however. If you're here because of her, move along. I have nothing to offer."

"I'm not here because of Belinda. I know you crossed over from that plane. It must've seemed like divine intervention when those doors started opening. You couldn't get back here fast enough, could you?"

The demon's red eyes narrowed. "What is it you think you know, *Romani*?"

Ah, well, he wanted me to know he could suss out information too. I kept my composure. "I know that centuries ago you ravaged the Indian Ocean side of the African continent. You moved from village to village, enslaving children, using them to wipe out the parents. I'm guessing that you fed off the children, who in turn fed off the parents. Using the kids was smart. By the time the parents were ready to admit something was wrong, it was already too late."

"That's one tactic that never goes out of style," he agreed with a toothy grin.

I kept at it. "You were banished by shamans." I tried to act bored as I moved along the hill line. "They couldn't destroy you, so they sent you to another plane. Was that before or after they saw the runes on the beach and realized how much trouble they were in? That's what tipped us off to the danger, by the way. Your compulsion to leave the runes as a warning was ultimately your downfall."

"Kwame." The demon's gaze was dark. "That was my one and only mistake. The villagers whispered about him, said he was powerful. I knew he wasn't powerful enough to take me. I should've killed him right away, but I played with him … and that gave him the time to come up with a plan."

"And that derailed your plan," I said.

"I won't make the same mistake twice. Imagine my surprise when I landed back in my world, and on an island, no less. My takeover couldn't have been easier because of that."

"Right. That's why you were just raging about losing a third of your army."

"Look around, girl." His voice dripped with disdain. "You're woefully outnumbered. My army is big enough to wipe your pathetic conglomeration off the map. Really, Romani, what were you thinking coming here alone?"

Galen appeared on the opposite hill just as the demon finished its question. His gaze was dark as he cleared his throat to draw the demon's attention. "She's not alone."

Beside Galen, Lilac moved to the front of the group and brandished her hellfire weapons. Hadley stood between Lilac and Galen, her hands blazing. Booker remained close to his girlfriend, his eyes keen. There was a dare there, and one look at the demon told me that he hadn't anticipated this move.

Despite his surprise, the demon was not ready to admit defeat. "Do you think this army is big enough to take out mine?" he bellowed.

"We're nowhere near done," Luke announced as Cole's team arrived on the third hilltop.

Nixie, at the front of the group, immediately threw a pouch into the air. Cole blasted the pixie dust with his fire magic and it scattered across the hills.

"*Vasta*," Nixie intoned in the language of her people, the children who had been hit with the dust freezing in place thanks to the pixie magic. Unfortunately, no matter how hard she tried, she couldn't hit all the children. There were at least twenty who remained unaffected. To my surprise, they didn't scramble to protect the demon. In their shock at our arrival, escape was the only thing on their minds, and they raced toward the water, where the sirens awaited them.

"This isn't your world any longer," I said as I began to descend the hill. I raised my hands, my fingers sparking with magic. "You should've stayed on the other plane. You could've lived out your days there."

"That wasn't living," the demon hissed. He looked perplexed as he peered in the direction the children had fled. "Come back, you cowards!" His voice was laced with panic.

"Let them go," I ordered, carefully picking my way between the frozen children as I closed in on him. I had to keep his attention on me. The children wouldn't stay frozen forever. "You've already lost. Don't compound this defeat with a massacre."

"What defeat? You're the one who has lost." The demon's face screwed up in concentration. He was summoning the children from their pixie sleep. Nixie's magic couldn't hold indefinitely without hurting them. "Kill," he ordered the waking children. "Kill, kill, kill!"

I hurried forward and slapped my glowing hands to either side of his head, forcing my way in.

The images made my knees grow weak. Village after village falling. Small faces going slack with death when he finished feeding off them. Bodies discarded in the African jungles as he moved on to the next village. No remorse. Very little joy. He was a killing machine who had been dulled by time.

That would all end today.

"*Glacio*," I ordered, my voice coming out in a rusty growl.

The spell had no effect on the demon. Instead, he laughed, not even making an attempt at slapping my hands away. "Are you trying to control me, Romani?" He laughed even harder. "Why do you think you have the power to stop me? You're nothing but a spot of fluff on the wind. You can only see what I want you to see."

I tried harder. I needed to keep him focused on me for a few more seconds.

"Look all you want, Romani," the demon barked. "Try to find a weakness. There is none. Your attack has failed. I cannot be stopped!"

Behind me, the children had broken from the pixie dust. I heard Nixie and Dolph yelling as they tried to corral the kids without hurting them. I kept my gaze on the demon's red eyes.

"Technology might be different. Times might be different. Women might be able to fight, when before they were relegated to being protected and locked away for childbirth in huts. I am still the apex. I won't be shifted to another plane again. I'm prepared. There's nothing you can do to stop me."

His ego grew with every passing word, and he was feeling full of himself now, which is exactly as I wanted him.

"I will take this island," he said. "I will feed off every being here and then move on. With each move, I will grow stronger. I know what to expect from this world. The people are as dumb as ever. Those on the mainland are non-believers. I will be able to take them as I go. It will be glorious."

"You sound pretty sure of yourself," I growled as I dug in harder. He hid nothing from me. He was right. There were no weaknesses to be found. I knew something he didn't, though. "What makes you think you can overcome all we have to throw at you?"

"Pixies are all flash and no substance." He shot Nixie a predatory look. "They are delicious, though. Shifters are of no consequence. Sirens — yes, I know they're in the water — cannot touch me. I have no equal on this island."

"You mean another demon," I surmised.

"Other demons aren't my equal. I am unique."

"Are you sure about that?" I asked when the figure I'd been waiting for moved in behind him. "Are you absolutely certain no one is your match?"

"As certain as I am that I will take this island by morning. You've all ensured that by opening yourselves to my army. You won't kill them, so they'll contain you. They'll feed off you, and by doing so, they will fulfill me."

He was a smug bastard, and I was ready to be done with him. "Let's test that theory." I let him see what I could see, Lilac standing directly behind him, by projecting the image with my mind.

His gasp was more of a grunt as he turned, but he was too late to protect himself. Lilac, her hellfire weapons at the ready, slammed her burning blades into the demon's chest. Her eyes blazed, matching his smug delight with her intensity, and she looked feral as she twisted her blades.

"*You*," the demon gasped. He was still on his feet, but clearly weakened. "You're like me but not pure. We can work together."

"I think I'm good," Lilac gritted out as she twisted again.

The demon still didn't fall.

"You're strong, girl of fire," the demon rasped, "but not strong enough to end me. This is merely a delaying tactic."

"Not quite," I replied as a war cry went up from the west. I took a step back to give Nellie room as he moved in with his ax.

"What?" The demon barely got the question out before Nellie swung his ax ... an ax that wasn't of this world but another. Even though the demon believed he'd protected himself from every weapon on the island, he'd left himself vulnerable to those from other planes.

My hands, still on fire, gripped into fists as I watched the demon's head detach from his body. Lilac kept her swords embedded in the demon's chest until what remained of the body began to flake away, small flecks disappearing on the steady ocean wind.

It was over. In the end, it was the tried-and-true tactic that had worked after all.

"Ha!" Nellie pumped his fist as he danced, his dress fluttering in the wind. "I told you it would work. Even demons need their heads."

I rolled my eyes until they landed on Lilac, who was breathing hard. "When you're right, you're right." Lilac's hair was as red as the offering from a crayon box. She seemed to be having trouble controlling herself. "Lilac ... ." I could see inside her head, even from a distance. There were black splotches over her impulse control, and yet there were also healing white patches trying to cover the black. The healing patches had a voice, one I recognized.

"Sami," I murmured, smiling as I thought about the young mage we'd crossed paths with in Savannah. "Sami has been here."

Lilac's forehead creased as Booker moved in behind her and pressed his front to her back.

"Vent, Lilac," Booker ordered. His hair was wild from the fire roaring off her and yet he didn't back up. "Do it now!"

Lilac closed her eyes and did as he instructed. In her head, I saw the white healing patches grow. Sami had clearly been here. Not only that, she'd managed to imbue Lilac with a healing ability. With Booker's help, the half-demon could practically heal herself. I smiled at the realization.

"I didn't realize you'd met the fabulous mage from the Midwest," I said to Galen as he joined us.

He shot me a look. "Aric is my cousin."

"You should've told me that from the beginning. We know them."

Galen didn't look nearly as impressed as I felt. "While it's nice that everybody is having a good time, we have a bunch of kids fleeing into the forest. They're all confused and about to get lost."

I snapped back to reality. The celebration could wait. "Right." I flicked my eyes to Nixie. "You can track the ones who were affected by your magic?"

She nodded. "Yup. We should go after them before they get too far ahead of us."

"Then let's do it." I was all smiles as I stepped over the demon's body. "We're not done yet. Let's find the kids and reunite them with their parents."

"Does nobody want to congratulate me on killing the demon?" Nellie whined. "Come on. That was awesome."

Lilac, who was back to normal, snorted. "Oh, please. Poet and I did all the heavy lifting. You just swooped in and took credit at the end."

"A win is a win," Nellie insisted.

"If that's what you need to tell yourself."

CHAPTER 29

Twenty-Nine

The clean-up took us longer than I thought. It wasn't just finding the kids. Once we did that, we had to convince them that we could be trusted. I wasn't sure what they remembered. I was hopeful they would chalk up their bad memories to dreams at some point and let it go, but they were all shaky as we led them back to town.

The sirens helped corral them on the fairgrounds, and Galen sent word to the parents. Within twenty minutes of arriving back in civilization, the parents descended to claim their children.

"We still have the ones in the tent," Kade noted as I watched several tearful reunions play out.

I nodded. "Yeah. We have Mark, too." I blew out a sigh. It was after midnight, and I was exhausted. I wanted to put all of this behind us. "Let's do it."

Galen accompanied us to serve as a trusted face for the kids. When we walked into the tent, Caleb was shaking the bars so hard I thought he might actually manage to rip them apart. Seeing Galen did little to placate him.

"Are we under arrest?" Caleb demanded, fury evident.

"Not tonight," Galen replied as I opened the cage door. The children didn't immediately run for the exit. They were too frightened. Even Ariel, who had apparently been captured on the beach when I was taking a tour through Caleb's mind, didn't immediately come to me.

"I've got them," Galen said as he edged around me. "They don't know you." He used his gentlest voice to cajole them out, explaining that their parents were arriving at the fairgrounds, and they had to go to the front of the property to meet them. That was enough to have the kids fleeing the cages and hurrying out of the tent, murmurs spreading between them as they tried to figure out what had happened.

Caleb, who looked ready to bolt the second he saw an opening, was brought up short when Galen's hand landed on his shoulder. "What do you want?" he demanded. Even though fear practically rolled off him in waves, he didn't back down.

"You and I are going to have a talk," Galen replied in a low voice. I'd told him what I'd seen in the boy's head. "It doesn't have to be tonight — in fact, since everybody is so tired, there's no reason for it to happen right away — but we're going to talk. I'll come to your village in a few days."

"Why?" Caleb's face was blank.

"Your parents need to do better by you — and I might have a job opening."

Caleb's snort was derisive. "I have no interest in being a cop."

"That's good because you're not qualified to be a cop. And you're not old enough. You are qualified to sweep the floors and help clean the building, though." Galen flicked his eyes to me. "Structure comes in many forms."

I smirked as I watched him lead the boy out. The tent was now empty, except for Mark, who looked as if he was ready to wrap his hands around my throat.

"Why am I in a cage?" he demanded. "Is this your payback for me not allowing you to move here?"

I might've been exhausted, but that made me laugh. "Oh, Mark, I think it's time you and I had a talk too." I grabbed one of the chairs at the center of the tent and lowered myself into it.

"Do you think now is the time for this?" Kade asked. He'd been mostly silent since we arrived at the animal tent. I chalked it up to him being tired. I also knew he was leery. Cleanup was always the most difficult part of this job.

"I want it done."

"What do you want done?" Mark challenged. His sneer matched the one Caleb had fixed Galen with. I realized, not for the first time, that Mark's demeanor often mirrored that of a frightened child. It gave me pause.

"Let me out of here!" Mark shook the cage bars and lowered his voice to a threatening hiss. "If you don't let me out, I'm going to lodge a formal complaint with Max. You'll lose your job."

"That's where you're wrong, Mark." I kept my voice even. As much as I wanted to celebrate my victory, that wasn't what a true leader did … at least in public. When Kade and I returned to our hotel room in an hour I could dance to my heart's content. "Max and I have already had a long talk." I chose my words carefully. "You should know that I will be taking charge of the circus from here on out."

"Oh, really?" Mark snickered. "Max just gave you the circus, did he?"

"He still owns the circus. He still has a say in how it operates for the next year or so, before he retires, but I will be taking control of the day-to-day operations. *All* of the day-to-day operations." I wanted to make certain there was no confusion on that point. "Do you understand?"

"I won't let you move here," Mark insisted. "I won't live on this island."

"You won't," I agreed. "As for moving here, I think that's a distinct possibility." I flicked my eyes to Kade, and he nodded his assent. "We'll talk to the others, gather opinions, but this island is what's best for us. We can be ourselves here, live life out loud, so to speak. We won't have to hide in the shadows if we set up shop here permanently."

"You just assume my people want to move here. They don't."

"That's likely true." I said. "But they're not your people any longer, Mark. Once the vote has been taken — and I'm almost positive I know how it will go — we will pick a date to cease traveling operations." I'd given this a lot of thought and knew exactly how I would handle things.

"We still have a year on the road, contracts to fulfill," I continued. "But we won't be taking on new locations. The next year will consist of coming up with a plan for our final move."

"It won't be to this island!" Mark was shrill. "I will not live here. You can't make me."

My lips curved into a half-smile. "You assume you'll be invited, Mark. I can assure you, that's not the case."

"Is that a fact?"

"Yes." I made sure there was no doubt in my eyes. I wanted him to see that I meant business, just like I wanted the demon to see that I had control of the situation. "You won't be part of our final move, Mark."

"So you're saying I'll be out of a job in a year. Do you even know what that means for your precious circus? I'll tell you. It means the end. Max knows that. He won't allow it."

"I've already talked to Max." I refused to let emotion rule me. "Max is not only aware that you're not part of the plan going forward, he's signed off on it. Also, you won't be with us for the final year of traveling."

For the first time since the conversation began, Mark showed real fear. "Excuse me?"

"You heard me." I was firm. "This is your last day in charge of the midway. Actually, yesterday was your last day in charge of the midway because it's after midnight. As of right now, Cole is the midway chief."

Mark looked as if he wanted to rip the bars off the cage and tear my throat out with his teeth. "You can't just fire me."

"But I have."

"I'll go to Max."

"Go ahead. He's aware of my decision. He stands by it."

"You can't do this," Mark wailed.

"It's already done." I slowly rose to my feet. "Mark, you've never been part of the solution. Even when Max considered you for a leadership position, it was temporary. He wanted to motivate me to get it

together. Thankfully, I managed to do that myself, without his prod-
ding. You're not part of the future. You can't be."

"This circus is my life," Mark growled. "I won't be displaced."

"You should've thought about that before you were the world's
biggest turd on a daily basis," Kade offered dryly. "You had a chance to
make things better, but you chose to make them worse whenever the
opportunity rose. You're done, Mark. You shot yourself in the foot.
None of us have sympathy for you."

"Cole will take control of the midway. He'll treat your people better
than you ever did," I said. "They'll be off their games to start, but we'll
help him with the transition. Before long, they won't miss working for
you. In fact, they'll probably prefer their new boss because he's not a
tool."

"You can't just give my job to that … that … ."

I knew he was going to say something derogatory, and I fixed him
with a hard look. "You want to be very careful about what you say
next," I warned. "As it stands, we're going to give you six months'
severance. That's my decision. I can revoke it."

Murderous intent lit Mark's eyes. "I won't let you do this."

"It's already done." I opened the cage door, practically daring him
to attack me. "You know you can't win this, Mark. Don't even try."

"I won't let you beat me."

"See, that's your problem." I shook my head. "For you, it's all about
you winning. I need us all to win."

"My people will never accept this."

"I think you'll be surprised about what they're willing to accept." I
hesitated as I moved toward the exit. "You can travel back with us to
Florida. From there, you're on your own."

"I'll kill you if you try to pull this off," he seethed.

"If you threaten her again, I'll be taking over your contract negotia-
tions," Kade warned, fury obvious. "You're not in charge, Mark. You
never were. If you keep at it like this, I'll make sure you understand
just how mistaken you were."

"I'm not going to let you do this. This is my circus."

"No, it's my circus." I was grim as I regarded him. "You have a nice
day now."

. . .

KADE AND I HAD TO STAY AT THE FAIRGROUNDS until each child was claimed. By the time we returned to the hotel, we were limp rags with barely the strength to strip out of our clothes before climbing into bed.

"That was an eventful day," he murmured as he tugged me close, his eyes already closed.

"Yes, and tomorrow is likely to be just as eventful. But after that … ."

"After that we can start planning." Kade's voice was sleepy. "Not just for the circus. We can start planning a wedding. We can come up with a timetable for moving here. We should probably tap Max to talk to the DDA about that, just to be on the safe side."

I'd already come to that conclusion. "It's all coming together," I murmured.

"It's going to be great."

Briefly, my mind drifted to New Orleans, and what was likely to be waiting there for me. "It is going to be great." I meant it, for the most part. "Tomorrow is a brand new day."

"Technically it's today."

"Close enough."

His lips landed on my forehead. "I love you."

"I love you too."

"I can't wait to see how this all plays out."

That had me laughing. "Life is an adventure, right?"

"Especially this life." He kissed me again. "I wouldn't have it any other way."

Things were looking up. Sure, there was a shadow hanging over me, and its name was Sidney. But given what we'd been through, I had no doubt we would be smiling when we came out the other side.

"I'll see you for breakfast."

"I'll be the one holding your eggs."

I was already half asleep when gritting out my final words. "Sounds like a plan."

Made in the USA
Middletown, DE
06 November 2024

64059408R00154